CW00801446
ARROW'S EDGE MC

PRAISE FOR FREYA BARKER

Freya Barker writes a mean romance, I tell you! A REAL romance, with real characters and real conflict.

~Author M. Lynne Cunning

I've said it before and I'll say it again and again, Freya Barker is one of the BEST storytellers out there.

~Turning Pages At MidnightBook Blog

God, Freya Barker gets me every time I read one of her books. She's a master at creating a beautiful story that you lose yourself in the moment you start reading.

~Britt Red Hatter Book Blog

Freya Barker has woven a delicate balance of honest emotions and well-formed characters into a tale that is as unique as it is gripping.

~Ginger Scott, bestselling young and new adult author and Goodreads Choice Awards finalist

Such a truly beautiful story! The writing is gorgeous, the scenery is beautiful...

~Author Tia Louise

From Dust by Freya Barker is one of those special books. One of those whose plotline and characters remain with you for days after you finished it.

~Jeri's Book Attic

No amount of words could describe how this story made me feel, I think this is one I will remember forever, absolutely freaking awesome is not even close to how I felt about it.

~Lilian's Book Blog

Still Air was insightful, eye-opening, and I paused numerous times to think about my relationships with my own children. Anytime a book can evoke a myriad of emotions while teaching life lessons you'll continue to carry with you, it's a 5-star read.

~ Bestselling Author CP Smith

In my opinion, there is nothing better than a Freya Barker book. With her final installment in her Portland, ME series, Still Air, she does not disappoint. From start to finish I was completely captivated by Pam, Dino, and the entire Portland family.

~ Author RB Hilliard

The one thing you can always be sure of with Freya's writing is that it will pull on ALL of your emotions; it's expressive, meaningful, sarcastic, so very true to life, real, hard-hitting and heartbreaking at times and, as is the case with this series especially, the story is at points raw, painful and occasionally fugly BUT it is also sweet, hopeful, uplifting, humorous and heart-warming.

~ Book Loving Pixies

ALSO BY FREYA BARKER

ON CALL SERIES (Operation Alpha):

BURNING FOR AUTUMN
COVERING OLLIE
TRACKING TAHLULA
ROCK POINT SERIES:
KEEPING 6
CABIN 12
HWY 550
10-CODE

NORTHERN LIGHTS COLLECTION:
A CHANGE IN TIDE
A CHANGE OF VIEW
A CHANGE OF PACE
SNAPSHOT SERIES:
SHUTTER SPEED
FREEZE FRAME
IDEAL IMAGE

PORTLAND, ME, NOVELS:
FROM DUST
CRUEL WATER
THROUGH FIRE
STILL AIR

CEDAR TREE SERIES:
SLIM TO NONE
HUNDRED TO ONE
AGAINST ME
CLEAN LINES
UPPER HAND
LIKE ARROWS
HEAD START

EDGE OF REASON

FREYA BARKER

ISBN: 978-1-988733-43-2

Cover Design: Freya Barker

Editing: Karen Hrdlicka

Proofing: Joanne Thompson

Formatting: CP Smith

ACKNOWLEDGMENTS

I always seem to be thanking the same people, but that's because they ALWAYS help me put my books together. They put in time and effort and I'm very grateful to have them in my life.

Karen Hrdlicka and Joanne Thompson, my fabulous editing/proofreading team; and Deb Blake, Pam Buchanan & Petra Gleason, my beta readers for Edge Of Reason. Also, CP Smith for her amazing formatting talents!

They're responsible for cleaning up my messes and making me the book look pretty!

Then there are a group of folks who make sure my books get into your hands.

Stephanie Phillips of SBR Media, my agent; Debra Presley & Drue Hoffman of Buoni Amici Press, my publicists; as well as all the amazing bloggers, who help spread the word of every new book.

But arguably the most gratitude I have for you, my readers. With each new book published you get excited at the prospect of a new story and run out to buy it the moment it hits the market.

I thank you so much for supporting, encouraging, and motivating me!

Love you all.

EDGE OF REASON

Brotherhood and beer meets single mom and apple pie.

I am a riding contradiction.
A scholar, a cynic, a brother, and a biker.

My name is Trunk.
I'm smart enough to recognize the chip on my shoulder, and cautious enough to keep it right where it is.

I am a misguided romantic.
A mom, a daughter, an agent, and a survivor

My name is Jaimie.
I'm strong enough to look after my family alone, and too stubborn to accept I don't have to.

We make an odd couple—our differences obvious—but when hatred and danger threatens to destroy everything of value in our lives, we only get stronger.
Together.

EDGE OF REASON

1

Trunk

"How's he doing?"

Ouray is waiting for me in the hallway outside the small office I use. Both of us watch as the lanky teen, I just spent the past hour with, disappears into the clubhouse common room.

The kid's a hard nut and so far little I've tried to get through to Matt has been successful. In fact, haven't even begun to scratch the surface since the club brought him in three weeks ago.

He'd been found in the furnace room of an apartment complex in town, where he'd been spending his nights staying warm. The kid jimmied a basement window and used that to come and go. Judging by the nest he'd made for himself between two large water heaters, he'd been there for a while.

Matt was lucky he didn't start a fire. Luckier still the building happened to belong to Arrow's Edge. Although whether he thinks so remains to be seen.

The Arrow's Edge is unlike any other motorcycle club I've encountered in my years riding. Most of them are either purely recreational, like the one I rode with back in Denver, or involved in illegal activities. Although flexible with the rules of the law, for the most part the club runs a variety of legal enterprises. In addition, they provide a safe haven for street kids, giving them a roof over their heads, food in their belly, structure, education, and a sense of family.

The boys all have their own stories on how they ended up on the streets, some harder than others.

Exactly how Matt—if that's even his real name—ended up where we found him is still a mystery. The boy is slicker than an eel in a bucket of snot.

"Hard to tell. Kid'll do and say anything to make sure he's got food to eat and a place to stay warm. He's a con."

"Streetwise," Ouray translates.

"I'm guessing he's been there for a good while."

"No names? Parents? Nothing we can get our teeth into?"

I shake my head. Three weeks of one-on-one sessions and he's not given me a single piece of concrete information. The kid's an enigma and a serious blow to my professional confidence.

"I'll keep on him," I promise Ouray, the club's

president.

I'm as frustrated as he is at the lack of information. Most of the boys here are under guardianship of the club, either obtained from the parents, through the CPS, or through the court system. Not knowing who a kid is makes that difficult.

"I know you will," Ouray says, clapping a hand on my shoulder. "You sticking around for Christmas?"

"Momma made me swear to stick around for dinner tonight, but I told her I can't be here tomorrow."

Momma is the club's matriarch. She's the wife of the founding former president, Nosh, and the two of them are like the club parents to anyone affiliated. Momma is not one to mess with.

"Your sister's?"

"Can't miss my niece's first Christmas."

"I met your sister," Ouray shares, chuckling. "Thinking that's the right call."

A little over a year ago, I left a good job as a child psychologist, working mostly with kids on the autism spectrum at the Children's Hospital in Denver, tired of politics and lack of program funding. I jumped at the opportunity when I heard through a buddy that a Durango MC was shopping for a child therapist. Of course, I did my research to make sure the club was on the up and up—as I'm sure they did with me—but when all was said and done, I didn't waste any time moving my ass out here. Life has to be lived, and when given a chance to combine work and passion, only a fool would say no.

The cherry on that cake was, just a few months after I

left Denver, my sister followed me out here. At the time she was pregnant and single, but has since become a parent and found herself a man. Decent guy, although, he had to grow on me.

Growing up, Christmas was always something other people celebrated, but for Tahlula and me it was just another day to get through.

Now that she has a baby and a man, she's bound and determined to catch up for all those holidays spent alone. Which means my ass will be in her chair tomorrow, come hell or high water.

I follow Ouray into the common room where Matt already reclaimed his turn at the game station with some of the other boys. Normally they get just a couple of hours of screen time per day, but given we've had snow on the ground for the past three weeks or so, and the temperatures have plummeted, they've mostly been cooped up inside. Because Momma put her foot down and won't tolerate nonstop gaming, they're limited to the afternoons.

"Boys!" The old woman sticks her head out of the kitchen. "Shut that shit down and get cleaned up. Dinner in fifteen." The kids don't hesitate, not even Matt. He hasn't been here long, but he knows damn well who rules the roost. "Matt, you run out to the gym and round up the guys there."

I watch the boy give her a nod and hustle out the door. He seems more intimidated by the five foot five senior citizen than he is with my six foot four bulky frame. They don't call me Trunk for nothing. I make a mental note to see if I can get Momma to help drag some information from the boy.

"Need a hand, Momma?"

"If you could move the pool table parallel to the dining table? I think there's a board that fits over it against the side of the porch. We'll probably need the smaller tables too, if you butt them end to end, we'll have three large tables. Folding chairs in the shed in the back."

"On it."

"I'll give ya a hand," Paco announces, having just walked in.

By the time it takes us to haul in the chairs, lug the heavy table over, and shift the rest of the furniture around, Momma and Luna—Ouray's wife—are ready to set the tables. Large white linen sheets to cover the roughed up surfaces, topped with nice bone china, matching cutlery, and proper glasses that seem out of place in a clubhouse.

"Turn on the Christmas lights, will ya?" Momma asks Ouray, who is observing the activity from a stool at the bar.

I barely recognize the place. The cavernous space, with scuffed barn board on the floors and sparse well-worn furniture, looks festive. A large Christmas tree sits in the corner by the bar and lights are strung around the windows and doors. I've never known an MC to put so much stock in the holidays. Then again, other clubs don't have Momma.

Dinner is a raucous affair, which isn't a surprise with around thirty people at the table. Especially when a few of them haven't even heard of table manners. Momma strategically installed herself and Nosh, Ouray and Luna, and Ouray's second man, Kaga and his wife, Lea, at each of the tables to keep an eye on the young ones. The rest of the club members, along with a few hangers-on of the female persuasion, have pulled up seats wherever there was room.

Across the table from me, Matt seems to take everything in: the food, the talking, the laughter. He looks overwhelmed when his eyes meet mine. Maybe even lost in this sea of brotherhood and togetherness.

I know just how he feels.

JAIMIE

"I STILL CAN'T believe you're here."

I look over at Mom, who has her eyes peeled out the window as we drive through Durango's downtown district.

"Wait 'til the moving truck arrives on Monday," she warns with a quick smile my way before she directs her gaze back outside. "You'll be a believer then."

She was supposed to fly in yesterday morning, but all flights into Durango were canceled due to the large storm, which dumped another ten or so inches on the snowpack that had already accumulated over the past weeks. This morning—Christmas morning—she caught the first flight in.

Winter in Durango is nothing to sneeze at, and I'm grateful for the new tires on my sturdy, secondhand Honda CRV.

I left Denver about six months ago with nothing other than a couple of suitcases and my then six-month-old son, River. If not for the support of my friend and client, Tahlula Rae, and the amazing people in her circle, the past half year would have probably decimated me.

I am now the proud tenant of a gorgeous little home in a nice family neighborhood, beside the Animas River. Since I've worked mostly from home, I haven't had much need for babysitting, but that will change now my divorce is final.

That had threatened to become a long, drawn out affair when my ex contested the divorce from his prison cell. Thanks to Tahlula's savvy Denver lawyer, who pled my case to the family court judge just days after my ex's conviction, I was granted a surprisingly easy divorce. The decree arrived at the lawyer's office last week.

Mom started packing the day after.

"I can't believe how much he's grown," she muses, looking over her shoulder at River, dozing in his car seat.

"I know. I'm so sorry you've had to do with pictures and videos, Mom. It just wasn't safe for you or for us to visit."

Mom turns tear-filled eyes to me as she grabs my hand. "Not your fault, Belle."

She uses the nickname I gave myself at three years old, after a lengthy obsession with all things Peter Pan and Tinker Bell. I try hard not to get emotional, giving her a smile and a firm squeeze instead, quickly turning my eyes back on the road.

"We have about an hour to get you settled in, before

we're expected over at T's place."

"Are you sure she won't mind me tagging along?" I snort at her question.

"Mom, the woman threatened to fire me if I didn't drag you over there right away. T has decided to do Christmas big, with a living room filled with family. That's us."

"But she's never even met me," she protests.

"Doesn't matter."

"I don't even know what to wear. I've never met a celebrity before."

This time I laugh outright. "Mom, you'll never meet a more down to earth person than Tahlula," I enlighten her. "She's more likely to be wearing jeans and a tee covered in baby spit than some cocktail dress. Hell, I doubt she even owns one. Trust me on this. You'll love her. You'll get a kick out of Joan as well—her soon-to-be mother-in-law—who's the salt of the earth and as straight forward as they come."

"Who else will be there?"

"Autumn and Keith with their son, Aleksander. He's only six months older than River, so it'll be baby chaos. You can 'grandma' all day long. I think T's brother Trunk's supposed to be there as well."

I try not to think too much about Tahlula's massive, brooding, much darker-skinned half brother. Despite a few acts of kindness and a degree in psychology, the man seriously lacks in social skills. The few times I've bumped into him, he's done nothing more than growl at me, yet I still have an unhealthy fascination with him.

"Who would name their kid, Trunk?"

"His name's Titus, Mom. Everyone just calls him Trunk. You'll understand when you see him."

At home, I take Mom for a quick tour of the house, and show her the brand-new, small, but self-sufficient apartment above the garage, where she'll move once her belongings get here. For now, she's sleeping in River's room while he bunks with me.

My landlord, Ollie—who lives across the street and is married to Chief of Police Joe Benedetti—told me she'd had a fire in the garage last year. When they rebuilt, they added the nanny apartment, which I thought would be perfect for Mom. With two large windows in front, she'll have views of the river across the street, and the two smaller ones at the back—one in the bedroom and one in the bathroom—look out on the yard.

Mom, who has a bit of a green thumb herself, will be happier than a pig in shit this coming spring when she sees the garden.

I quickly pack a few changes of clothes for River, and one for myself, just in case, while Mom freshens up. Downstairs I grab the pumpkin and apple-rhubarb pies I baked from the fridge. Dessert had been the only thing I'd been allowed to contribute. Mom comes down carrying a large plastic container.

"What are those?"

"Sugar cookies." She smiles as I make a dive for the container. "You can have one, Jaimie," she admonishes me when I discover it filled to the brim with my all-time favorite Christmas cookies. She and I would spend a day every year, baking and decorating these holiday favorites.

"When did you have a chance to make these?" I ask, my mouth full. Luckily River is still sleeping in his car seat in the living room, or I'd have to share.

"On the weekend. Can't have Christmas with my girl without her favorite treats."

I round the kitchen island and wrap Mom, who is not much taller and equally rounded, in a big hug. "Love you, Mom. I'm so glad you're here."

"Me too, Belle, me too."

The first person I see when we walk into Tahlula and Evan's house twenty minutes later, is her brother. If it wasn't for the barely-there muscle twitch by his right eye as his gaze seems to travel through me, I'd swear I was invisible.

"Holy moly," Mom whispers behind me. "I see why."

Yeah. It's hard to miss the large, wide, and illegally good-looking black man leaning against the counter.

N
nw
ne
W
E
ARROW'S EDGE MC

2

TRUNK

FUCK.

She's as pretty as she was when I first saw her, despite the hell her scumbag of a husband put her through. Curves for days on her short frame, blonde shoulder-length hair, and sharp blue eyes that don't seem to miss a thing. Even the tow-headed baby she has perched on her hip doesn't do much to curb her appeal.

I've never really had preference for a particular set of looks, but hers seem to hit all the right buttons. Or the wrong ones, depending on your point of view. I've been with women of all shapes and sizes, all colors of the rainbow, and just about all walks of life—even dated a few for longer than the couple of weeks it usually takes me to tire of them—but none have stuck. I'm surprised at the impact seeing her again still has on me.

There's no mistaking it's her mom walking in behind her. The hair is dark—mostly gray now—but the eyes are the same, as are the generous curves and short stature. I wonder if she has the same sharp tongue I've heard from her daughter.

My gaze drifts back to Jaimie, who seems to have caught sight of me. Fuck.

"Take Hanna, will ya?" Tahlula shoves my niece at me and my arms come up automatically. "I need to say hello."

The baby snuggles against me with a blind trust I don't know I deserve as I watch my sister join Evan at the door, wrapping her arms around first Jaimie and then her mom.

She's claiming everyone as family now, my sister. There was a time, not that long ago, when it was just she and I. Now she has a fucking house full of people.

Blackfoot and his wife, Autumn, with their rugrat. Evan's mother, Joan. Even two of Evan's fellow firefighters, and Tony Ramirez, who's Blackfoot's partner with the Durango PD. Add to that her friend, Jaimie, and her mother. *Shee-it*, a fucking houseful. I'm getting claustrophobic.

"Want me to take her from you?" Evan asks as he walks up, reaching for his daughter.

"Nah, she's good."

Just because I don't fuss over the baby doesn't mean I don't like holding her. Even if the poor kid has red hair like her dad. Luckily, she's growing into her mama's good looks.

"Trunk, come meet Sandra."

I let my sister drag me into the living room, where I mumble what I hope is a polite "Merry Christmas" to Sandra, and limit myself to a nod to her daughter before sitting down, settling Hanna in my lap.

The next half hour is spent opening the kids' gifts. Tahlula insisted no presents for adults, thank fuck. The damn kids were challenge enough.

I lucked out at the Harley store on the south side of town when I popped in to grab a new beanie after losing the old one. Winter is hard on a bald head. I spotted the little tees on the rack near the cash and bought three. Two black and one pink, all with the Harley logo. The sales girl rolled her eyes when I couldn't give her any sizes, so I ended up grabbing ones that looked right and slammed them on the counter.

Apparently, I overestimated. Aleksander, Autumn and Blackfoot's kid, insisted on wearing it and it hangs down to his knees. Whatever. They can grow into them.

After presents, drinks are refreshed and the two boys sit down on the ground to check out some of their new toys.

I try to ignore the hum of conversation around me and get lost in thought, until I feel a tug on my jeans and look down. The little blond boy, who moments before was playing on the floor with Blackfoot's kid, is pulling himself up on my pant leg. His knees wobble and my free hand shoots out to keep him standing. His blue eyes are impossibly round in his face as he looks at me. Then he looks at Hanna, who's fallen asleep in the crook of my arm.

"Ba!" His little finger points at her. "Ba!"

"Baby,"

"Ba!"

"Yeah, that's a baby."

He wedges himself between my knees and reaches for Hanna. A pudgy hand closes on the sock that keeps slipping off her foot, and yanks it off. "Ba!" he prattles, shoving said sock in his mouth.

"Kid, you don't wanna make a habit of sticking other people's dirty socks in your mouth," I rumble quietly, plucking it from his fingers. "It's a nasty habit."

"Ba!"

"Exactly. It's gross."

"Ba–up!" His hand slaps my thigh. "Up!" he says again, stretching his arms toward me.

Without thinking, I reach down and lift him on my lap. He's immediately focused on Hanna, and I can just hold him back before he launches himself at her.

"Easy boy," I tell him, before settling him firmly on his side of my lap. "That's my niece you're throwing yourself at. She deserves a little more finesse, don'tcha think?"

"I can take River if he's bothering you." I look up to find his mother standing in front of me, barely hiding the grin pulling at her mouth.

"He's fine," I assure her, trying not to get lost in those amused blue eyes. To underline how 'fine' he is, the kid puts his thumb in his mouth and leans his head against my chest.

Jaimie's full grin is out, white teeth peeking out between pink lips.

Fucking hell.

"He's the baby-whisperer."

I roll my eyes at my sister's comment. She first called me that a few weeks ago when Hanna fell asleep on my chest after a fussy crying spell.

"I can see that."

"He may scare grown men, but is a big ole' softie with kids," Tahlula feels necessary to add.

"That's it," I announce firmly. "Collect your spawn. I need some fresh air."

Hanna's still sleeping like the dead when her chuckling mother plucks her off my lap, but River loudly protests when Jaimie reaches for him. I breathe in a whiff of vanilla when her hair falls forward over her face as she scoops up her son.

I'm out back, pulling on a cigarette, when the door slides open and Blackfoot steps out. Luke, my sister's dog, who is sniffing around the yard, lifts his head.

"Got another one of those?" I silently hand him the pack and my lighter. "Fuck, sometimes I forget how good that first hit is," he says, inhaling deeply.

"When'd you quit?"

"Years ago. Only time I miss it is when I'd like an excuse to escape a crowded room."

"I hear ya. I'm not one for crowds myself. I carry a pack in case of an emergency."

Blackfoot chuckles at that before he falls silent. The

two of us watch the dog mark his territory, occasionally taking a drag. "More snow coming," he finally says, and I look up at the overcast sky.

"Looks like."

I feel his eyes on me. "Get any more info on that boy?"

Arrow's Edge sometimes called in help from local law enforcement to get a background on some of the kids we pick up. Some of them run away from home after something as simple as a disagreement with their folks, or getting into some trouble with the law. Those kids are usually reunited with family after mediation by the club. The tougher ones are those where kids are running from a violent situation. In those cases, we get more involved.

Our latest kid, Matt, is a bit of a challenge and Ouray asked Blackfoot to run his picture and his first name, to see if anything would pop up. Nothing has, and Matt's not talking.

"Nothing. I tried again yesterday, but he's locked up tight. Thinking of asking Momma to have a go. He seems a little more responsive to her." I take a final drag before dropping the butt into the tin my sister left out here for that. She caught me flicking my butts into the yard and climbed up one end and down the other, before getting me the can.

Blackfoot follows suit. "Anything you come up with, let me know. I'll look again."

"Will do."

"You ready to go back in?" he asks me with a grin.

Through the sliding door I take in the packed house. Joan and Jaimie's mother are in the kitchen, setting out food, and I just catch a glimpse of Evan heading down the hallway toward the bedrooms, probably putting the baby to bed. In the living room Tahlula throws her head back, laughing at something Jaimie says, a sound I can hear out here.

She seems right at home in the crowd. Ironic, given not so long ago we were both loners, preferring our own company to that of others. Remnants of a fucked-up childhood.

Tahlula has moved on. Me, not so much.

"Fuck, no," I growl before opening the sliding door.

Jaimie

I'm not sure how I ended up sitting across from him.

They moved some of the furniture aside to expand the dining table, with drop-in panels to facilitate the eleven adults, while I was in Tahlula's office, putting a very tired River down to sleep. By the time I walked in, it had been the only chair available, between Mom and Tony Ramirez, and directly opposite Trunk.

Mom appears to be having a good time over dinner, bonding with Evan's mother over a common love of gardening. They lost me when they started discussing the best types of soil for growing tomatoes and my eyes wandered. Right into Trunk's almost black ones, intently focused on me.

Yikes.

I produce a smile, which promptly has his gaze drop to my mouth before turning away. Well, then. Ignoring the pang of disappointment at the lack of response, I turn to Tony instead.

"So what's your story? Are you a born and raised Durangoan or are you an import like me?"

The man is gorgeous and he knows it. He turns his thousand-watt smile on me and my hand grabs the edge of the table not to go weak at its force. "Import," he answers in his smooth baritone. "I'm originally from Boulder, where I grew up before I ended up in Denver. Worked for the DPD for about six years before I moved here."

"Which district?"

"Three. Washington Park area."

"No shit? That's where I'm from. You must've already known your chief, Joe Benedetti. He worked in District Three, as well." I'd just come by that information after having dinner across the street at Ollie and Joe's place a couple of weeks ago.

"He's a friend. In fact, I'd like to think I had a hand in bringing him here."

Over my pies we reminisce about all the great coffee shops, pubs, and restaurants in Washington Park, when Tony suddenly asks, "There's some great spots here too, though, have you been out yet?"

"Nah, hands full with my son. I'm more of a homebody these days."

"That's a waste of a beautiful woman," he says, tilting his handsome head to one side. "You should come out with me. I can show you the good spots around town; we can have some fun. What do you say?"

I'm not sure if I'm imagining it, but I swear I hear a growl from across the table. I turn to find Trunk glaring at the detective as if he's ready to rip his head off. What the hell?

"Did you say something?" I ask him, and his gaze slides to me. Before I can identify the heated look in his eyes, something impassive slides in its place.

"Yeah," he says, pushing back from the table suddenly. "I should get going."

"Already?" Tahlula speaks up.

"Got stuff to do."

Followed by a choir of goodbyes and see-you-laters, Trunk lumbers to the front door, his sister behind him. I watch him shrug into a heavy down winter coat, while T engages him in a whispered conversation. Grabbing her by the back of the neck, he pulls her close, whispering something in her ear, to which she wraps her arms around his middle in a hug.

Conversation around the table has picked up again, but my eyes are still on the two of them until Trunk catches me watching and I quickly turn away. A second later the front door opens and Tahlula calls out, "Jaimie! Your SUV is blocking his truck."

Shit, I forgot I was the last to pull into the long driveway.

I quickly get up, grab my keys from my purse in the hallway, and join them at the front door, shoving my feet in my snow boots.

"Just give me the keys," Trunk grumbles, holding his hand out.

"I've got it." I keep them in my hand as I put on my coat.

"Jaimie, gimme the keys."

I send him a glare, still a bit stung by his repeated dismissal. "I said, I've got it. I thought you were in a hurry to get out of here? You'll be on your way faster if I move it myself."

He clasps a hand in the back of his neck and takes in an obvious deep breath. "Fine," he finally bites off, yanking a beanie over his scalp. He kisses the top of his sister's head and walks out the door.

"I'll be right back," I tell Tahlula, before following him. I hear the door shut behind me.

It's dark, but the moon reflects a beautiful blue light off the still-pristine blanket of snow. Ahead of me, Trunk climbs into the cab of his GMC truck; I feel his eyes burning through the window as I pass by.

I can't figure out what his issue is with me. Annoyed, I stomp to my SUV, get behind the wheel, and give the engine a minute to warm up before backing out. I pull off to the side and wait for his truck to back up.

With only his front wheels in the driveway, his truck stops and I watch as he gets out. What the fuck now? Stalking over to my driver's side, he knocks on the window.

"You're stubborn," he informs me when I roll it down.

Immediately my annoyance flares into anger. "That's what you got out of your truck to tell me? I'm stubborn? Coulda saved you the trouble. Been that way all my life, so you're not telling me anything new. Now if that's all, I don't wanna keep you from whatever is so damn important on Christmas you'd bail on your sister, but have a merry one." With that I close my window.

Next thing I know, my door is yanked open and Trunk shoves his head inside.

"That was rude," he rumbles, and I can't help it, I burst out laughing.

"I was rude? Seriously? Dude, you invented the word with your grunts and glares. I guess I must've done something awful to you in a previous life, 'cause I can't figure out what your beef is with me."

"No beef."

"Coulda fooled me," I scoff.

"No beef," he repeats, leaning so close I'm almost bent over the center console. "But you are a distraction I could do without."

Shocked, and frankly stung again, I watch as he backs out and slams my door shut. A few moments later I see his taillights disappear down the road.

I take in a few deep breaths before pulling the CRV back in the driveway, my hands shaking on the wheel.

Son of a bitch.

3

TRUNK

"SURE YOU DON'T wanna stay?"

The woman, Lynette or Lisette or something like that, clearly had other plans for tonight, given the way she's plastered against my side. Some heavy floral scent wafting up from her irritates my nose. The memory of a subtle hint of vanilla, much more appealing to my senses, suddenly hits me.

New Year's Eve party at the clubhouse is only for adults. The boys are all bunking at Momma and Nosh's house on the backside of the property.

Yuma, their son and the club's sergeant at arms, had been in charge of tonight's diversion, which means I'll have to thank him for the octopus currently wrapping herself around me. Lynette or Lisette—whatever the fuck it is—is one of the exotic dancers Yuma considers appropriate entertainment.

Ouray just shrugged and sat down on the couch, pulling Luna on his lap to watch the show. Admittedly, the girls were pros, but it's becoming obvious they're pros at more than just dancing. I don't pay for women and I don't share them. Not that I care if others do, it's just not my thing. I glance over at Yuma, who has two of the girls draped over him and doesn't seem at all bothered one of them is pulling his business out of his jeans as she buries her face in his lap. That does it for me.

I turn to Paco, who's manning the bar and appears uninterested in the action on the couch. In the year or so since I've been here, I've never seen him with a woman. The only brothers I know are in any kind of relationship are Kaga, who's married to Lea and has twin sons, and Ouray. The others will occasionally bring someone to the clubhouse, but you rarely see them a second or third time.

"I'm heading out."

"Man, it's not even midnight yet," Paco points out. "You're not crashing here?"

"Nah. Just had a couple of beers and I've got stuff to do tomorrow."

I untangle myself from Lynette or Lisette—or whatever—who pouts annoyingly. "Aren't you gonna wish me a happy new year?"

"Plenty of guys here, I'll leave that for one a them," I point out, stepping out of her reach and lifting my chin at Paco. "Later." He raises his beer bottle in greeting.

By the time I reach the door, the woman's already planted her booty on Honon's lap. Guess she likes her guys big. He's probably the only brother I'd think twice about ever taking on. The motherfucker is taller and probably outweighs me by a good forty pounds.

Outside the cold air hits me. Winter here sure is different from Denver. Especially up in the mountains. I don't think I've seen the ground around my house since the first snow started falling about a month ago. The road outside the compound gets plowed, as does the road to my place, at least partway. The plows turn around about two hundred yards from my house, which is why I bought the GMC truck before winter. I can hook on a blade and clear a path to my front door myself.

Only a dusting of snow covers my earlier tracks when I pull into my driveway. Aside from the single porch light I usually flick on before I leave, the house is dark.

I'd hate to think of my sister still living up here. She and the baby would be cut off from the world. Granted, I wasn't exactly on board when she hooked up with that cracker, Evan, but in hindsight I'm glad. He got her to move into his place in town, and I bought her place from her.

It's pretty quiet in the summer, but that's nothing compared to the utter silence of winter up here. The almost permanent blanket of snow absorbs what little sound there is.

By the time I kick off my boots, and toss my coat on the couch, it's five minutes to midnight on the kitchen clock. I can either go to bed and sleep into the new year or watch the countdown on TV. I might be able to catch some of the fireworks in town below from my back deck.

I'm flicking through channels to find one of the Denver networks, when my phone rings. Tahlula's name appears on the screen.

"Thought you'd have something better to do than bug me on New Year's Eve," I grumble, answering the call, but I'm hiding a smile.

My sister has always been the first, and frequently the only, to wish me a happy new year. A tradition stemming from childhood, when our mother would be mostly passed out from whatever festivities she'd taken part in the night before. Doesn't matter where we were, doing what, but by the time the clock hit midnight; we'd be side by side, either in person or on the phone.

This year, now that she has her own family, I thought for sure it would be the end of that tradition.

"Nope." She pops her P and I can hear the smile in her voice.

"Your man asleep already?" I ask, as on TV the countdown to the new year begins.

"He's grabbing me a blanket. We're on the front porch waiting for the fireworks." *...Eight—Seven—Six...* "Where are you?"

"Just got home."

...Four—Three...

"Love you, Brother."

"Ditto, Sis."

...One—Happy New Year!

"Happy New Year."

"Same to you." I hear the dull thud of fireworks in the distance.

"Evan says Happy New Year too."

"Back at him."

"Trunk?"

"Yeah, Sis."

"You okay?"

"I'm good."

"Still coming over tomorrow? I guess it's 'later' now."

"Is there gonna be a crowd?"

I hear her soft chuckle. "No crowd. Just you and Joan."

"I'll be there. Go watch the fireworks."

"Okay."

I tuck my phone back in my pocket, go to shrug on my coat, and shove my feet into a pair of old sneakers. Grabbing a beer from the fridge, I head out the sliding doors to light a smoke and watch what I can see of the fireworks.

I briefly wonder if Jaimie is watching them too.

Jaimie

"Happy New Year, sweetie."

I'm in the kitchen, waiting for the coffee to brew, when Mom walks in from the breezeway between the garage and the house.

The holidays have been rather hectic, with Mom getting in on Christmas and us spending most of that day at Tahlula's place. Then we had River's first birthday on

Saturday, the twenty-eighth, for which we had a little party here with the usual suspects: T and Hanna, Autumn with Aleksander, and even Ollie popped in.

Tahlula surprised us with the news she was pregnant again, adding to it she and Evan would be tying the knot in a simple ceremony at the courthouse on January seventeenth. When Autumn started talking showers and the like, she was quick to point out they don't want any hoopla.

We were alone in the kitchen when she asked me to be her maid of honor, which brought tears to my eyes.

Mom's stuff arrived in the big truck the day before yesterday, and with the help of Evan and some of his buddies, Mom was moved into her apartment by dinnertime. We were up there quite a bit, putting away her stuff and putzing around.

Finally, last night, we ended up spending New Year's Eve watching a movie on the ridiculously large TV in my living room, and had plans to stay up for the countdown. Instead we barely made it to eleven o'clock before we called it a night. Both of us tuckered out.

"Same to you, Mom." I quickly embrace her in a tight hug. "I'm so glad you're here."

"Me too, honey." She smiles at me before her eyes scan the living room. "Where's my grandson?"

"Still asleep." The words have barely left my mouth when the baby monitor crackles with his early morning babbles. "I stand corrected."

"Why don't you grab him, and I'll get some pancakes going for breakfast."

I lean in to kiss her cheek. "Sounds like a plan."

Twenty minutes later, we're sitting at the small dining table, River in his high chair trying to spear pieces of pancake with his plastic fork.

"Have you decided yet?" Mom asks, and I glare at her from under my eyebrows.

I know what she's referring to, but apparently she's done dropping hints. "No," I answer, a bit curtly.

Mom overheard Tony Ramirez suggesting to take me out on the town at Christmas dinner. She'd also been privy to the repeat of his offer after I came back inside, still utterly confused by Trunk's words and actions. I'd been teetering between flattered and royally pissed to have been called a distraction, and didn't trust my judgment, so I brushed him off with a, "We'll see."

"He seems like a charming man: handsome, an officer of the law at that. What's not to like?"

"I didn't say I don't like him, and I can't deny he's good-looking, but it's the charming part that has me on the fence." Not to mention the fact I'm more drawn to the rough looks and taciturn, mostly grouchy, demeanor of my best friend's brother. But I keep that to myself. "He's smooth, Mom. Too smooth. I get the sense he's looking for a quick distraction…" There's that word again. "… and not for the long-term complexities of a single mother with a toddler and a moving truck full of baggage."

"Pshaw." She flaps her hand and leans over the table. "Nothing wrong with the occasional *distraction*." She adds air quotes. "We all need a little something-something on occasion."

I clap my hands over my ears but can't stop the semi-hysterical giggle that bubbles up. "For Pete's sake, Mom. I'm mentally traumatized as it is. No need to add to that."

Mom snickers at my antics and helps River direct a piece of pancake to his mouth. "I loved only one man in my life," she shares, referring to Dad, who died much too young of cancer twenty-two years ago when I was just sixteen, "but that doesn't mean I became a nun after he passed away. Do you remember our neighbor when we lived on South York Street? Mr. Jackson?"

"La-la-la, I don't want to hear any more," I warn her. I don't want to know about my mother and the burly carpenter next door, who always smelled of sawdust.

Mom shrugs. "I'm just saying."

I'm still battling the visuals when I'm upstairs grabbing a quick shower, while Mom keeps River busy in the living room. I try to visualize Tony with me instead, but he keeps morphing into someone else. Dammit.

If I didn't know any better, I'd think my mother planned it when, just as I come down the stairs, my phone rings.

"Hello?"

"Happy New Year, darlin'." There is no mistaking the smooth sound of the detective's voice and my eyes immediately dart suspiciously to my mother.

"Same to you, Tony," I return, watching as Mom's head whips around, happy surprise on her face. I turn my back on her and wander into the laundry room off the kitchen for some privacy.

"What are you up to?"

"Not much. I think we'll have a lazy day."

"Mmm," he rumbles. "What about after you have your lazy day? There's live music at the Irish Embassy Pub on Main Street tonight. Wanna come?"

"I don't know."

"Oh come on," he pushes. "Keith and Autumn will be there, and I'm sure Joe and Ollie will show up. It's a New Year's tradition. No strings. Just a fun night out."

I'm waffling. I don't want to give off the wrong impression but the way he makes it sound, it's a gathering of friends and not a date. Through the crack in the door, I catch Mom in the kitchen trying hard not to look like she's listening in.

"Jaimie?"

"Okay, fine. What time should I be there?"

"I'll pick you up."

"Or … can always catch a ride with Joe and Ollie, that's probably easiest," I quickly suggest.

There's a brief silence on the other end before he repeats, more firmly, "I'll pick you up at eight."

I guess I can give him that, since he's not pushing for dinner or anything. Maybe it is just about listening to music with a few friends. "Eight is good." It'll give me time to get River bathed and in bed before I head out.

"See you then. And, Jaimie? I'm looking forward to it."

There it is, the sign I should've said no, but before I can bow out, he's already hung up.

"Don't worry about us," Mom says, as soon as I step out into the kitchen, not even bothering to hide the fact she was eavesdropping anymore. "We'll be fine. I'll sleep on the couch until you get home, or don't get home at all. Either way," she quickly adds when I throw her an exasperated look. "You go have fun."

"You do realize I'm thirty-eight years old, right, Mom?"

Her eyes narrow on me. "Of course. How could I forget? Every one of those years is mapped out on my face in wrinkles. I'm old, I worry, I want you to have fun. What's wrong with that?"

I raise my eyes to the ceiling and pray for calm. I hear her. I may not have understood that concept when I was younger and not a mother myself, but I get it now, annoying as it may be.

"Nothing, Mom," I concede, before changing the subject. "Wanna watch college football?" It's an old tradition, dating back to when my dad was alive. New Year's Day was spent in front of the tube, catching as many of the six college bowls as possible.

She seems to think about it, her index finger tapping her lips. "You know, I think we should change it up this year. Maybe a nice Hallmark movie instead? Something romantic to get you in the mood for your date?"

"Mother!"

"All right, already. Keep your panties on." She throws me a sneaky grin. "For now, anyway."

N
nw
ne
W
E
ARROW'S EDGE MC

4

Jaimie

"YOU LOOK LOVELY," Mom says when I come down, and I almost want to rush back upstairs to change when I see hope flicker in her eyes.

I don't want to give off the wrong impression, to her, or to Tony.

Other than mom-jeans or yoga pants, easy-to-clean tees and sweatshirts, and a handful of dreary office suits, I don't have a lot of choice in my wardrobe. I already wore my go-to dressy pants and fitted sweater at Christmas. The only other thing suitable in my closet is this rust-brown wrap dress, with long three-quarter sleeves and generous cleavage. Paired with my brown, high-heeled boots, it accentuates every goddamn curve.

"I'm not done," I tell Mom, and dive into the coat

closet in the hallway, coming up with my cropped jean jacket and quickly shrug it on. “There,” I announce. “Now I’m done.”

Apparently Mom is not exactly on board with my last minute addition. “Don’t you think that spoils the effect of the dress?” she suggests with as much tact as she can muster. Which isn’t saying a lot.

“I’m going to see live music in a bar with friends, Mom, not dining at a fine restaurant with a date.”

“Is he picking you up?” she fires back, undeterred.

“Well, yes, but—” I don’t get to finish my thought.

“Then it’s a date,” she firmly concludes.

Whatever. If she insists on deluding herself, I can’t stop her. A sharp rap on the door lets me know it’s too late for that anyway.

“If River wakes up, just give me a call, okay, Mom?”

“We’ll be fine. I raised you and you’re still breathing, aren’t you?”

“I know, but—”

“Jaimie Lynn Belcamp, open that door,” she orders, using my full name like she used to when she wanted me to know how serious she was.

I roll my eyes, much like *I* used to, and open the door.

He looks good, in a short navy blue peacoat and dark jeans. Very put-together. Very *GQ*. Very smooth. I’m trying to imagine him with baby spit all over his pressed dress shirt. I can’t.

I also can’t ignore the flowers he’s holding out to me.

“You look lovely,” he unknowingly echoes my mother’s words. Unlike my mother, though, his eyes get stuck on the sliver of cleavage still visible between the edges of my jacket. In his defense, he catches himself and his eyes shoot straight up to mine, the hint of a blush on his face.

"Thank you," I mumble, trying to avoid my mother's meaningful, 'told-ya' looks as I hand her the flowers to put in some water. Do friends bring each other flowers for a casual night out? I've been out of the game for a while, but I'm pretty sure that's not standard procedure.

"Ready for My Sticky Fingers?" I believe my mouth falls open and I hear my mother's gasp behind me. Tony looks between us, confused, until he finally clues in. "The band! That's the name of tonight's band."

Leaving my stupefied mother standing in the doorway, I quickly hustle Tony to his car in the driveway.

"I'll check in with you later, Mom, I won't be too late," I call over my shoulder, before Tony opens the door for me and I settle in the passenger seat. He climbs behind the wheel and blows out a deep breath.

"Well. That was embarrassing," he mumbles, as he backs out onto the road. Suddenly the whole situation tickles my funny bone and I snicker. "Not helping." His disgruntled words only make it worse and before long I'm laughing out loud, tears running down my face.

"I'm sorry," I manage when I can breathe again, sneaking a peek in his direction. The corner of his mouth pulls up in a smirk.

"Don't be." He suddenly chuckles. "You should've seen your face. For a second I thought you were going to slam the door in my face."

"The thought may have crossed my mind."

"I'm usually smoother," he says wistfully.

I twist in my seat to face him. "Can I be straight?" He quickly glances over and nods before turning his eyes back to the road. "I thought this was to be a few drinks with a group of friends? The flowers…"

"Too much?" he asks with a flick of his eyes.

"They're lovely, but they make me feel like maybe we're on different pages. To be blunt, I may be in the market for a new friend, but not for any romantic entanglements."

The knuckles of his hands on the steering wheel turn white, and it takes a moment before he responds, but he does it with a smile. "Can't fault a guy for trying." He shrugs as he pulls into a parking spot along Main.

"I totally get if you wanna take me back home," I offer, but to my surprise he turns to me with his eyebrows raised.

"Are you kidding?" He turns off the engine and unbuckles. "The Irish offers half-price wings when there's live music. Can't miss out on those."

Glad for the lighter note, I let him help me out of the car and even slip my arm through his as we walk to the pub.

TRUNK

"I WANT YOU to walk me down the aisle."

For the sake of Evan's mother, who is sitting right across from me at the dinner table, I've been biting my tongue. Otherwise, I might have had a thing or two to say about the fact my sister got herself knocked up so soon after the scare she had when Hanna was born.

I've been sitting here with my eyes on my empty plate, listening to the surprise wedding plans, while I try to wrap my head around the barrage of news over dinner. However, when Tahlula makes that suggestion, my eyes shoot up to meet hers.

"What?"

"You heard me," she sasses, but her eyes are shiny.

Fuck, I hate crying. Especially from my sister.

I open my mouth to answer, but no sound comes out. Clearing my throat I try again, "You want me to give you away?"

"You're the only one who can," she says, scoring another direct hit to my soul. "You're my family."

Shee-it.

"Guess I can do that, Sis, but I'm not wearing a tux, or freakin' wedding colors, or any 'a that bullshit," I grumble.

"Deal, and thank you."

Tahlula's smile is bright, and something relaxes inside me. She's happy. In all those years when it was just us; I would've given an arm to see a smile like that on her face. Now she is, even though it fucking took another man to put it there.

I glance over at Evan, who only has eyes for my sister. Sucker is so far gone, it's a miracle he remembers his own damn name. Good man, though, even if I do hate to admit it.

Hanna chooses that moment to make herself known, her angry cries don't need a baby monitor. She has a good set of lungs on her.

"I'll get her," I announce when Tahlula starts getting up, happy for a break from all the sappy wedding talk.

My niece looks nothing like me. Bright red hair and pale skin versus my own black hide. It's hard to tell we're related. Our mother was African American, but Tahlula and I are from different fathers. Mine black, and as far as we know, my sister's sperm donor was Caucasian; her skin's a lot lighter.

Hanna, well, she looks white, except maybe for her mouth and the tight curls that are starting to form in her hair. Those, and her golden-brown eyes, are all her mom's.

"Hey, girl," I mumble walking into her room.

Her little legs are kicking furiously and her arms reach for me when I lean over her crib to pick her up.

"Feeling left out?" I settle her on my arm and it only takes a second to register the smell. "You're killing me, baby," I complain. "That better not have gone up your back, or I'm calling your mother."

Luckily, the damage is minimal as I make quick work of her dirty diaper and carry her downstairs.

Tahlula nurses her in the living room while the rest of us clear the table. When the dishwasher is loaded, I announce I'm heading out.

"Where are you off to?"

"Meeting up with a few guys before I head home," I answer my sister's question.

"Oh, would you mind dropping me at home?" Joan steps out of the kitchen, drying her hands on a towel.

"I said I'd take you, Ma," Evan reminds her.

"I know, but if Titus is leaving, he'll be practically driving by my front door anyway. No need for you to get all dressed up and go out in the cold."

Evan's mother insists on calling me by my given name. Something I'm surprisingly okay with. From her anyway.

"I'll drop ya off. No problem." I walk over to the couch, planting my fists in the seat on either side of Tahlula, bringing my face close. "Proud to walk you down that aisle, Sis."

"I know." She smiles up at me and I kiss her forehead before dropping my eyes to Hanna, who looks to be half-asleep again.

"She's growing on me," I mumble, kissing her red hair.

"Liar. You're completely smitten with her."

I straighten up, trying to hide a grin. "I don't do smitten."

"Whatever. Get out of here," Tahlula waves me off.

A few minutes later, I climb behind the wheel; Joan is already buckled into the passenger seat.

"You remember where it is?"

"Right, then second right. Fifth house on the left."

"You've got it." She smiles at me before glancing out the window. I've barely made my first right when she speaks again. "You'll have to forgive an old lady for interfering, but why on earth don't you have a nice girl?

You're handsome, smart; you do respectable work. And no woman worth her salt would miss that soft side you're trying so hard to hide."

Anyone else I would've told off or ignored, but this will be my sister's mother-in-law and a nice lady to boot. I don't have the heart to do either.

"Just not my thing, Joan."

"Bullhickey." I glance over at her vehemence. "It's everybody's *thing*. Man is not an island, my dear boy. The world is a big beautiful place, all you need is someone to show you."

"Haven't seen a lot of beauty, Joan," I tell her, pulling up to the curb outside her house.

"Then maybe you haven't been looking well enough," she counters without hesitation. "Beauty was sitting right across from you at Christmas dinner, and you missed it. You also missed her looking at you. Open your eyes."

In the time it takes me to figure out what she's talking about—or rather who—she's already getting out of the truck. I quickly follow suit and hurry to join her on the sidewalk, offering her my arm, even as my thoughts drift to Jaimie.

On her front step, she puts a hand on my shoulder for balance before lifting on her toes so she can kiss my cheek.

"You're a good man, Titus."

"Have a good night, Joan," is all I can think of to say back.

Even as I walk back to my truck, I feel her words warming me from the inside out.

I hit the intersection by Main Street and sit there, undecided, part of me wanting to head north toward Jaimie's house. When a car honks behind me, I take my foot off the brake and turn south instead. A few of my brothers are waiting. I'll have that beer and, if it's not too late, maybe after I'll take a detour by her house.

Lady Luck is smiling on me when a parking spot opens up right across from the Irish.

JAIMIE

"WANT ANOTHER ONE?"

Tony has to lean down to me, his lips by my ear so I can hear him over the loud music.

The band is good, with lots of great covers of popular eighties' rock, but my ears are not as receptive to the high decibels as they once were. My head is spinning, although admittedly not only from the volume in here.

I lean back and twist my neck so I can talk directly in his ear.

"I should probably pass."

What can I say? I'm a lightweight. The two glasses of wine I had over the past couple of hours have fast gone to my head. I've already been giggling stupidly at the banter around the table, but can't seem to stop myself. No need to embarrass myself further.

"'Scuse me." I push against Tony's shoulders when I suddenly need to pee. He immediately steps aside, steadying me with a hand in the small of my back when my legs take a minute to stabilize.

Holy shit.

"I've got her," I hear Autumn say, and I turn to smile at her, almost losing my balance again. With her arm firmly around my waist, Autumn guides me to the ladies' room in the back. "Are you gonna be okay?" she asks, when I stumble out of the stall beside her and over to the sink. I have to hang on with one hand while splashing cold water on my face with the other.

"I'm good as long as I hold onto something," I assure her, sounding more confident than I feel. "That must've been some potent wine."

"They serve big glasses here," Autumn says, as she joins me by the sinks to wash her hands. "And you had four of them."

"Four?" I wince at my own piercing volume. Definitely drunk.

"Don't you remember?"

"Shit. I remember two. Only two. No wonder I'm so…"

"Hammered?" She snickers, slipping her arm around me again. "We all need to let loose every so often, girlfriend. I'm just glad I'm not you tomorrow morning."

I groan and roll my head on her shoulder as she pushes open the door and guides me through.

"I've got her."

My head snaps up at the familiar rough voice. Unfortunately, that sets off a dizzy spell and I feel my knees buckle. Autumn's arm around me is replaced by Trunk's massive ones, as he slips one around my waist and the other behind my knees, lifting me clear off the ground.

"What are you doing with my date?"

Uh-oh, I can't quite open my eyes to confirm, but I'm pretty sure that was Tony's voice. I open my mouth to protest the term 'date' but quickly close it when I'm hit with a wave of nausea.

"Taking care of her." I snuggle deeper into Trunk's arms, the vibrations of his deep rumble soothing.

"Like hell. I came with her, I can take her home."

Oh my, Tony sounds really pissed.

"You let her get pissed out of her brain on your watch, I think you've done enough."

Okay, I don't think I like that comment, but I'm too comfortable to do anything about it. I vaguely hear someone in the background say, "Let it go, Tony," and the next thing I know a blast of arctic air hits my exposed skin.

"Just a sec, Little Mama. I'll get you warmed up in no time."

That sounds really good. My mind is trying to conjure up ways he might accomplish that as I hear the beep of a car lock.

"I can walk."

"Now she tells me," he grunts, hoisting me into what I think is the cab of his truck. "Here, take this."

I don't know what he put over me but it's warm and smells of him. In seconds I'm drifting, the last thing I hear Trunk's voice.

"Lord, you try me."

5

Trunk

I LOOK BESIDE me where Jaimie is passed out; her head tilted back, her mouth partly open, sawing logs.

Oddly it doesn't take away from her appeal. At all.

I'd clocked her the moment I walked into The Irish to meet up with Honon and Paco for a few beers. She'd been completely oblivious to me; she was facing the stage and bobbing her head to the music. She was sitting at a table with the Benedettis, and Keith and Autumn Blackfoot. Keith was the only one who spotted me coming in. I didn't see Tony Ramirez until he came from the back—bathroom probably—and took a seat right next to her.

If it wasn't for Paco waving me over to the bar, I might've acted on the surge of anger boiling my blood. I managed to engage in some conversation and tried to enjoy the music, until I noticed Ramirez get real cozy with her. I was already off my stool when she suddenly pushed him off, and aided by Autumn, stumbled to the bathrooms in the back. That was enough for me.

The porch light is on when I pull in next to Jaimie's Honda in the driveway, and I can see the flicker of the TV through the living room window. Her mom is still up.

Jaimie doesn't even wake up when I open the passenger door and reach in to unbuckle her. She moans a little and snuggles her face in my neck when I lift her out.

The front door opens when I step on the porch.

"Trunk? What's wrong with her? Where is Tony?"

"She needs her bed, she's wasted," I limit myself to explaining.

Sandra steps aside and waves me inside with my load. "Is she okay?"

"Nothing a good night's sleep and a fistful of ibuprofen in the morning won't fix." I head straight for the stairs and carry her up. Jaimie isn't a big woman, but she's not exactly light either. The muscles in my arms are burning with the strain.

Her room is surprisingly sparse, no knickknacks on the dresser or mountain of pillows on her bed. It smells like vanilla. *Fuck.* Sandra comes in behind me as I drop her daughter on the mattress. I plan to beeline it out of here when she suddenly blinks her eyes open and clenches a fist in my shirt.

"Trunk? What…"

"You're home. Go back to sleep, Jaimie."

I remove her fingers from my sleeve and back out of the room when her mom starts peeling off her daughter's sexy as fuck boots. I need to get out of here.

"Thank you!" Sandra calls after me as I pound down the stairs.

When I pull the front door shut behind me, I take in a deep breath, welcoming the frigid air. It goes a long way to clearing her scent from my nostrils. I can ignore my hard dick a little longer. Not like I don't have enough experience with that.

Instead of heading home, I turn back toward The Irish. I left my brothers without explanation—although I'm sure they didn't miss my dramatic exit—and I should probably clear the air with Jaimie's friends. I'm still pissed at Ramirez, but I'd be a crap psychologist if I didn't realize that has more to do with me than it does with him.

Fuck.

Jaimie

"I've been trying to get in touch with Tahlula all week. I need to talk to her about her manuscript. Is everything okay?"

I glance in the mirror at my reflection. The dress T and I picked for me to wear clings to every one of my curves, and not for the first time, I'm having second thoughts. Thank God it's a deep navy blue, instead of some light pastel. That would've been much worse.

"More than okay, Karen," I tell Tahlula's editor, Karen

Dove. "She's getting married today. She's had her hands full trying to pull off a wedding on such short notice."

"Married? Holy crap, how come I haven't heard of this?" She sounds a little perturbed.

"It's a small affair. A courthouse wedding with family and a few friends," I quickly appease her. "They're not even going on a honeymoon, not with Hanna still so young, so things will probably just return to normal after the weekend. I'll let her know to call you, okay?"

Mollified, she answers, "Sure, that's fine. I just wanted to talk through a few final points before I send her the edits back."

"Great. Did you get the artwork for the cover sorted?" I refer to a conversation she and I had before Christmas after Tahlula rejected the first cover design. In the mirror, I see the door to my bedroom opening as Mom carries River inside. My face breaks open in a smile at the sight of my son. Mom managed to wrestle him into a tiny dress shirt, dark jeans, and tiny cowboy boots on his feet.

"I'll have something for her to look at after the weekend."

"That's good, thanks, Karen. Look, I have to get going or we'll be late. I'll let T know you called."

"Wish her all the best."

"Will do." I hang up and turn around. "He looks adorable," I tell Mom, who rolls her eyes.

"Like putting an octopus in a straight jacket," she complains before giving me a once over. "You look stunning."

I look down and run my hands over my dress. "Don't

you think it's too revealing?"

"You should flaunt those curves God graced you with," she says firmly.

Never mind my curves have curves. I feel like a stuffed sausage in the Spanx I'm forced to wear, in an attempt to smooth them all out. "I could do with a few less."

"Nonsense. I bet that boy, Trunk, would have a thing or two to say about that."

I roll my eyes. Ever since I got hammered out of my brain a few weeks ago—I wince at the memory of the massive hangover the next day—Mom seems to have forgotten all about Tony and is actively pushing Tahlula's brother on me.

I haven't seen or heard from him, and actively worked at keeping it that way.

The whole incident had been embarrassing, in hindsight. It was bad enough Tony called the next day, wanting to know how I was doing and apologizing for not keeping a better eye on me. I reminded him that was not his responsibility, but my own. Normal people wouldn't get blotto after four glasses of white wine, and frankly, before I got pregnant with River, neither would I. Then Autumn called as well, and Ollie stopped by with some ginger tea she claimed would help.

I've been keeping a low profile since, but today I'll have to come out of hiding, and looking at my formfitting, navy blue outfit, I'm doing it in a rather spectacular way. Not sure what I was thinking saying yes to this dress.

"We should get going."

"I know, I just need to put on some lip gloss and I'm

ready."

We just made our way downstairs when there's a knock at the door. One of the Benedetti boys is standing on the porch with a box in his hands, a sheepish look on his face.

"Hey, Mrs. B. Dad told me to come apologize to you. This box was left in front of our house a few weeks ago, but I was late for soccer practice and put it in the garage. I kinda forgot about it. Dad just found it on the workbench. I'm so sorry, I hope it wasn't important."

I take the small box from his hands and see my name on the label. "I'm sure it wasn't, Mason. Don't worry about it."

"Okay, Mrs. B. Sorry again." The kid hops off the porch and jogs down the driveway and across the road.

"What's that?" Mom wants to know.

"Don't know." I shove the box in the hallway closet and grab my purse. "We're going to be late."

"You look beautiful."

She does. Tahlula's gorgeous skin is set off against the ice-blue pantsuit she picked. I'm a little jealous at how stunning she looks.

"You're gonna make Evan drool."

T chuckles. "Honey, I don't need clothes for that."

"*Shee-it*, Sis. Don't need to hear that crap."

I remind myself to breathe. Trunk looks beautiful too. His massive form is poured into a sharp navy suit, and crisp white shirt, making him look so different from his usual jeans and leather.

The moment his eyes find me, I turn to Tahlula. "I should head out there." I quickly kiss her cheek, and without another look for her brother, I slip by him.

Thank goodness the only ones walking down the aisle will be the bride and her escort, so I can sneak down the side and take my spot at the front, where Evan is already waiting with Hanna in his arms and Cap, his best man, by his side.

The doors at the back of the courtroom open and all heads turn. I should be looking at the beautiful bride, but my eyes keep drifting to the man accompanying her. They stop right beside me and I hear him rumble, "Be happy, Tahlula," before kissing her forehead and turning to Evan to take their daughter.

The official portion is short but sweet, and after congratulations and a few snapshots outside the courthouse, we all troop to the Hilton along the Animas River for dinner and the reception.

"How is he holding up?" I ask Mom, who's been keeping River occupied.

"He's fine, but if you want, I can take him home," she offers.

"You don't need to. Tahlula arranged for babysitting right at the hotel. She didn't want to be too far from Hanna, since she's still nursing. Ollie's daughter, Trinny, is looking after them. She'll have Aleksander as well, so River will have his buddy to play with."

We barely find our seats, after dropping River off with

Trinny, when the bride and groom are announced. My heart aches a little at how happy they look when they walk in. Hand in hand and smiling wide, as Evan twirls his wife around. Strains of Ed Sheeran's "Perfect" fill the air the moment they hit the dance floor.

They do little more than sway and stare into each other's eyes, but it's so sweet, I have to brush away a stray tear. Suddenly Cap is standing in front of me, his hand out.

"They want us up there."

Right, wedding party duties.

I let him lead me onto the dance floor and try to follow his lead. A bit of a challenge, since the man appears to have two left feet and no rhythm. I'm concentrating so hard not to get my toes stepped on; I don't notice that the dance floor has filled up.

"Mind if I cut in?"

I look up, startled at Trunk's gruff voice.

"Thank, God," Cap mumbles in a pained voice. I should probably be offended, but I'm too busy noting Trunk's large hands replacing Cap's. An electric current spreads from where he touches the small of my back and my hand, which he presses against his wide chest.

Unlike his predecessor, Trunk can move, and despite my inability to speak, my feet effortlessly follow his around the dance floor.

We still haven't spoken when Ed Sheeran morphs into the next song. People around us leave, but Trunk's dark eyes keep me in place.

"You're beautiful."

I feel the vibration of his deep timbre down to the tips of my toes, and I almost stumble with the impact of his words. His arm tightens, pulling me flush against his body and my fingers curl into his biceps in response.

I've heard people wax poetic about the world disappearing, but I've never quite experienced it. Until now.

Those eyes, I might've thought hard and judgmental before, are now soft and warm. Hot, even. They make me believe his words.

"If you would please return to your seats, the first course is about to be served."

The DJ's voice is like a bucket of ice water.

I feel almost bereft when Trunk's arm disappears from around me, but he keeps my hand firmly in his as he takes me back to the table, and to my surprise, takes the seat next to mine. I'm not sure what is happening, but when I look up, I see both my mother and Joan smiling as if they just shared a secret.

"Titus Maximus Rae," Tahlula teases from the other side of the table. "I thought you said you didn't dance?"

"Shut up, Sis," Trunk growls at his sister who grins at him, unimpressed.

Under the table, he keeps a firm hold on my hand until dinner is served, then he lets go, giving my knee a squeeze before he digs into his meal. It takes me another minute to realize I'm the only one not eating and I quickly grab my fork.

What just happened?

TRUNK

THE MOMENT I see that fool blundering all over Jaimie's feet on the dance floor, all my good intentions blow right out of the water.

Fucking hell.

I knew I'd ventured too close to the edge when I brought her home from the pub. I'd even gone back to clear the air with her friends after virtually kidnapping her from under their noses. They seemed mostly amused, which annoyed me, except for Ramirez who was put out and let me know it, which pissed me off.

Honon and Paco thought the whole thing was hysterical, and spent the next half hour ribbing me, until I threw a few bills on the bar and stalked out of there. For the second time that night.

Shee-it, the woman had me all turned upside down. So I steered clear.

Until today.

I didn't think seeing her would have quite the impact it did. That dress helped. Those innocent eyes, over those sinful curves, almost did me in. Good thing she beelined it out of there before I could make a fool of myself in front of my sister.

I stopped to have a smoke outside when the couple made their grand entrance, only peeking in a few minutes later to find Evan's boss stumbling all over Jaimie.

Those blue startled eyes looking up at me, her pink lips falling open when I turned her in my arms. Suddenly, none of my reservations mattered much when she felt so perfect against me.

Over dinner, I touch her as much as I think I can get

away with. I even drag her back on the dance floor a time or two, something my sister apparently finds hilarious.

Although Jaimie eventually starts taking part in the conversation around the table, she's yet to say a single word to me.

"I'll drop Jaimie later," I tell Sandra, who just mentioned being ready to go home.

"Perfect, I'll just grab River and take her car," her mother announces.

"Excuse me," Jaimie speaks up sharply, and all heads turn her way. "You're talking about me like I'm not even here." Her first dirty look goes to her mother, but the next is reserved for me.

The fire shooting from her eyes has me instantly hard. Fuck, call me a fool, but I love that sharp tongue of hers.

"I'm perfectly capable getting myself home. I'm thirty-eight, not twelve. I don't need my mother and…" She seems momentarily lost for words, before finishing with, "…whatever you are, making plans for me."

"Okay," her mother drawls, with an air of patience. "So you want to leave now too?"

Jaimie swings her head around and bulges her eyes at her mother. "I didn't say that."

Sandra throws her hands in the air. "Fine, figure it out by yourself, I'm getting River and heading home in your car. Come or stay, whatever you decide."

Jaimie sputters under her breath as her mother says her goodbyes. "I'll stay until they cut the cake," she finally says. "I won't be long."

Not long turns out to be another couple of hours

exercising patience for me, until I can finally escort her to my truck and help her in. The moment I slide behind the steering wheel, I lean over, wrap my hand around the back of her neck, and pull her close, covering her lips with mine. She gasps into my mouth and I take the opportunity to taste her deeply.

Fuck me, she even tastes like vanilla.

Her tongue is tentative as mine boldly sweeps her mouth, but one of her hands has found its way to the back of my head, holding me close. The sharp sting of her nails on my scalp tells me she's as much into this as I am.

When she moans softly down my throat, I break away from those sweet lips. I have no choice; otherwise, I'll have her fucking riding me in the middle of the parking lot.

"Holy shit," she mumbles, touching a few fingers to her swollen lips.

"Yup."

I press the heel of my hand against my dick, willing it back into submission before I start the engine. Fat chance of that happening.

Shee-it.

N
nw
ne
W
E
ARROW'S EDGE MC

6

TRUNK

"YEAH," I SNARL into the phone.

My eyes stay on Jaimie, who is still breathing hard from the scorching kiss I just planted on her.

"Are you still in town?" Ouray's voice sounds rushed on the other end.

"Yeah. Why?"

Jaimie starts squirming, but I use my free arm and hips to keep her pinned against the wall next to her front door.

"Security company called, silent alarm is going off at the gym. Cops are en route, could you meet them there? Bubba is on his way, but he's coming from Cortez. You have a key, right?"

I do have a key. Most of the brothers do. We have

workout space in one of the garages at the compound, but in the winter months it gets pretty cold in there, so we head into town. I do most of my workouts during the night; I don't sleep a lot.

The gym is owned by the club, as is the yoga studio next door, and they're only a few minutes away.

"I'll check it out."

I end the call and stuff the phone back in my pocket, before slipping a hand up Jaimie's spine and into her hair. A slight tug brings her head back and I slam my mouth over hers, sweeping my tongue between her lips for a last taste.

"I gotta go," I mumble against her mouth when I come up for air. "Be in touch."

I'm already walking to the truck when she calls out.

"Wait!" She shakes her head to clear it before focusing squinted eyes on me. "What the hell happened? What are we doing here?"

"Don't have time for that now, James. Like I said, I'll be in touch."

Something tells me she doesn't like my response when she throws me a dirty look before letting herself inside, immediately turning off the outside lights. No time to worry about that now.

There are two patrol cars in the parking lot when I pull up to the building.

"Are you Trunk?" one of the officers asks when I get out of my truck.

"That'd be me. What've we got?"

He walks ahead of me to where the bottom glass panel

on the door to the gym has been knocked out. Glass is everywhere. "Stay behind us while we clear the place," he says, pulling open the door that was left unlocked.

I follow them inside. Before I have a chance to flick on the lights, I can already smell the wet paint.

"Jesus."

Every wall, including the large mirror where the weights are stacked, is covered in red paint. Splashes, lightning bolts, tags and what looks like a fist with the middle finger extended.

"Check this out," one of the officers walks up to the boxing ring, where a huge red puddle is spreading over the canvass.

"Shit. Must've been more than one," I suggest, amazed at the amount of damage done in what couldn't have been that long between the alarm going off and the cops getting here.

"Two or three at least. Bunch of punks, probably. We've had some vandalism around town. May be the same kids."

"Hey, Conley!" the other officer yells from the back room. "Looks like they left out the back. Found a can."

Twenty minutes later, another patrol car has joined the first two outside the gym, and a female officer is taking pictures and collecting evidence, when Tony Ramirez walks in.

"What've we got?" he directs at Officer Conley after only a nod my way.

It's not that he and I were ever what you'd call friends, but it's clear I'm not his favorite person right now. Not that I give a fuck.

While Conley fills Tony in, I slip outside to have a smoke. I pull out my phone to send a quick message to Kaga, when Bubba's ancient Volvo 244 pulls into the parking lot.

Bubba Williams is a former heavyweight boxing champ who manages the gym for Arrow's Edge.

"Fuck me," he growls, taking in the broken glass in front of the door.

"Wait 'til you see the inside." I crush the butt under my boot before following him in.

"Sonofabitch." The other man stops in the middle of the gym, his eyes on the floor of the boxing ring.

"Bubba." Tony comes walking from the back of the building and shakes the hand of the big black man. It shouldn't surprise me they know each other. A lot of local first responders prefer this gym to the two larger ones on the south side of town. "Have you had any troubles lately? Anyone come in and give you a hard time?"

"No more than usual."

"Any idea—"

Bubba holds up his hand to cut Tony off and tilts his head to the side. "Hear that?"

I concentrate on listening, but all I hear is a sporadic ticking in the overhead pipes or maybe the ductwork.

"Water running," he clarifies. "Where's that coming from?"

We spread out to check any taps or toilets in the locker rooms and the small kitchen in the back. "Nothing in here," Tony concludes.

"There's a tap at the back of the building," Bubba suggests, already moving to the back door.

Outside, the female officer is walking around with a flashlight, looking through the brush. She looks up when we step through the door.

"Hey, watch where you're going."

"It's okay, Smith," Tony calls out from behind me. "Have you noticed any water running?"

The woman cocks a thumb over her shoulder. "Not sure where that hose is leading, but it's feeding into something. I assumed an irrigation system or something."

Bubba is already on the move and curses loudly. "Those fuckers!"

The plain garden hose looks like it was shoved in a vent at about shoulder height on the back of the yoga studio next door. Bubba yanks it out and I quickly turn off the tap.

"Do you have a key?" I ask him and he holds up his key ring.

There are a couple of inches of water on the floor when we walk in, and the hardwood floor moves under our feet.

"I'm calling Ouray," Bubba announces, pulling out his phone as I splash through the water to the back room, where I find a kitchenette with one of those stackable washer/dryer units against the far wall. The hose behind it feeds right to the vent visible on the outside.

"What do you think?" I ask Ramirez when I step outside. "Look like just some kids to you?"

He shakes his head slowly.

"If I were you guys, I'd keep an eye out."

Jaimie

I'll be in touch, my ass.

I feel like a goddamn yo-yo, being reeled in only to be flung away again. Been there, done that, and I didn't even get a T-shirt.

I knew he'd be bad for me. I just knew it.

When he literally swept me off my feet, like some kind of movie hero, and carried me out of the bar, the thin shield I was holding up already started cracking. Granted, I kept a low profile after that embarrassing episode, but he was nowhere to be seen either.

Then the wedding, that's where he figuratively swept me off my feet; first on the dance floor and later with those soul-melting kisses. Only to disappear again.

Tahlula and Evan got married almost three weeks ago. *Asshole*. Nineteen days since he pressed me up against my own damn porch and mauled me stupid—not that I'm counting.

Luckily, I've been able to stick close to home, busy updating Tahlula's website, dealing with a decent backlog in emails, and scheduling social media posts for the next few months. Unfortunately, I have to venture out this afternoon, and it's snowing like mad.

Tahlula has a conference call with her entire publishing team about the upcoming release of *Mens Rea.* She wants me there, which means I need to shovel the damn driveway so I can back my Honda out.

The past few snowstorms Ollie plowed my driveway, but she's not home. She, Joe, and the kids are off for a few weeks in the Bahamas, visiting Joe's parents, so any snow clearing is on me.

I dive down into the hallway closet to dig out my boots.

"How about pork chops for dinner?" Mom calls from the kitchen.

"I don't care, Mom," I snap, irritated as I pull stuff from the bottom of the closet that has become the catchall for stuff without a proper home. Newspapers, River's baby carrier he's long outgrown, an old diaper bag, a box, a sweater, and about ten pairs of flip-flops—as well as my boots.

I toss everything back and am about to return the small box to the closet when I remember Joe's son, Mason, dropping it off last month. It had been delivered to their place by accident. I toss it on the hall table instead and shove my feet into the boots.

"You know…" Mom comes walking out of the kitchen and stops a few feet from me, her hands on her hips. "You've been in a foul mood for weeks. Snapping at me, impatient with River, grumbling and scowling the rest of the time. What on earth has gotten into you?"

Suddenly flushed with guilt, I run my hands over my face. I know she's right. "I'm sorry, Mom, it's just…"

"That boy? Trunk?"

I snort. "Uhh, hardly a boy, Mom."

"I saw you, you know. The night of the wedding. Didn't mean to spy, but I heard a phone ringing outside and looked out the window."

I blush at the thought my mother was a witness to

that carnal kiss. It stole my breath and did a few other things to my body besides. "It was just…it didn't mean anything."

"Bullhickey! You don't fool me."

"Mom, I've gotta go," I dismiss her, reaching for the door. "Otherwise, I'll be late."

"So pork chops then," she calls after me, and I can't help smile.

I give her a thumbs-up before I walk out the door.

It's coming down good. I pull the hood of my jacket up and tug on my gloves before making my way to the garage to grab the shovel. There has to be at least ten or so inches piled on my Honda already.

It's backbreaking work and I'm already sweating buckets underneath my coat, when I hear the sound of a car door closing and then footsteps crunching up the driveway.

"Gimme that."

The next moment the shovel is yanked from my hands, and Trunk's big form starts clearing the drive without even giving me a look. The heat underneath my thick coat ratchets up a notch and I swear steam starts coming from my ears.

"What are you doing here?"

He tosses a big pile of snow in the front yard before turning to me. "Tahlula called me. She said you were heading to her place for work, and she was worried you might not get out of your driveway." As if that is satisfactory explanation, he turns his back to me and goes back to work.

"So you're only here because your sister sent you?"

His shovel stops mid-scrape and he drops his head between his shoulders. "*Shee-it.*"

"What makes you think I want you here if you don't wanna be here?"

He slowly turns around. "Been busy."

"That's nice," I snap. "But I don't really care." I step around him, snagging the shovel from his hands and attack the snow. "I've got this."

"Jaimie…"

"Don't 'Jaimie' me, Trunk. Let's just go back to ignoring each other."

I push a pile of snow off to the side and turn back to the driveway, when I find him standing right in front of me. He grabs the shovel from my hand and tosses it in the snowbank, snagging me around the waist with his other arm.

"You—" That's all I manage before his mouth slams down on mine. The hard, closed-mouthed kiss is as effective as the hungry one from weeks ago was. My hands grab onto his biceps for stability, and his groan vibrates against my lips when my fingers dig in.

"Fuck, James," he mumbles when he lifts his mouth.

It takes me a minute to find my equilibrium, but once I do, I don't hesitate hauling back and punching him squarely in the gut. It's like slamming your fist into a brick wall.

"Fucking hell," I yelp, tears stinging my eyes as I shake the pain from my hand. Then I twist from his hold and run back to the house before I make even more of a fool of myself.

"He's an asshole," I tell Mom, who looks up when I come storming inside. I kick off my boots and shrug out of my coat before taking the stairs two at a time.

By the time I get out of the shower, I've had my little private meltdown and quickly dig my phone out of my jeans pocket. My call goes straight into voicemail.

"T? I'm running a little late. Just start without me, I'll be there as soon as I can."

When I get downstairs, River is awake and playing on the floor.

"Mama!" he cries out when he sees me, stretching out his arms to be lifted.

"Hey, kiddo." I snuggle him in my arms, when Mom walks up.

"What was that all about?" she asks, taking River from me.

"He drives me mad, that's all," I share, grabbing my purse, and putting on my coat and boots. "I shouldn't be more than a couple of hours."

"Go. We'll be fine."

I kiss River's head, Mom's cheek, and walk out the door.

Both my SUV and the driveway are cleared of snow.

N
nw
ne
W
E
ARROW'S EDGE MC

7

TRUNK

"WHERE WERE YOU?"

Ouray is waiting outside, having a smoke, when I drive up to the compound.

Tensions have been high these past weeks. The vandalism to the gym and the yoga studio had only been the start of a series of what appears to be targeted problems plaguing the club.

We'd still been cleaning up the paint and water damage when Justin—the manager at the Brewer's Pub, another of the club's businesses in town—called to let Ouray know the inspector had just shut the restaurant down for a host of critical health violations. Everything from unexplained rodent droppings in the bins of dry foods, reports of food poisoning from diners, to a sewer back up, had left a big damning Public Health Inspection warning on the front doors of the restaurant. In all its years in operation, the Brewer's Pub had not received as much as a warning before.

The last drop in the bucket had been a cockroach infestation at the River's Edge Apartment building, also owned by the club.

Within a month, the Arrow's Edge's reserves—already limited during the winter season—have been decimated. The short-term cost of clean up brought the club to its knees, and there's no telling what the long-term impact might be.

In short, we're scrambling, to the point there's talk of pooling some of our personal resources to keep the club afloat. Despite attempts at keeping the problems from the young ones currently in our care, the unrest among the brothers is filtering through to them, which is where I come in.

"Had a stop to make before coming in," I answer without further explanation. "What's the latest?"

I calmly wait out a scrutinizing glare from Ouray, until he finally let's his eyes drift off. "Nosh caught two of the boys sneaking out of the kitchen after breakfast, half the damn pantry in their pockets."

Hmm, the natives are getting restless. It makes sense for street kids to go look for the security of food first. I get it.

"Who?"

We currently have five boys ranging from nine to fifteen living here. Matt was the latest addition. The other four kids already have their club names. It's a tradition Ouray started back when he took over the hammer many years ago. A way to make the boys feel included, part of the tribe. It also serves to let them have a fresh start, one without the trauma some of them endured since a very young age that may be attached to their given names. Matt is a rare holdout. The teenager has a chip on his shoulder the size of Texas, and aside from his disinterest in securing a club name; we still don't have much information on how he ended up on the street. The kid isn't sharing, and so far, we haven't been successful digging into his past.

Probably part of why I fully expect him the first to be named.

"Ezhno and Istu," Ouray lists, surprising me. "I already had a talk with them. They're in my office doing schoolwork."

Istu I can see. The youngest, he's also the one who still scarfs down his meals like it's his last one. Most of the kids do that initially, until they start believing there's always a next meal. Istu doesn't believe yet.

Ezhno is a surprise. He's probably the quietest of the bunch. Solitary but observant. There isn't much he misses, but it's difficult to gauge what he does with all that information.

"Mind if I use your office?"

He waves his hand. "Be my guest."

When I walk into the clubhouse I see Ahiga and Matt sitting at the dining room table, books open in front of them.

Most of the kids are shuttled to the public school in Durango daily. Ahiga is hearing-impaired and for lack of better options for him locally, he's being home-schooled. Matt's legal status with the club is still uncertain, so we can't enroll him in public school yet. Since he and Ahiga are about the same age, he tags along in Ahiga's program. With ease, from what I understand. The kid is bright.

His eyes dart up at me the moment I walk in the door, only to drop back to his workbook without any reaction.

I sign a *Hello* to Ahiga when he notices me. I'm pretty decent using ASL, and have no problem holding a conversation. Sign language has come in handy working with some of the autistic children in the hospital program in Denver.

The two pantry-raiders look up with guilt advertised all over their faces when I walk into Ouray's office.

"Boys. Wanna put those pens down for a minute and come sit here?" I point at the worn leather couch against the wall. Both boys comply, and I wait until they're squirming uncomfortably in their seats before I pull one of the visitor chairs around and sit down facing them. "What's the deal?"

Istu looks sideways at the older boy, who is staring at the tips of his sneakers. "We was hungry," he says, turning back to me.

I sit back, cross an ankle over the opposite knee, and fold my arms behind my head. "Huh. Hungry? Didn't Momma just feed you guys a big breakfast like she does every morning?"

"Well…yeah, but what if we got hungry later?"

"*Shut up,*" I hear Ezhno whisper under his breath before he darts a furtive glance my way.

Dropping my foot back to the ground with a thump, I lean forward with my elbows on my knees, pinning the older boy with my eyes. "You missed a meal since you came here, Ezhno? Ever? You think Momma's gonna let you go hungry? Ever?" My only response is a shrug of his shoulders.

I get the sense I won't be able to get more than that out of him. Rather than try to push the issue now, I decide to let both boys stew for a bit longer.

"Just so you know, it won't be up to me to decide on consequences for your actions—that's up to Momma and Ouray—but I can tell you that honesty goes a long way." I send each of them a firm look. "I'll be in my office across the hall for the next hour, should either of you want to come clean. Choose wisely."

"Any luck?" Ouray is waiting in my office.

I shake my head. "I could probably get Itsu to talk, but I don't want to pressure him. I get the sense this isn't just about pilfering food from the pantry."

"I'll talk to Wapi," Ouray suggests. "See if he's picked up on any talk."

Wapi is one of the two prospects assigned to the boys' dorm, a repurposed barn between Nosh and Momma's place and the clubhouse. He and Shilah rotate weeks supervising the boys during the night.

"Let me know. Any news on what's going to happen at the apartments?"

"Exterminator is scheduled to tent the building and

fumigate this weekend. I'm looking at twenty-two fucking tenants and their families displaced from their home for two to three days. Aside from the cost of the exterminator, the cost of alternate lodging for the tenants is costing a whack. I wouldn't be surprised if the bill attached to this latest clusterfuck is over twenty grand."

"Shee-it. Anything I can do, brother?"

He runs both hands over his face. The man has aged ten years over the past few weeks. "Stay on top of the boys, will ya? We've got enough shit piling up from outside the club, don't need any here at home."

"No problem, Chief."

I watch him leave the office; his shoulders slumped. I wouldn't want that kind of responsibility on mine. Good thing he has a family to go home to at night.

My thoughts immediately jump to Jaimie, and all the ways I'm fucking things up with her.

I end up waiting two hours—time spent doing a lot of soul-searching—but when the boys still haven't shown by five, I get up and close my office door behind me.

My turn to face the music.

Jaimie

"Is everything okay?"

I'm quickly jotting down the last of the details worked out during the long conference call, when Tahlula turns to me. She'd already been on the call when I came in, so we haven't had a chance to chat.

"Fine," I answer a little cautiously. I don't exactly feel

like sharing all the conflicted feelings I have around her brother.

"Did Trunk get there in time to dig you out?"

To hide the flush suddenly heating my face, I bend down to tuck my notepad and pen in my purse. "He did."

"So?"

I take in a deep breath before plastering what I hope is an impassive expression on my face and sit up. "Sorry, what?"

The knowing grin on Tahlula's face is a warning. "Girl, you do realize everyone witnessed what happened at my wedding, right?"

"It was just a dance." I don't bother denying I know exactly what she's talking about.

"Is that what you've been telling yourself? Let me enlighten you then; it was the first time I've ever seen Trunk dance. With anyone. Anywhere. At any time." She clearly punctuates each statement until I'm rolling my eyes.

"All right, I get it. He doesn't dance." I lean forward over the table, tapping my index finger on the table. "Well, he was dancing with me, and then he was kissing me in his truck, and on my porch, and then he disappeared without a word for three fucking weeks, T. And *then*, he shows up at my house because *you* sent him, takes over without even a howdy-doo, let alone an explanation to what the fuck happened with him saying he'd be in touch. You know what he did? He kissed me *again*... asshole. What am I supposed to do with that, T?"

A throat clears behind me and my head whips around

to find Evan leaning in the doorway to the office. "Don't mind me," he says, lifting his hands defensively before turning to his wife. "Hanna's having a nap and I'm running out to the store. Do you need anything?"

"No, babe. I'm good."

"Jaimie? Anything?" I just shake my head. "For what it's worth; my brother-in-law may have been shortchanged in social skills and is tragically lacking in finesse, but his heart is big and in the right place."

When he disappears, Tahlula puts a hand on my arm. "He's right, you know. Trunk looks like an ogre, and half the time acts like one too, but he's a good man. It's not really my place to tell you what drives him, but I hope you'll give him a chance."

"Okay, *now* I'm annoyed you guys are messing with my perfectly good snit," I grumble, standing up and slinging my purse around my shoulder. "I'm going home. Mom's making pork chops."

"Pork chops?" Tahlula does her best to hide her grin.

"Don't laugh. Mom's serious about her pork chops, so I can't be late. I'll talk to you tomorrow."

Her lusty laugh follows me down the stairs and out the door.

Sometime during the afternoon it stopped snowing. Traffic is still light, though, and it doesn't take me that long to pull onto my street. I almost slam on the brakes when I see the big black truck parked by the curb in front of my house.

Sonofabitch.

So much for a quiet night of pork chops and

contemplation.

I'll hear him out, but then he'll listen to me, and God forbid if he tries to shut me up with that lethal mouth of his.

He's sitting on the couch when I walk in, River standing by his knees. Trunk's dark bald head bending low to my son's blond one. Mom is in the kitchen, a smile teasing her mouth as she looks at me.

"Mama!"

"Hey, kiddo. Give me a minute, okay?" Apparently River doesn't want to wait a minute. He drops to his hands and knees and races over while I'm still taking off my coat and boots. He started walking just after Christmas but still prefers crawling when he's in a hurry, like now.

I toss my gloves and coat on the hall table and bend down just in time to scoop him up. His little hands clap on my cheeks when I kiss his little face.

"Miss me, kiddo?"

"Mama."

"Yes, baby. Mama is home."

His little legs start pumping. "Da, da."

"You want down?" I set him on his feet and keep hold of one hand. He toddles immediately back to the couch, where Trunk is watching our every move with those dark, ebony eyes.

"I asked Trunk to stay for dinner," Mom announces from the kitchen. She doesn't even have the decency to turn around so I can burn her with my glare. It slides right off her back. "Dinner coming up. Maybe you want to get him a fresh beer?"

My eyes dart to the coffee table where an empty bottle is sitting, evidence he's been here a while. Great. He's still looking at me when I glance over, his face is as impassive as ever, but I swear his eyes are amused. I have to squash the urge to stick out my tongue at him.

I do as Mom asks and fetch him another beer. When I hand it over, his fingers purposely brush over mine and an involuntary shiver runs up my arm. Our eyes lock, but when Mom announces food is on the table, I yank my hand back and pick River off the floor, carrying him to his high chair.

Mom does most of the talking during dinner, with mostly monosyllabic responses from both Trunk and me.

"It was good, Mrs. Belcamp. Thanks."

"You're welcome, and call me Sandra," Mom says, her smile bright as she gets up from the table. "Now, if you kids wouldn't mind cleaning up, my grandson and I have a date with *Jeopardy* up in your bedroom. Don't we, buddy?"

Before I can launch a protest, Mom lifts my son from his seat and disappears upstairs with him. I'm left with Trunk, who raises an eyebrow at me.

"What do you want, Trunk? Why are you here? Again?"

"I fucked up," he says, pushing back from the table and stacking the empty plates before carrying them to the kitchen.

Okay, I have to admit that's a pretty strong start, so I grab at the serving dishes and follow.

"Shoulda called. Shit went nuts at the club, and I didn't."

"Not sure that helps your case," I warn him, opening the dishwasher and stacking in the rinsed plates he hands me.

"Don't bust my balls, James. I'm trying. The shit at the club, it's starting to look serious. It's impacting everyone, including the kids. Everyone's on edge."

"Can I make a suggestion?" He nods, handing me the cutlery. "Why don't you try telling me what's going on here? What do you want with me? Because to be honest, my head is spinning. One minute you're up in my space, and the next moment you're gone." He leans a hip against the counter and crosses his arms over his chest, but he listens intently. "I've been a convenience before, Trunk. It doesn't feel good, and I don't—"

I promised myself I would not let him shut me up with another kiss, but when his big hands cup my face and he touches my nose with his, before brushing his lips over mine, I'm putty in his hands. "You're not a convenience. You're not. As for what's going on; fuck if I know, but I can't seem to stay away from you. I don't know if that's an answer that'll satisfy you, but it's the only one I've got. This, sitting down for a family dinner with a woman, is new to me. I'm discovering I like it. I like a lot of things about you."

My hands come up to grab his wrists, and I lift on my toes to press a soft kiss to his mouth.

"It's a good answer, Trunk."

He blows out a hard breath.

"Well, thank fuck for that."

8

Jaimie

"HOW ABOUT WE just do the New York one? You could fly in the night before, and head out after the signing. We'll take care of everything else."

I called Karen the moment I finished reading her email. She'd mentioned sending me a detailed schedule for the release of *Mens Rea* next month, but she never mentioned anything during the conference call about back-to-back bookstore signings. Four of them: Boston, New York, Baltimore, and Washington DC.

I told her right off the bat that wouldn't fly with Tahlula, which didn't appear to surprise her. She was probably aiming for the New York one all along, hoping we'd agree to the lesser demand if she started high.

"You know I can't make decisions like that without

consulting her first."

"Sure, but maybe remind her of her contractual obligations regarding promotion." There it is; the not so veiled threat. I swallow a sharp retort. "Our team could work with just the one appearance at the Union Square store if we did a morning and an afternoon session. Schedule a few interviews in between. A one-day deal, in and out."

"I'll talk to her." That's as much of a commitment I'm willing to make.

The travel isn't a big deal for me, I have Mom to take care of River, but T is still nursing Hanna and for her it would be more complicated.

"I'll need a firm answer by tomorrow afternoon, so we can set this up."

"You'll have it. Talk to you soon." I quickly end the call before I'm tempted to show her the sharp side of my tongue.

I pull the release schedule up on my laptop and try to fit in the trip to New York. It'll make for a tight fit, but it's doable. The next month is going to be hectic.

I mentioned as much to Trunk the other night, when he asked me out on a date. It had been a bit of a surprise. He didn't seem like the kind of guy to do the whole dating thing. When I mentioned that, he told me he never took the time before. He seemed to get by just fine with quick and easy hook-ups he shut down the moment expectations exceeded what he was willing to invest. Which apparently had been limited to time in bed.

His honesty had been a little disconcerting. My own

dating life before marriage had been active enough, but I'd never been what could be considered an easy lay. A guy had to invest some time and attention before I'd think about sleeping with him. Not necessarily a good girl, just selective as to who I wanted to share my body with.

"I'd like to earn that right," he'd said, making my panties melt on the spot, before asking me out for dinner this weekend. Tomorrow night in fact.

Dinner I could do, but I warned him that time is not always my own with a young child and the current work demands around his sister's upcoming release. He assured me he could be patient: that the promise of having me naked in his arms would be enough.

I had my doubts around that.

The possibility of getting naked with Trunk has been at the forefront of my mind ever since, and the closer we get to Friday, the more antsy I become. Mostly because I don't know how far he'll take things, given the chance, or how far I'll allow him to go. I don't seem to have much restraint when he has his hands on me.

"Jaimie!"

"Up here," I call out to Mom. Luckily River, who is napping in his room on the other side of the upstairs landing, is a heavy sleeper.

She sticks her head around the door to my office. "I was just tidying up downstairs and found this." She holds out the box I last saw on the hall table before I tossed my coat over it.

"I keep forgetting about that."

It's addressed to me, but there's no sender, just an Amazon logo on the side of the box. I grab the scissors off my desk and slice through the tape. When I pull out the packing material and see what's inside, it takes me a moment to register, before I fling it on the floor.

"What is it?" Mom bends over to pick up the box at her feet. "Is this some sick joke?" She holds up the toddler-sized camouflage pajamas sporting 'Daddy's Little Hunter' on the front.

Not hearing a word from my ex or his lawyer since our divorce became official had made me complacent, indulging in the wish for that chapter of my life to be over. One look at the package brings home how foolish I've been.

There is no doubt in my mind it's his doing, despite the fact he'll likely spend the rest of his life in jail. He's been found guilty from possession of illegal firearms to attempted murder, and everything in between. On top of that, the FBI is still looking into their suspicions around the militant nationalist group he was involved with. Despite the poor state of my marriage, I'd been absolutely clueless and beyond shocked to discover the revolting ideology he subscribed to. Not to mention the sick realization he'd been leading a double life almost the entire duration of our marriage.

"Rob?" Mom guesses accurately before she starts digging through the box. "There's an envelope."

"Put it down, Mom," I say urgently when she tries to hand it to me. "Put it down on my desk." I immediately pick up my phone and dial Keith Blackfoot.

"Do you remember when it was delivered across the street?"

Special Agent Gomez has been letting Detective Blackfoot do most of the talking until now.

"It must've been early January. I remember the Benedetti boy saying it had been in their garage a few weeks already, and he brought it over the day of Tahlula and Evan's wedding. I didn't look at it too closely because we were already late." I look at the box on the coffee table. "What I don't get is why it would have my name and address, but it was dropped off across the street? How he has my address to begin with?"

"Not sure," Blackfoot answers. "Let me give the boss a call." He gets up and steps outside.

"Anything you can think of that might've triggered this?" Gomez asks when door closes behind the detective.

"River's birthday," Mom pipes up.

"When was that?"

"Three days after Christmas," I confirm.

"That could do it," he mumbles, using a pen to turn the card he carefully fished out of the envelope to face him.

> Bone of my bones and flesh of my flesh,
> remember he is MY blood.
>
> My son,
> take your hunting gear, your quiver and bow,
> and go out in the field to hunt some game for me, then
> wash your feet in the blood of the wicked.

TRUNK

"I GREW UP in Denver with my mother and my sister. I never knew my dad. All I know is he was black, but my sister's father was white."

I keep an eye on Matt as I share a little of my upbringing, in a last ditch effort to get the kid to talk. Maybe if I can see a reaction to something I tell him, I can wedge open that door.

So far, no reaction at all. Fuck, but the kid is tough. Time for the heavy stuff.

"My mother was an addict and a drunk. She couldn't hold down a job, other than spreading her legs when she needed her next fix. There were periods of time when she tried to be a parent, but most of the time the parenting was up to me. We moved around a lot. Most of the time she was able to find a roof over our heads, but there were times we lived on the street."

A tiny spark of interest shows in his face, but he quickly slides the impassive mask back in place.

"I'm not gonna tell you what all I did, but I was doing my part bringing in money—or food—from the time I was eight years old. When I was fourteen, I stole a car from a neighbor in the trailer park we'd been living in for a while, so I could drive my mother to the hospital. A john had beaten the crap out of her."

That earns me a wince. Going in for the kill.

"I'd just turned eighteen and my sister was fifteen when we found her lying on the couch. She'd overdosed and choked on her own puke."

Immediately his eyes dart out the small window, avoiding mine, but I see a muscle in his jaw ticking.

"You have a mom, Matt? Is she waiting for you?"

A knock at the door draws a loud curse from me. Wapi sticks his head inside.

"You best have a damn good reason," I bite off.

"Ouray says it's urgent."

Fuck.

I glance at Matt, who turns his head to me, a triumphant grin on his face. *Jesus.* I just spilled my guts, could stand to lose my license to practice after the unorthodox treatment tactics, and the kid thinks it's funny.

"We'll pick this up later, Matt." Wapi steps aside to let him pass. "Where is Ouray?"

"Office."

Ouray is sitting at his desk when I walk in. "Have a seat."

"What's up?" I almost add he interrupted a near breakthrough with Matt, but swallow it. In hindsight, I may not have been as close as I'd hoped.

"I just got a call from Joyce Mangiane, from Child Protective Services in Monticello. You'll remember we've worked with her before." His eyes drift out the window as he continues, "Three days ago, a boy was found in a local park. Unconscious and severely beaten. He's since woken up, but they have no idea who he is or where he's from, and the kid won't talk."

My hands are clenched in fists at the thought of someone beating up a child. It sickens me. I'm not sure why Ouray is telling me about a kid in Monticello, but

I'm sure he has his reasons. I don't have to wait long.

"Joyce says local police have been unable to match him with any missing child reports, and questioning him is almost impossible. Any time someone tries to approach him, he becomes like a caged animal. Joyce wants our help. Yours, specifically."

"Why?"

"Don't fuckin' take this the wrong way," he says, leaning forward on his desk, "but you're the only black child psychologist she knows."

"And?" My fists clench even harder.

"And…" Ouray drawls. "The kid's black. Some of his injuries suggest the attack may have been racially motivated. Joyce thinks he's more likely to open up to you."

"Shee-it."

"Need you to head up there tonight, Trunk. That kid's got no one he trusts. So terrified they have to restrain and sedate him so they can treat his injuries."

"How old?"

"She's guessing he's seven or eight."

"Sonofabitch," I bite off.

"Yeah."

I push up from the chair. "Tell her I'm on my way."

"Thanks, brother. Booked a room for you at the Inn at the Canyons."

Glancing up I raise an eyebrow. "Presumptuous." Ouray grins and shrugs his shoulders in response.

The snow starts falling when I'm on my way home to pack a bag, and my thoughts immediately go to Jaimie with a pang of regret. I won't be able to take care of her driveway. I should also let her know I likely won't be able to make our dinner date for tomorrow night.

It takes me a few minutes to grab my stuff at home, lock up, and head back out on the road, which is getting worse by the minute. "Call Jaimie." I instruct my hands-free.

"Trunk?"

"Yeah. Look, something urgent's come up and I have to head out of town for a while. Not sure how long I'll be, but I'm not gonna be able to keep our date tomorrow night." I'm met with a pregnant silence. "James?"

"Whatever. That's fine." She sounds almost distracted. "I've gotta go, River just woke up."

Before I even get a chance to say goodbye, she's hung up. I immediately call the club, and Ouray answers.

"Need a favor."

"You've got it. What do need?"

"Weather's getting bad. Can you send one of the prospects to shovel the drive at 247 Animas Place?"

"Jaimie's place?"

"I'll get Wapi out there as soon as the worst is over." He pauses for a minute. "Jaimie. So it's like that, is it?"

"Whatever," I growl.

Ouray's laugh booms over the speakers as I reach to end the call.

9

Jaimie

I DIDN'T SLEEP much last night.

When Gomez and Blackfoot left, they took the box, the gift, and the card with them, but the message is burned in my brain. So fucking creepy.

Keith found out from Joe Benedetti that they often received packages for their former tenants, and the delivery guy may have automatically dropped it off with them when nobody answered the door here.

That's one mystery solved, but it doesn't explain how Rob would've found out where I live. Because the box was from him, there's no doubt about that. Gomez pointed out it wouldn't have been that hard, if someone made an effort.

I thought I'd been pretty good at closing down my life

in Denver, but I guess there were some things I hadn't considered. I didn't exactly go into hiding—something I have a feeling I may come to regret—I just didn't expect for him to make the effort to find me. Not from jail. Not when the divorce was already finalized. To what point?

The note, though. It's clear he's not as done with us as I thought he was.

If that wasn't enough to keep my mind churning all night, Trunk called. I'd been happy to hear from him, but that was short-lived when he told me—telegraph style—he couldn't do dinner because he was heading out of town. The disappointment was sharp and immediate. I didn't have a chance to ask for an explanation since he was in an obvious hurry to get off the phone, and I never had an opportunity to tell him about the package.

I'm still bleary-eyed when I hoist River on my hip and make my way downstairs, where I can hear Mom rambling around in the kitchen.

"Morning, sweethearts." She comes over to kiss my cheek and the top of River's head, before taking him from my arms. "Have you seen that snow outside? It must've continued through the night. I had to shovel the breezeway, it had piled up against the door."

"I could've done that, Mom."

She slips River in his high chair and hands him a sippy cup. "I'm not helpless, you know," she says with a stern look my way, reminding me how I came by my independent streak.

"I'll head out after breakfast and start digging us out."

"Oh, you don't have to." She smiles over her shoulder

as she pops bread in the toaster. “Someone is already working on it.”

“What? Who?”

I’m already moving to the living room window to check outside, a butterfly of hope spreading its wings. Sadly, my first glimpse of the much too lean figure, dressed in all black, shoveling my driveway squashes it instantly.

“I’ll be right back,” I call over my shoulder as I shove my feet into boots and don a jacket before heading outside.

I can barely see his eyes from under the beanie pulled low on his head. “Mornin’”

“Uh, yeah, morning. Can I ask what—”

“Trunk.”

“Sorry?” I stop in front of him, planting my hands on my hips.

“You were gonna ask what I’m doin’ here. Trunk wanted your drive clean so he sent me.”

“Oh. Well, that’s very kind of you, uh…”

“Wapi.”

Fucking weird name, but what do I care? I’m too busy being annoyed.

“Okay, Wapi. As I was about to say, it’s very kind of you, but I can take it from here.” I go for the shovel but he moves it out of my reach.

“Not a big deal. I’ll just finish it up.”

“Actually, that won’t be necessary. I’ve got this.”

“Ma’am,” he says, clearly trying to stay polite but making me feel ancient in the process. “If it’s all the same to you, I'd like to get this done. Don't wanna get my ass kicked and risk losing my chance at getting patched into the club."

"Ass kicked?" I'm shocked, and more than a little concerned. I got the impression the MC was not into violence, but I guess I was wrong.

"You've seen Trunk?" he asks with a grin. "No one wants to mess with that brother. I won't be much longer and then I'm outta your hair."

It's clear the man-child won't be deterred, so I simply nod and turn back to the house, where I stop and call out to him, "Perhaps you can pass on a message for me? Take that shovel with you and tell Trunk to stick it where the sun don't shine."

His hearty chuckle follows me inside.

"What was that all about?" Mom wants to know when I stomp into the kitchen.

"I don't wanna talk about it."

She wisely doesn't say anything else after my snippy response and slides an omelet in front of me, but she does it with a tiny smile tugging at her lips.

I cave when I'm halfway through my breakfast.

"He irks me."

"So I gather," Mom says, without even looking up from her plate. Also annoying.

"I get maybe five words of highly unsatisfactory explanation on why he cancelled our date tonight, but he apparently had enough time left to call in the troops to clean our driveway."

"The gall of the man."

I shoot Mom a sharp look, but her head is turned to River, feeding him a bite.

"I never know whether I'm coming or going with that man. One minute he has me convinced he's interested, but it's clear he doesn't have a very long attention span. I don't need that kind of aggravation in my life. I had that once, I'm not volunteering for it again."

"Oh, would you give it up?" Now it's my mother's turn to speak sharply and I look up surprised. "How can you even compare the two? When was Rob ever thoughtful enough to make sure you could safely get out of your driveway? The man would take off for weeks—even months—at a time, without a single thought for your well-being. Last I remember is you risking your neck on that godforsaken ladder, trying to clear the downspout in the spring, all because he was too busy to take care of that. Do I need to give you more examples?"

"No." Duly chastised, I put my fork down and shove the plate away. I've lost my appetite.

"Look at me, sweetheart." She waits until I do before reaching across the table to put her hand on mine. "Does Trunk seem like the kind of man who would ever have you climb on a wobbly ladder?"

"Maybe not, but it's not like I can't do those things myself," I sputter.

"Anyone who spends five minutes in your presence knows you can do those things yourself, and then some. But that's not really the point, is it? The point is he cares enough so you wouldn't have to. I get your cold feet, Jaimie, and I'm not saying Trunk couldn't do with some training when it comes to how to treat you, but you'll never get that if you don't give him a chance instead of focusing on his shortcomings."

I really hate it when Mom makes sense. Almost as much as when she puts me in my place. I'll be forty in less than two years, and still she has the ability to make me feel two feet tall.

"From what little I know about him and Tahlula, they haven't exactly had the best of examples in their lives. Maybe cut him a little slack."

I pull my hand from under hers and get up, taking the dirty dishes to the kitchen.

"I'll think about it," I say stubbornly.

Mom rolls her eyes.

By the time my phone screen shows Trunk calling, after I get into bed that night, I've convinced myself maybe I should.

Trunk

I DIDN'T THINK there was anything that could bring down my opinion on humanity lower than it already was.

Apparently I was wrong.

In the past twenty-four hours, the only information I managed to get from the little boy in the hospital bed was his first name—Ezrah—and he was only eight years old. I managed to glean that much through barely distinguishable mumbles, hand gestures, and a lot of guessing. His poor face was so badly battered; it was difficult for him to talk.

Joyce Mangiane, the CPS caseworker, had made the right call.

Ezrah's initial reaction was to struggle against his bindings, but I sat down so I was more at eye level with him, and started to softly talk to him. I can't remember what I rambled on about, but it seemed to calm him down after a while.

I never used the room Ouray got me last night, but tonight I need a mattress. My fucking back is broken, sitting on that damn stool beside the kid's bed.

Ouray got an update on the way to the Inn at the Canyons, but I waited until after I had a quick shower and was lying down before calling Jaimie.

"Hey."

I wasn't expecting the soft voice. In fact, I wasn't even sure she'd pick up, and at the very least had been prepared to get a strip torn off me. Getting sweet Jaimie is a nice surprise, one that is immediately noticed by my Johnson as well. Although she makes me hard, whether she blows bubbles or spits nails. My dick is an equal opportunity cheerleader.

"How are ya, Little Mama?"

"I'm okay. You?"

"Better now."

"How so?" I hear the rustle of fabric and imagine her lying in bed.

"This mattress is the shit and I'm talking to you."

For a few seconds she's dead silent, and I wonder if that was too much information. *Shee-it*, I don't know what the fuck I'm doing.

"Oh. I, uh…thank you for sending someone to do my driveway," she finally says, a little uneasy.

"Would've done it myself, but I'm in Monticello."

"Monticello?"

"Yep. Wouldn't a cancelled on you if it wasn't an emergency."

She seems to think on that too before answering. "I thought you were—"

"Bailing. I figured." I take a deep breath to get rid of the tight feeling in my chest. "I wasn't. Not anymore. Woulda called you sooner, but I just got out of the hospital. Ouray got a call from someone he knows with Child Protective Services. A kid was found earlier this week, hurt bad, but not talking. They thought I might be able to help. Fuck, Jaimie, you should see him, his face is so swollen he can barely see out of his eyes."

"What happened?"

Her question is filled with compassion, warming me. I fold an arm behind my head, suddenly eager to share it all.

"Boy's name is Ezrah, just eight years old. He was found unconscious and covered in blood in a park. Someone not only beat the crap out of him, but he has burns on his arms and torso and that sick fuck carved a swastika on his chest," I grind out.

A sharp inhale precedes her soft, "Oh my God, you've got to be kidding me."

"He's black, Jaimie. Just a little, eight-year-old black kid. Some days I just don't get what this world is coming to."

At the discovery of the mark cut in his skin I almost lost my shit, but I had to keep it together for the boy. It's a relief to be able to talk about it. Unfamiliar, but a relief.

"I don't either," she says, and I'm reminded she's just recently been introduced to that particular underbelly of society. "Trunk?"

"Yeah, James."

"Is he going to be okay? Ezrah?"

"Gonna do what I can to make sure he is. First step is to find out who he is."

"No parents?"

"Dunno. No one seems to be looking. No reports of missing kids matching his description. His clothes are at least a size too small, and he cut the toes out of his sneaker so they'd fit."

"Street kid," she concludes.

"Looks like."

"Will you guys take him on at Arrow's Edge?"

"If no one shows up claiming him, we likely will. For now, he'll be in the hospital for a while. Kid's got some healing to do yet." When she falls silent once again, I prompt her. "Jaimie?"

"Are you gonna stay 'til he's released?"

"Couple more days, I think. Depends on how things go. I'll drop in when I get back to town, if that's okay."

She apparently finds that funny. "You're asking? I didn't realize you knew how."

"You bein' a smartass?"

"Me?" She chuckles, followed by a loud yawn and a mumbled, "Sorry."

"Tired?"

"A little."

"I should let you go. We'll talk when I get back. Get this dating thing back on track."

I hear the smile in her voice when she answers, "I'd like that."

"Good. I think there's something going on at the clubhouse next weekend. If I'm back, I want you to come." Fingers crossed Yuma isn't in charge of entertainment again.

"The clubhouse?" She actually sounds excited at the prospect, and I briefly wonder if I didn't just jump the gun on that.

"It's nothing special, so don't expect too much. I'll be in touch."

"Don't say that if you don't mean it." At her quick admonishment, I'm reminded I told her those exact words before and didn't follow through. That's not gonna happen again.

"I mean it. Get some sleep."

"Night, Trunk. Look after Ezrah," she says softly.

"Will do, Little Mama."

N
nw
ne
W
E
ARROW'S EDGE MC

10

Jaimie

I HAVE BEEN spinning my wheels this past week, haven't had my head in the game.

River was teething, which means he's been fussy, particularly at night. Then Mom was hit with a short but particularly nasty bout of stomach flu. She kept to her apartment for days for fear of contaminating River or me.

I had my hands full looking after the two of them during the day, but at night my mind would start churning. Thoughts around that more than disturbing note, trying to figure out what the hell to make of it.

The only highlights have been a couple of calls from Trunk. He's been keeping me up-to-date on the progress with the little boy. The good news there is Ezrah is healing physically, but they haven't been able to glean any more information from the boy. Nothing to give them any indication who did this to him.

I purposely haven't shared anything with him about the box or the note. What would be the use? The man has enough on his mind.

This morning I received a text from him, saying he expects to be heading home sometime later this afternoon. It was the kick in the butt I needed to get myself back on track.

"Mom? Are you okay with River for a bit? I need to see Tahlula to go over a few things with her."

"No problem. Would you be able to pick up some groceries? Cupboards are empty."

I'm not surprised, I haven't been out of the house in what seems like forever.

"Yes. Can you make a list and text it to me?"

"On it."

I kiss the top of River's head, bundle up, and grab my bag before heading out into the cold. Jesus, that's a shock to the system after being cooped up inside for so long.

There's only a thin layer of snow on the CRV, but I'm more concerned about the car starting after sitting idle so long. I probably should've at least let the engine run a time or two over the past week. Luckily it turns over right away and within minutes I'm on my way.

"I LIKE THIS one." Tahlula taps one of the printouts of

proposed ads I brought for her to look at.

"Me too," I confirm. "I'll send it back to them right away. They're hoping to snag a few prime spots for release week."

"Sounds good. What's next?"

"New York."

T rolls her eyes. She's not a fan of public appearances. "Do I have to?"

"I think so. They're already conceding to one signing, and however many interviews we can squeeze into a single day, but technically they could demand a lot more from you."

"Fine. Confirm with them. I guess I'll start pumping."

"You could always bring Hanna," I suggest. "Maybe Evan wants to come as well?"

"Not likely," she states, snorting. "I think he'd rather visit a proctologist than NYC."

"What she says," Evan contributes from the kitchen, making me laugh.

"Anyway, I'd rather keep my family as far away from the spotlight as I can," T points out, and I can't blame her for that. She's experienced firsthand how scary the spotlight can be. There are crazies everywhere.

"Let me check with Karen how we are for flights. We'll try to fly out as late as possible the day before and head back immediately after you've fulfilled all your obligations."

"Fine," she grumbles before her face lights up. "Have you heard from Trunk?"

"I…uh…may have. Why?"

She grins wide. "Good. I just wanted to make sure. His birthday is coming up in a few weeks, it's his forty-fifth and I want to surprise him, but I may need your help."

"For what, exactly?"

"To keep him distracted but close to home while I plan this."

I raise my eyebrows. "What on earth makes you think I have that kind of power? You're his sister, you should know better than anyone, nothing and no one will keep your brother from going exactly where he wants to go."

She smirks. "I bet you could."

"You're giving me way too much credit here, T."

"And I think you're giving yourself too little. I watched him looking at you at my wedding: bewildered, yet intrigued, like he wasn't quite sure what to make of you but couldn't wait to find out."

"We'll see." I resolutely close my notebook and gather my things. "I should get going. I have a shitload of groceries to get: this past week cleaned us out."

"Glad everyone's feeling better."

"Me too," I agree.

Snow is just starting to fall when I walk out. More snow. It's already March and we've had snow on the ground almost since early December. I hope it doesn't carry through to April, as I'm told is possible. I know it's in part because of this past week being stuck at home, but I'm getting a serious case of cabin fever and can't wait for spring to show.

I'm not the only one hitting the City Market on a Friday

afternoon. Everyone in town seems to have picked this time to stock up for the weekend, and it takes me about an hour to fill my cart and make my way through the line at the cash register.

The short drive home is already treacherous, with visibility near zero and the roads jammed with rush-hour traffic. I heave a sigh of relief when I turn onto our relatively quiet street.

Mom has the door open when I walk up with the first load of groceries.

"It's getting bad already," she comments, taking the bags from my hands. "I just watched the forecast, they're saying eight to ten inches tonight with the possibility of another five before morning."

"Lovely," I grumble. "How was River?"

"Tired himself out. He fell asleep on his play mat. I just covered him up and left him there."

I peek over her shoulder to see a little bump under the quilt on the floor beside the coffee table. My boy probably needs to catch up on the sleep he lost this past week. I could do with that myself. "Let me quickly get the rest inside."

I'm on my third trip back to the car when a familiar truck turns into the driveway. My stomach does a little flip as it pulls up beside my Honda, and Trunk gets out. I barely have a chance to register how good he looks before I find myself pressed between my SUV and his hard body, his mouth already hungry on mine.

I'm overwhelmed, both by his size and his voracity as he eats at my mouth like a starved man. A deep groan rumbles from him when I tangle my tongue with his. I experience a full-body shiver when a cold hand sneaks under the back of my coat and down my waistband, fingers clenching my ass cheek. He immediately pulls back his hand and his mouth. I whimper at the loss of contact.

"Sorry," he mumbles against my lips.

"Don't be."

His hand curls around the side of my neck, a thumb lifting my chin, and his molten dark eyes are right there, searching mine. "Shoved my hand down your pants in full view of your neighbors during a snowstorm, Jaimie, I coulda used a bit of restraint."

"Did you hear me complain?" I challenge him and his eyes narrow.

"Gettin' you naked is about all I can think of. Don't tempt me." He lifts his eyes over my head and releases his hold. "Your momma's waiting."

"Shit." I quickly straighten myself.

"Go inside, James, I've got this." He almost shoves me out of the way to grab the last of the groceries.

Mom is indeed standing in the door opening, grinning from ear to ear as I walk up. She fans her face.

"Phew…that was something else."

"Mom," I warn her in a low voice, pushing her inside.

She's not wrong, though.

Trunk

She tastes better than I remember.

Dayum, I'm glad I came here first. Goes a long way to easing the ache I felt leaving Ezrah behind in Monticello. Just because I agreed with the general consensus the club may not be what's right for the boy yet—he's too fragile physically and emotionally—doesn't make walking away from him any easier.

I had no choice. First of all, Joyce found him a nice African American foster family. I met them and no matter how hard I tried to find fault with them, I couldn't. Ezrah took to the woman instantly. He still barely speaks, only single word answers to direct questions, but he shuts down the minute you ask anything about what happened to him or where he came from.

It's clear he isn't local to Monticello: the black population is less than a quarter percent and was easily vetted. Even for all of Utah the percentage of African Americans is less than two, which makes it all the more amazing Joyce was able to find the couple.

The second reason I had to come home was some more unrest at the clubhouse. I talked to Ouray yesterday, who mentioned a few fights had broken out between the boys that even his son, Ahiga, got mixed up in. The man sounded almost defeated. It's been a tough couple of months for the club, which is probably why it's best Ezrah's not coming back with me.

"Good to see you, Trunk." Jaimie's mother smiles like the cat that got the canary when I walk into the kitchen with the groceries. Jaimie is nowhere to be seen.

"Sandra."

"No pork chops tonight, but how does lasagna sound?

I've got plenty."

My mouth waters. Whatever she has on offer is better than the fast food I've been living on this past week. "Sounds good to me."

"What sounds good?" Jaimie asks, coming down the stairs with River on her hip.

"Trunk is staying for lasagna."

"Is that so?" Jaimie glances at me, a smirk on her lips, before she drops her eyes to her son, who looks like he's ready to jump from her hold. She lifts him in front of her. "You want Trunk to stay for dinner?"

"Unk!" The kid pumps his little legs like he's got somewhere to be.

"Trunk," Sandra repeats, grinning at the boy.

"Dunk!"

Fuck. I'll take it. I reach out and barely manage to catch him when he launches himself at me. One hand immediately slaps against my cheek, while the other hooks onto my bottom lip. "Easy, Lil' Brother. Let's you and me find something else to beat up. Leave the women to sort out the kitchen."

I grin when I hear Jaimie's shocked gasp behind me. I like her any way she comes, but I like her best all riled up.

I build River a block house, which he takes great pleasure in knocking down, giggling harder each time I try to do it again. At some point a beer is set on the coffee table, and I look up to see Jaimie's round ass move as she walks back to the kitchen. The ass that felt mighty fine in my hand. I catch Sandra eyeing me with a smile on her face, and I quickly redirect my attention to River.

It's shocking how comfortable I am in this white picket fence house, with these two women, and this little tow-headed boy, who seems to think I hung the moon.

I'm glad I warned Ouray I wouldn't be in 'til late tonight, because I have no intention of leaving here anytime soon.

Jaimie

I STAYED TO help Mom in the kitchen, only so I could watch and listen from a distance to the interaction between the two guys in my living room.

Trunk's patience seems endless and I chuckle a time or two at my son's peals of giggles every time he lets his destructive little fists fly. When he eventually quiets down, Trunk reaches for the remote and scoops River up in the same move, settling him on his lap as he turns on the TV.

Their heads are bent close, my son's nearly white downy one almost touching Trunk's bald, dark, much bigger one. A sigh escapes my lips.

"That salad is not gonna toss itself," Mom whispers behind me. Caught, I quickly return my attention to dinner.

Over lasagna, Trunk fills us in on Ezrah and the couple who stepped up to take him in. I detect a wistful tone to his voice as he describes leaving the boy in their care. I'm starting to see the soft center to this intimidating, rough man his sister alluded to. In the way he talks about the boy, in how he handles my son, and in the attention he's shown me.

River ends up wearing most of his dinner. I quickly whisk him up to give him a bath, while Trunk starts gathering the dirty dishes, telling Mom to go watch her show. By the time I come down—my son settled in his crib upstairs—I find the two of them on the couch, battling it out over *Jeopardy*. I could never keep up with Mom, but she seems to have found a worthy opponent in Trunk.

My mother yawns dramatically when the program's credits roll. "I'm wiped. I think I'm heading upstairs to read a bit."

I roll my eyes in response. "Subtle, Mom."

"Well, it would've been if you hadn't pointed it out, Jaimie," she snaps back, suddenly wide-awake. To Trunk she says with a saccharine smile, "Careful of those claws, my dear." I snort at her endearment for him. "She may look sweet, but my daughter can be stubborn like a mule and prickly as a porcupine."

"Thanks, Mom."

Trunk chuckles, a good sound that rumbles from deep in his chest. "That's what I like about her, Sandra," he says, and I watch as my mother melts on the spot.

"Me too," she admits, before giving me a saucy wiggle with her fingers and heading for the side door.

"What are you doing over there?" Trunk asks when Mom closes the door behind her. "Get your ass over here."

I badly want to tell him how I feel about being ordered

around, but not as much as I want to feel his strong arms swallow me up. Which is exactly what he does when I sit down beside him. My butt barely touches the seat when he lifts me easily onto his lap.

"Whoa. Not wasting any time," I mutter breathlessly.

"Done enough a'that."

A statement he underlines by sliding his large hand under my sweater. His rough palm stroking the skin of my bare stomach raises goosebumps all over my body.

"Cold?" he asks at my barely suppressed shiver.

"Not in the least," I confess, wrapping my arms around his neck as I raise my lips to meet his.

Full, strong, and yet surprisingly soft lips slide seductively over mine. His long fingers pull down the cup of my bra and have no trouble finding my tight nipple, tugging it firmly. I gasp and he seizes the opportunity to slide his tongue in my mouth.

Where our kiss in the driveway had been urgent—almost frenzied—this one is languid and exploratory.

My senses are filled with his taste and touch, and the feel of his hard body against mine.

Hard all over, I discover when I shift restlessly on his lap. He grunts when I do it again, quickly adjusting my position so I'm straddling him. He rolls his hips underneath me as his hands slide up my back, easily releasing my bra. I'm too focused on the feel of him, the size of him between my legs, to notice when he quickly releases my mouth to divest me of my sweater.

My head falls back as I rock my hips on the hard ridge, while his mouth closes on one breast, massaging the other in his large hand.

I curve my fingers around the back of his head, and holding him close, feeling my body gear up for release.

"Wait," he rumbles, as his mouth lets go and he forces his head back against the couch, looking up at me.

"I don't wanna," I tell him, my fingers digging into his shoulders for purchase.

"One second," he insists, as he pulls down my zipper with one hand while shoving the other down my waistband in the back. "Shee-it, James. So wet for me."

The long fingers of his right hand trail down my crack, easily sliding inside my channel, while his left thumb zeroes in on my clit. My body ignites on contact, pulsating and shaking with my release. I let myself collapse breathlessly against him, my face buried in the crook of his neck.

"You blow me away," he rumbles, his lips brushing my ear. "So fucking tight. So fucking responsive."

"I'm sorry," I mumble, a little embarrassed.

"For what? Setting off like a firecracker at my touch? Do you know how fucking hot that is?" I lift my head. "Amazing," he adds when my eyes meet his.

"It's been a while," I confess.

"Yeah?"

"Guess I lost my attraction once I became pregnant."

Maybe not the best time to bring up my bigoted, racist, maniac of a husband, while sitting half-naked on Trunk's lap. His fingers tighten on my hips, and I curse myself for even bringing it up, when his lips curve in a smile.

"Knew he was a fucking idiot. Didn't realize how

much of one until now." He tags me behind my neck and pulls me down for a hard kiss. "Hop off, Little Mama."

"But what about…?"

"Not when I'm expected back at the clubhouse tonight. No way I'm gonna hurry once I get inside you. It'll hold. Now hop off."

"I could—"

"James—killing me here, baby. Hop on off."

"Bossy," I snap, scrambling off his lap and grabbing my sweater off the floor, yanking it over my head.

He stands up as well, adjusting himself in the process. "It's who I am."

"I know. I'm trying to decide whether I like it or not," I confess, making him smile wide.

I think my heart stopped in my chest. It's the first time I've seen him full-out smile, and it's devastatingly beautiful. He has dimples. How the fuck am I supposed to resist those?

"You like it," he rumbles.

I'm afraid he's right.

11

TRUNK

"YO. TRUNK, ARE you even listening?"

Shit. No, I wasn't.

I was reliving the tight squeeze of Jaimie's pussy around my fingers. It had taken everything out of me not to roll her over and bury myself inside her body. Those tits, her scent, the little gasps as she reached for relief; she was fucking magnificent. My dick is still hard.

I look around Ouray's office and see the other four men's eyes on me. "What was that?"

"I asked if you had any thoughts, but now I'm not sure I wanna hear them," Ouray shares, making some of the guys chuckle. He shushes them with a single look. "The boys, any suggestions on how to handle them? It's like someone put something in their Cheerios, for fuck's sake. Momma had to take Elan into the emergency room with a gash on his head that required twelve stitches. From Istu whacking him with a five-pound weight this morning." He bulges his eyes out at me, before sitting back, crossing his arms over his chest. "Three days ago, Ezhno kicked the PlayStation against the wall—broke the damn thing—and yesterday my son swung at Matt when they were on kitchen duty together. Nobody will fucking fess up to what went down."

"Where are they now?"

"Elan is with Momma and Nosh, Ahiga is at home with Luna, and the other boys are in the barn with Wapi and Honon keeping an eye out."

Yuma snorts loudly. "I still think it's ridiculous we have to put a brother on babysitting duty."

"Yeah?" Paco jumps in. "Would you rather those boys end up doing each other harm and CPS jumping all over our backs?"

"I'm just saying, we already have brothers watching the gym, the restaurant, and the Riverside Apartments around the clock. We've got fourteen brothers, three cubs, two senior citizens…hardly enough to cover all our businesses *and* those damn boys." The cubs he's referring to are the club's prospects.

"What do you suggest then, Yuma?" Ouray asks sharply. "Those businesses are our bread and butter and someone is doing a bang-up job shutting us down."

"You don't know that," the younger man says defensively.

"Fuck's sake, are you blind?" Paco loses his cool.

"Almost twelve years smooth sailing and then suddenly, in the time span of a few weeks, shit goes down at every single one of our locations? You know damn well that's no coincidence, brother."

"All I know is this club used to mean something. We had respect both in town and with the other MCs. Nowadays, we're nothin' but a laughing stock." With that he storms out of the room, slamming the door behind him.

Things are going to shit in a hurry. Not only outside of the club but inside as well.

I ignore Yuma's dramatic exit and lean forward, my elbows on my knees.

"Who stands to benefit if the Arrow's Edge falls apart at the seams?"

I've only been with the MC for a little over a year, so I haven't seen them running anything other than legal businesses, but I also know there was a time they were on the wrong side of the law. Ouray had a lot to do with turning the club around when he took the hammer.

I wouldn't have patched in otherwise. Not that I'm an angel—Lord knows I've skirted boundaries and even crossed them in my life—but only if I could morally justify my actions, if not legally. Gunrunning and drug trafficking don't qualify, keeping the town clear of outlaw MCs, or other criminal elements moving in, by any means necessary absolutely do.

"Too many to count," Ouray says, running a hand through hair that's already standing on end. His stress is showing. "We control the south end of the most direct route north through the Rockies. It's not the first time—and I'm sure it won't be the last—someone wants to either suck us in or wipe us off the map. Discord in our ranks doesn't just play into the hands of whoever is behind this, but of every fucking trafficker out there."

The room falls silent for a few moments before Kaga, who has been silent so far, speaks up. "We need to pad our ranks. Get some fresh blood in. I have an idea I've been toying with for a while that may benefit some of our boys too."

"Which is?"

"I have a buddy in Grand Junction. Road name's Brick. He's a mechanic and runs his own business. He's been talking about a change of scenery. We've got lots of room here, what if we invited him up here? See if he'd be interested in setting up a shop here? It could be another source of income, a draw to pull new blood in."

"I don't know," Ouray mulls. "With all the shit flying right now."

"I think it's a good idea," I voice. "Not just from a business perspective, but also for the boys. Something constructive for them to invest time in. Let them dick around with old cars, under supervision. Learn something. Call it professional development or some fucking thing like that, but having them jointly fix up some old clunker would go a long way to building their team spirit. Fuck, maybe we can see if this Brick would run apprenticeships for kids who show a knack."

"I like it," Paco contributes, but all our eyes are on Ouray.

"All right. Kaga, get in touch with this Brick guy and feel him out. If not him, maybe he knows someone else who might be interested. Paco, talk to some of the other brothers, see if you can come up with something we can do to draw interest in the club. I don't know what—maybe a fucking open house or whatever—but think of something. It's already March and everyone is gagging to get out on the road, let's make use of that." Then he turns to me, his face dead serious. "And you, find out what the fuck has gotten into those damn kids, including my son."

"What about Yuma?" Paco wants to know.

"I'll take care of Yuma. Also, remember we've got a few guys from the Moab Reds swinging by this weekend. Party tomorrow night, but I don't want any of our shit to be on display."

"Got it, Chief."

It's already after midnight when we break it up. There are only a few brothers hanging around the bar, Yuma is not one of them.

"Beer?" Paco asks me.

"Yeah, give me a minute."

It's too late to call Jaimie, but I can send her a text to remind her of tomorrow night.

***Me:* Pick you up at 8 for club party.**

Too long a wait if you ask me, but I'm gonna need time with the boys to see if I can get them back in line. I should probably crash here tonight; I can worry about clearing my driveway tomorrow.

I've barely sat down on the barstool when my phone pings.

***James*: Bossy. Thnx for the driveway btw.**

I smile at her message. When I left her earlier the snow had stopped, and I quickly cleared the few inches that had fallen before getting in my truck.

***Me:* You like me bossy. Why r u up?**

The sound of her incoming text is immediate.

***James*: River. Teething.**

***Me:* Poor lil' dude. Poor Little Mama. Try to sleep.**

***James:* Trying to. Hard when someone's blowing up my phone.**

***Me:* 'Hard' and 'blowing' in one breath? You're cruel.**

***James:* LOL. You're easy.**

***Me:* For you, yes. Night, James.**

***James:* Night, Titus Maximus Rae.**

I chuckle at her use of my full name, undoubtedly thanks to my fucking sister.

"Fuck you've got it bad, man," Paco teases, grinning as he slams a bottle on the bar in front of me. "I didn't even know you were capable of smiling."

"Shut the fuck up," I fire off, but I do it with a grin on my face.

JAIMIE

"ROUGH NIGHT?"

I turn my bleary eyes on my mom walking into the house.

"I ended up keeping him in my bed. Easier than getting up every hour on the hour."

"Ouch," she says, sympathetically. "Why don't I keep him tonight? Give you a break? My bed is big enough, or we can move the playpen up there."

The thought of a full night's sleep is enticing. There's also my date for tonight. I almost feel guilty even considering pawning my son off for the night, so I have my hands free. So to speak.

"Actually," I start, looking at my mother from under my puffy eyelids. "I forgot to mention, I have a date tonight."

"Trunk?"

"Ma! Of course Trunk. Not like men have been knocking down my door."

"You're a beautiful woman, Jaimie. That nice detective noticed. I bet others have too."

"What I am is a single mother of a toddler, who doesn't really have the time to date. Hardly appealing."

"Bullhickey. Doesn't seem to bother Trunk. I'll be happy to look after River so you can have a little fun. You're due."

I get up from my chair and walk up to her, giving her a hug. "You're the best, Mom."

It's Saturday, but that doesn't mean a day off. Not in this industry. I managed to send off the confirmation for our upcoming trip to New York, and Karen got back to me this morning with a proposed itinerary.

She's booked us to fly out this upcoming Friday afternoon, returning twenty-four hours later. The schedule is jam-packed, and I wonder if it wouldn't be wiser to stay until Sunday. With the transfer in Denver it'll be between six and seven hours of travel time both ways. Doesn't leave much time for sleep or breaks. I grab my phone and dial Tahlula.

"Have you seen Karen's email?" she asks right away.

"That's what I'm calling about. I think we should tack on another night. Come back Sunday."

I listen to her sigh deeply. "I don't want to."

"I realize that, but you're gonna be dead on your feet with the schedule the way it is. I know you don't want to leave Hanna that long, but you have another baby you need to think about."

"You know I don't like it when you make sense, right?" she complains. I hear some rustling in the background and then suddenly Evan is on the phone.

"Jaimie? Could you book me and Hanna on whatever

flight you guys end up on?"

I chuckle. "You sure you wouldn't rather I book you an appointment for a rectal exam?"

"You're a sick individual, woman," he retorts with an audible shudder.

"My work here is done. Tell T I'll send her over the information as soon as I have it. You're a good egg, Mr. Biel." I grin at his responding grumbles before ending the call.

I spend the afternoon finalizing details and making sure I have announcements for the signing next Saturday posted all over Tahlula's social media. It would be a waste of a trip if no one showed up.

Now I'm standing in front of my closet, a towel wrapped around me, wondering what the hell one wears for a party at a clubhouse. It doesn't sound like a place you'd get dolled up for, not that I'd remember how to do that anyway, but I do want to look good. Resolved, I grab my least mom-style pair of jeans off the shelf and pull a navy wrap sweater off a hanger.

Mom sticks her head around the door just as I'm assessing my outfit in front of the mirror.

"Stop fussing," she orders when she sees me tugging at the sweater. The cleavage is a little more generous than I remember from the pre-River days, but then so are my breasts.

"I look like a walking fruit basket," I grumble. "I should put a tank top on underneath."

"You look lovely as you are," Mom says firmly. "Besides, there's no time to change, your date is being entertained by your son, but I'm sure he'd rather see you."

"He's already here?"

"You were in the shower. Shouldn't keep him waiting even longer."

I roll my eyes, ignore her snicker, and I slip by her to head down the stairs.

"SO WHAT SHOULD I expect?"

Trunk glances over. "Expect?"

"From this party."

I shouldn't be surprised Trunk seemed to appreciate the deep V of my sweater. He allayed any doubts I might've had by pulling me close with one arm and sliding his hand down to my ass. Then he kissed me thoroughly, right in front of my mom and River, who was happily perched on his other arm.

Right before we left, Mom mortified me by pointedly telling Trunk my son would be sleeping in her apartment tonight, and therefore we didn't have to worry about waking him up. Before she had a chance to say anything else embarrassing, I grabbed Trunk's hand and pulled him outside.

I was so busy being annoyed with my mother; I didn't get nervous until just now, driving through the gate and into the compound.

"Just a party. Some drinking, probably food—knowing Momma—friends, music."

"Will Luna be there?" I'd met Ouray's wife at Tahlula's wedding and liked her a lot. She could be my skinnier, tougher, kick-ass sister.

"Yup. Can we go inside now or do you have more questions?"

I narrow my eyes on him, but that just makes the corners of his mouth tilt up. There are the dimples, and there goes my snit.

"Fine."

The light of a cigarette flares up in the shadows under the overhang when we walk up, and my hand clenches in Trunk's.

"Nice piece." The disembodied voice sends chills down my spine, and Trunk goes rigid beside me.

"Don't know who the fuck you are, but you may wanna rethink that comment." Trunk moves partially between me and whomever is out there, and coward that I am, I curl my hand in the back of his coat, getting a little freaked out. So far this isn't my idea of a good time.

The glowing tip of the cigarette arcs through the air and lands right in front of us, sizzling in the snow. The man steps out of the shadows and stops with his back to the door.

"That how you treat your guests?" he snarls. "Your prez needs to teach you some manners, *boy*."

I feel tension crackling off Trunk and quickly wrap both my arms around his waist, grabbing on tight. I'm under no illusion I can hold him back, but at least I'll have tried.

"Chains." Ouray's firm voice sounds behind the guy.

"Your beer's getting warm, my friend." He steps out, throws an arm around the man's shoulders, and turns him toward the door. "I'll be right in."

The moment the door closes behind the guy, Ouray turns to us with his hands held up.

"What the fuck, brother?" Trunk growls, his body still tight with tension.

"Chains is an asshole, especially when he's been drinking, which he's done since he got here. He's also vice president for the Moab Reds, and since I'm still not clear why the fuck they wanted this visit, I'd prefer to save any bloodshed 'til later."

"Excuse me," I blurt out, finally letting go of Trunk's waist, but now he throws an arm around me. "Could we maybe do away with bloodshed altogether? I've kinda been looking forward to this date."

Ouray grins wide. "Nice to see you again, Jaimie. Come on in."

N
nw
ne
W
E
ARROW'S EDGE MC

12

Jaimie

"YOU'LL GET USED to it."

I'm not so sure, as I take in the man introduced to me earlier as Yuma head off down the hallway at the back with his arms around two giggling females. It doesn't take a whole lot to imagine what they'll be up to.

"Is that normal?" I ask Luna, who winces a little at my question.

"For some of the guys it's hard to let go of the old ways, which was basically live hard and live free. What you saw there is an example of the live free part. There'll be times—usually well after Momma calls it a night—when they don't even bother finding an empty room." She shrugs and smiles at me.

I'm not a prude—I don't think—but I'm not sure I'd

like an audience, let alone extra participants. "It doesn't bother you?"

"No. Not anymore. I know now Ouray may not have issues being buck-ass naked in front of his brothers, but he there's no way he'd allow strange eyes on me. My other concern was the women, but I've learned they are here by choice."

I look across the large room at Trunk, leaning against the bar, deep in conversation with Luna's husband. "Did he…?"

"Trunk? Not that I know of," she says, clueing into my train of thought easily. "Not that I've been witness to anyway."

"Refills?" The young guy who Trunk had sent to shovel my driveway, stops by our table.

"Water for me, Wapi. Thanks," Luna tells him.

"I wouldn't mind one more, but after that cut me off." He grins before heading back to the bar.

"Not a big drinker either?"

"Not exactly," I admit with a wince, remembering the last time I was drinking wine. Two glasses will be my new limit. Especially if I want to keep my wits about me.

"I was going to ask you, did my boss get in touch with you?" Luna asks, and my gaze darts immediately to Trunk who is still standing by the bar. "Don't worry. I don't make it a rule to share details about my work with my husband, let alone anyone else here. It's better for Ouray's peace of mind if I don't. He tends to be a little protective."

"I haven't told Trunk yet," I confess. "What I know

about Trunk, he'll flip his shit. I'm kinda hoping it was an isolated incident I can forget about. I've certainly been trying."

"Understandable. Well, on the plus side, what we've discovered is not news. The pj's were purchased from an account with Amazon in your ex's name. He didn't exactly make an effort hiding that fact. To put your mind at ease, we're keeping close tabs on him. He makes any moves, we'll know about it before you do."

"Guess I was naïve thinking he was gonna just let us go."

I feel a tingle down my spine and my eyes drift to the other side of the bar, where Chains, the guy who accosted us outside, is staring at me despite the redhead draped all over him. He lifts his beer in my direction when he catches me looking, and I immediately turn away.

"Talk about someone else who freaks me out," I confess.

"Chains? He's a piece of work."

"You wanna steer clear of him," Wapi mumbles, as he sets my glass in front of me.

"What he says," Luna confirms when he returns to his spot behind the bar. "The president for the Moab Reds is a contemporary of my husband's. Ouray respects Tink, which is the only reason he opened the doors to Chains and his buddies."

I resist the temptation to look back in the man's direction and focus instead on Trunk, who is making his way over here, Ouray right behind him.

"Gettin' hammered again, Little Mama?" he asks,

pulling out a chair beside me.

"You're making it sound like I do that all the time," I snap, bristling. "It was one time, Trunk. Once." I notice too late his eyes are sparkling with amusement.

Ouray chuckles as he lifts his wife from the chair, before sitting down, pulling her onto his lap. Her muttered objections go unheard. It's my turn to snicker when she rolls her eyes at me.

I'm having fun, listening to the other couple sharing some stories, while I'm nursing my glass of wine, Trunk's hand warm under my hair at the back of my neck. We dance a few times, my body pressed so tight to his it's on fire. Doesn't take much to imagine what this man could do to me without the layer of clothes separating us.

We've just returned to the table from our last foray to Eric Clapton's "Layla" when Chains approaches the table, the redhead teetering right behind him. Trunk immediately stiffens, and I can feel the tension coming off both Ouray and Luna. Under the table I put my hand on Trunk's leg.

Instead of stopping, he walks right past us to the pool table with only a glance in our direction, almost to make sure he has our attention. There he pushes the woman rather unceremoniously over the table, tugging up her skirt and stripping down her barely-there panties.

"Fuck me," Trunk growls beside me and my hand curls into his muscular thigh.

I'm mesmerized by the sight of Chains kicking her legs apart, freeing himself from his dirty jeans, and with deft movements rolling on a condom before lining up his cock and plunging inside her. His eyes are on me the entire time.

"Easy, brother," Ouray rumbles when Trunk suddenly surges to his feet.

"Unless you want a confrontation on your hands, *brother*," Trunk sneers. "Get rid of that fucker and call me when he's gone. Until then, we're outta here." He pulls me up by the hand and starts moving for the exit, keeping a tight hold of me.

"Uh, Trunk?" He doesn't slow down so I try again, but a little louder, yanking my hand from his. "Trunk!"

"What!" he snarls, swinging around, his eyes blazing with heat. Just not the kind I like seeing.

"Before you haul me out there in sub-zero temperatures, I'd like my coat, and if it's not too much trouble, my purse." It's out of my mouth before I consider this may not be a good time to get sassy.

"Don't be smart with me, Jaimie. Not fucking now."

I'll admit, the narrowing of those onyx eyes on me is a little intimidating, but I stand my ground, folding my arms over my chest. "And I'm not about to go anywhere without my stuff."

"Here you go," I hear from behind me, and I turn to find Wapi holding out my things.

"Thank you." I may have put a little too much gratitude in my words.

"For fuck's sake," Trunk mutters, as I shrug on my coat and throw my purse over my shoulder.

"See you later, Wapi. That was very nice of you." I smile big at the guy, who shakes his head before turning back to the bar. Next thing I know I'm pulled out the door by Trunk. This time I let him, I know I've made my point.

TRUNK

I HAVE TO rein my temper in before I trust myself to start the truck.

That fucking dirtbag, his eyes on my woman while he's hammering his dick into some willing pussy. The message couldn't have been clearer.

Disrespect.

For me, but also for Jaimie. The first is nothing new to me, but the second I won't stand for. It's for her sake I dragged her out of there. She's had enough filth darkening her life; she doesn't need more.

She's ignoring me, looking out the side window, and staying silent all the way to her place, which is not unwelcome.

I wasn't kidding when I told her "Not now" earlier. After spending the whole fucking day trying to get the boys to tell me what the hell is up with them, my patience had already been stretched to the limit. Not having anything to give Ouray, who's been looking for an answer, didn't help my mood. The introduction of that misogynistic, racist piece of shit has been the fucking cherry to my day.

"You know," Jaimie says softly when I pull into her driveway. "A person only has as much power as we're willing to give them."

I open my mouth to warn her off, but close it again when I realize she's got a point. Shutting off the engine I turn, tagging her behind the neck, and pulling her close. "How'd you get so wise?" I mumble against her lips opening willingly.

I taste the remnants of her wine, mixed with her own enticing flavor, as my tongue encounters hers. Her hands seek out the smooth skin of my scalp, scraping gently, and I swear the heat in the truck goes up by twenty degrees in seconds. "James," I caution her, pulling away.

"Don't stop," she mutters, pressing her mouth back to mine.

"Not fucking you in the driveway," I manage. I set her firmly back in her seat and take her in. The blonde hair I've been able to muss up in just minutes, the deep pink, pouty lips, and the sexy flush high on her cheeks. "Invite me in or send me home, Little Mama."

Her eyelids slide halfway down over those baby blues as she sinks her teeth in her bottom lip. "Are you gonna boss me around?"

Smartass.

"Depends. You gonna invite me in and find out, or send me home?" With some satisfaction I note she squirms a little in her seat.

"In," is all she says, opening the truck door.

Shee-it.

I'm on her the moment the front door falls shut behind us, pressing her against the wall, a knee between her legs and my tongue in her mouth. Fucking hell, she ignites like a fire, scoring her nails in my neck, her tongue meeting mine stroke for stroke. Who'd have thought the innocent looking, blonde nymph would light up like that?

I grind my cock into her heat when she wraps a leg around mine. When she mewls down my throat, I know I have to slow things down or she'll have me coming in my fucking jeans.

"You're stopping again," she snaps, her lips full and slick, and her eyes full of fire when I take a step back.

"Rather not waste a load in my jeans," I grunt, grabbing her hand and pulling her to the stairway.

"Charming," she mumbles, as I push her ahead up the stairs.

Watching that lush ass at face level isn't helping my control, and by the time she leads me into her bedroom, I'm already pulling her top up from behind. She lifts her arms, freeing the sweater, and turns to face me when I fling it on the floor. Her hands go straight for my shirt, shoving it up my chest. I reach behind me, grab a handful of fabric between my shoulder blades, and pull it over my head. Her hands are already exploring.

"Jesus, Trunk, look at you."

"I'd rather be lookin' at you." Putting my money where my mouth is, I reach for the zipper on her jeans and strip them down, dropping on my knees in front of her. Her belly is soft when I bury my face there, inhaling her hot scent. Dipping my tongue in her belly button, my hands dig into the globes of her ass. I feel her skin pebble as I drag my tongue down to her pubic bone over the silky scrap of fabric.

"Lie back, James." She shuffles backward until the

mattress hits her knees and lies down, spreading her legs immediately. Fuck yeah, the crotch of her panties is soaked. "Hope you're not attached to these," I mumble, ripping the lace band at her hip.

"Trunk!" she protests, raising herself up on her elbows, just as I lift her legs over my shoulders.

"Hush." I spread her pretty pink folds open with my thumbs, and taste her with my tongue.

It doesn't take much before her thighs are quivering and her hips are lifting off the mattress. I slide two fingers inside her, and suck hard on her clit, making her jerk under my touch as she comes.

She's still recovering when I'm already scrambling to my feet. I dig in my pocket and pull out a condom, sticking it between my teeth as I kick off my boots and socks, and strip down my jeans.

The moment I tear the foil, Jaimie's head pops up and her eyes track down my body until they get caught on me rolling on the condom.

"Holy shit," she mutters.

"Bra off, baby."

Without moving her eyes from my dick, she reaches behind her and lets the bra fall down her arms, releasing those large perfect breasts.

I bend over her body, and shove my hands under her, scooping her right off the mattress. Her arms automatically circle my neck, and her legs wrap around my hips. Her soft flesh engulfing me.

"Trunk…"

"Titus. When I fuck you, call me Titus."

With my hands under her ass, I take a few steps until her back is braced against a wall. Then I slowly lower her on my dick. So fucking slick. Warm. Tight. I squeeze my eyes shut, fighting the urge to pound inside her when she whimpers.

"You good?"

"Mmhmm."

"Words, James," I grunt.

"Less talking, Titus. Fuck me already."

Shee-it, she makes me hot when she's snippy. I ease out, brace my legs, and thrust back inside, deep and hard. I do it again, and then again, until I leave my head out of the game and let my body take over.

N
nw
ne
W
E
ARROW'S EDGE MC

13

JAIMIE

WHEN I ROLL over to check my alarm clock, I discover I'm tender in areas that had been ignored for too long. Although, to be honest, I might well have been tender this morning anyway given last night's gymnastics and the size of my exercise partner.

A satisfied smile steals over my face. Being on the short side has been an annoyance my whole life, until Trunk showed me all the ways our height difference can be used creatively. I can scratch a few of my secret fantasies off my list.

He left last night—or rather, earlier this morning—explaining he wants to be at the clubhouse when the boys get up. Apparently their young charges have been giving the club some trouble lately, and Trunk is eager to get to the bottom of it.

I want to use today to figure out what I'm going to pack for New York. Travel clothes are easy, but it's the command performance outfits I'm struggling with. I still have my office wardrobe—drab skirts and pants suits—but most of those I don't fit into anymore after having River. It's been ages since I've shopped for clothes; the last time was when I was pregnant. Maybe Mom wants to go.

I can hear her putzing around the kitchen downstairs and swing my legs over the side. Time to get my lazy ass up. I'm glad no one is here to witness my short walk to the bathroom. Waddle is more descriptive. I could probably use a nice hot shower to ease those aches.

Fifteen minutes later, I walk into the kitchen—a little less tentatively—and am greeted by my son's excited squawks.

"Hey, my buddy," I coo, lifting his jumpy little body out of the high chair. "What has you so happy this morning?"

"I could ask you the same thing," Mom comments, lifting her coffee to her lips to hide a smile.

"Trust me, you don't wanna know." I grin when she rolls her eyes.

"Unless the reason for that smirk on your face is the fact you've had a stellar night's sleep like your son—no—I really don't want to know."

I lift my fingers to my mouth and pretend to zip my lips, before blowing a raspberry in River's neck, making him giggle as he grabs onto my hair. "Easy, kiddo." I carefully pry his little fingers open. “You’re gonna have me as bald as Trunk if you don’t watch it.”

“Unk!”

“Exactly. Now finish up your cereal while Mommy gets some coffee, okay?” I slip him back in his seat and get myself some fuel to face the day.

“Want me to cook you some breakfast?”

“No. You don’t have to do that every morning, Mom. I’ll grab some cereal.” I grab a bowl from the cupboard. “I was thinking of going shopping today. It’s actually a nice day to get out. Are you game?”

“You’re asking me? Of course I am. What are we shopping for?”

I sit down beside my son, across from Mom. “I don’t really have anything appropriate to wear for my New York trip. I want something fun, not like the mom-clothes I’ve been schlepping around in.”

She eyes me across the table, on eyebrow slightly raised. “Is this about New York, or about Trunk? That man better take you as you are, or—”

“Ma. It’s about me. I feel the need for a change. Trunk couldn’t care less what I wear, in fact, he probably prefers it to be nothing.” I chuckle when she slaps her hands over her ears, and I wait until she pulls them away. “I want the outside to match the inside. It’s been so long since I’ve done anything fun for me.”

She reaches over and squeezes my hand. “Then that’s what we’ll do.” Turning to River she says, “And you, my boy, will get your first good husband training.”

“He just turned one,” I point out, my mouth full of

cereal.

"Never too young to start," Mom shares sagely.

I'm just clearing away the dishes while Mom is up in her apartment getting ready, when there's a knock on the door.

"Unk!" River was playing on the living room floor, but is now watching the door eagerly. I wonder if I should worry about the obvious preoccupation my son has with that man.

Instead of Trunk, it's Ollie at the door, looking unreasonably tan and healthy for winter.

"Haven't seen you since you got back. You look like you've had a fabulous time." I step aside and wave her in.

"It was amazing," she gushes with a smile. "Fuck, but it's cold to be back."

"Unk!" River cries crawling over.

"Shit," Ollie claps her hand over her mouth. "I didn't see him there. Joe always tells me to watch the swearing." I realize she thinks he's copying her f-bomb.

"Actually, that's his version of 'Trunk,' I think he was hoping it might be him."

"Trunk? As in, the dangerously hot hunk who happens to be Tahlula's brother, Trunk?" I shrug and grin. "Get the frick out of town. I was kinda thinking last year, when he showed up to help you move in here, you'd look cute together." Cute is not exactly the term I would use in anything relating to Trunk, but I don't bother telling her that. "So I guess he's been here enough for River to have bonded?" She gives my shoulder a shove. "Now I know whose truck was in your driveway last night. Joe was ready to come over and knock on your door. I'm glad I was able to hold him back."

Ollie is known for having a tendency to run off at the mouth, so I just wait until she takes a breath.

"Yes. Thank you. Yes, and so am I, because that could've been embarrassing. But," I add quickly. "It's all pretty new."

"New? He was eyeing you even back then. That was last summer." I'm ridiculously tickled at that bit of information, but force the self-satisfied grin down. Ollie doesn't need any encouragement. "It was at his sister's wedding things changed, wasn't it? I knew it!"

"Knew what?" Mom catches Ollie's last words as she walks in from the side door.

"Hey, Mrs. B. I'm talking about your daughter and that gorgeous man. If I didn't have one already at home, I'd be jealous."

"They make a gorgeous couple, don't they?"

I roll my eyes up to the ceiling, hoping for deliverance from the two of them almost having us married off.

"Actually, the reason I popped over…" Ollie finally shares, "…is to see if you'd like to come over for dinner this coming Friday? I found a massive pot roast in the freezer I'm planning to cook."

"Mom probably would," I volunteer. "But I won't be able to make it. I'm flying to New York on Friday. Just for the weekend, it's for work," I clarify.

"New York? That's exciting."

"It is, although I'm not sure I'll see much of it. We were

actually heading out to do some preparatory shopping. I want some new clothes for the trip. Any suggestions?"

"You'll find your standard places—T.J. Maxx, JCPenney, etcetera—in the Durango Mall. If you want something a little more unique, I would try Main Avenue. There are a ton of little boutiques close together downtown. Depends on what you're looking for."

"Unique," Mom answers for me.

TRUNK

"YOU'RE FREAKING ME out."

Paco catches me in the hallway outside of my office.

"The fuck did I do?"

"I just got used to the fact that scowl you usually wear is not nearly as threatening as it appears. You fucking smiling, though? You look like a serial killer, brother. Knock it off."

I wasn't aware I was smiling, but I know why. Suddenly it makes sense why Istu was looking at me funny earlier. Maybe that's why he decided to share what happened in the gym the other day.

Perhaps I should smile more often. Chances are good on that; if it's up to me I'll be fucking smiling every day.

"Get used to it," I fire at Paco.

"Jesus, another one down for the count," he grumbles. "Chief wants to see you in his office."

Ouray's door is open so I walk right in.

"Close it behind you." I do and sit down across from him. "This is about last night."

I was wondering if he'd address Chains. I haven't seen any sign of him this morning. "Okay."

"Just so you know, I had to hold my wife back last night from ripping off Chains's dick and shoving it down his throat, or I would've followed you out to clear the air."

I chuckle at the visual. It's not hard to imagine Luna going off on the asshole. She's a spark plug. "No worries."

"Pulled Chains into my office after. The bastard was smug. Said he'd stopped by to offer help; he'd heard we'd run into some trouble and had a proposal for me."

"He did, did he?" My tone drips with sarcasm.

"Mmm. In exchange for housing a couple of his men and the use of the old storage barn north of the compound, he'd be willing to pay handsomely. Enough we wouldn't have to be dependent on our businesses to keep us going."

"I'm guessing he didn't volunteer why he needs his men here or what he's planning to store."

"Course not. I'm about to give Tink a call. I'm curious why he sent his second-in-command with such an offer. He knows we're not into anything that can't stand the light of day."

I'm surprised they'd even approach the club, knowing Ouray is literally married to the FBI. "How stupid is that guy? He knows who your wife is, doesn't he?"

"Sure he does. That's not a secret. Difference with guys like Chains, they feel so goddamn superior, women have no power in their world."

Neither apparently do people of color, but I keep

that to myself. "You should've let your wife at him last night," I suggest. "He would've experienced firsthand the kind of power women hold."

Ouray chuckles, probably remembering not too long ago Luna managed to knock me on my ass in the boxing ring. I got her down—by sheer body volume—but damn, small as she is, the woman can kick ass.

"Nothin' woulda pleased me more, but knowing Chains, it would've resulted in war. And that, brother, is something we're not looking for or equipped to handle these days."

"So how was it left?" I want to know.

"I'm supposed to think on it for a bit."

"Are you?"

That question earns me a narrowed glare. "I'm gonna pretend you didn't just ask me that. I need time to figure out how to fuckin' say no without it causing serious problems for us."

"Gotcha."

"That's why I wanted to talk to you. You're a psychologist, but you're also someone who's dealt with punks like him before. I need a way outta this mess without making the Moab Reds a full-blown enemy of the club. 'Preciate if you'd give it a thought."

"Sure," I agree, even though I don't have a fucking clue how to handle this. I'm positive the smile I was wearing earlier has worn clear off by now.

"Anything new on the boys?"

"Just finished talking with Istu about the incident with the weight. He shared a bit. Boys have been pickin' on him and Ezhno recently."

"Why?"

"He's not saying." He doesn't really have to. It doesn't take too much imagination to see why those two may have been singled out. Istu is clearly of Asian descent, and Ezhno is at least partially black.

"Color," Ouray concludes.

"My guess."

"That can't fly."

"Agreed."

"Did he mention any other names?"

"Elan is obvious, but he didn't name anyone else."

"I want you to talk to Ahiga next. I want to know what has him riled up. He won't talk to me or Luna. He's been holing up in his room, doesn't even want to come to the clubhouse anymore."

I want to tell him it's not unusual behavior for a teenager, but I get a sense he already knows that, but is worried all the same.

"Maybe it's easier if I go to your place?"

Ten minutes later, Luna shows me inside their house. It's actually across the road from the compound, overlooking Chapman Lake.

"Thanks for doing this, Trunk."

"No problem, but weren't you a trained forensic psychologist?"

She smiles. "Yeah, except my son doesn't give a rat's ass his mom has a degree. As far as he's concerned, I'm being typically intrusive and overprotective."

"Gotcha. Where is he?"

"Up in his room. He may pretend to be asleep. He's good at that."

"I remember that trick. I also know a trick or two to make sure he's awake. You have a problem with wet sheets?"

She starts snickering. "Do what you must."

I leave her grinning at the base of the stairs and head upstairs.

There's no answer when I flick the light switch outside his door; I open it anyway. He's facedown on his bed, a pillow pulled over his head. I walk over and try to pull it away, but his hands are curled in the sides, holding it down. Like hell he's sleeping.

The bathroom is right across the hallway. I grab the glass sitting by the sink and fill it with water before I return to his bedroom. He doesn't appear to have moved, but I can see the tension in his lean muscles. I raise the glass over his back and slowly tip it.

The moment the water hits his back he flips over, an angry scowl on his face.

"What the fuck!" he signs angrily. "*What was that for?"*

I calmly put the glass on his nightstand before answering him. *"That was for being a punk and mind your language."* I pull over the desk chair and sit down, leaning forward. "*Now, I'm gonna be here as long as it takes for you to tell me what's been going on with you. Your parents are worried, and I don't blame them. You're not acting like yourself."*

"I'm fine," he gestures.

"Then how come you're up here pretending to be asleep? I know something is going on with the boys. I'm not an idiot. I think you know something about that."

"I don't know what you're talking about."

I take a deep breath trying to ignore his attitude. *"What made you swing at Matt? He been picking at you too?"*

It's a wild guess, but when his eyes flit up to mine, I know I'm at least getting warm. Istu never pointed a finger at Matt, but there's something off with that boy, and the problems didn't start until the club took him in.

Ahiga just confirmed my suspicions.

14

TRUNK

"WHERE ARE YOU?"

I'm in Jaimie's driveway and her SUV isn't here. I was on my way home, when I had this sudden urge to see her, and drove over.

After talking with Ahiga—who finally admitted Matt pissed him off by mocking him, but didn't want a big deal made of it—I briefly stopped into the clubhouse. Ouray was holed up in his office with Yuma and Kaga, so I ended up having a beer at the bar with Wapi and Honon.

It gave me a chance to observe the boys interact while playing what, I assume, is a new game system. They seemed a little subdued, but that may have been because Momma and Nosh were sitting a few feet away, ready to jump in if things got out of hand.

At some point, Kaga came down the hall and went straight for the bar to fetch some fresh beers. He mentioned in passing they'd be a while yet, but there'd be a club meeting tomorrow morning at eleven, so after my beer was done I said my goodbyes and headed out.

"Why?" Jaimie wants to know.

"Because I'm in your driveway and your car's gone."

"I'm out shopping. Well, technically I'm done shopping, but we stopped for a bite to eat. You should've let me know you were coming."

"How long you gonna be?"

"Just paying the bill. We shouldn't be too long."

"I'll wait."

I use the time to check in with the family who took in Ezrah, just to see how the kid is doing. According to his foster mom, he's healing well, but has trouble sleeping and still won't talk about what happened to him. When they try to bring up the subject of his attack, he shuts down and stops talking altogether.

"He's mentioned you once or twice," she shares. "Asking where you are, when are you coming back, that kinda thing."

Fuck, that burns. I hated leaving him, but it was the better choice, and that hasn't changed. No way I'd want him anywhere near the current tension in the clubhouse. That doesn't mean I can't go see him.

"I'm gonna try and come visit this week, maybe next weekend. Don't mention anything to the boy, I don't wanna disappoint him if it doesn't work out."

Not long after I end the call, Jaimie's SUV pulls in

beside me. Before she has a chance to get out, I already have the back door open and pluck a sleepy River from his car seat. The boy snuggles into my neck with a softly mumbled, "Unk."

"I've got him," I tell Jaimie, who's waiting with a soft look on her face. "I'll grab those later," I add when her mother opens the back door on the other side and starts reaching in for the pile of bags.

"Have you eaten?" Sandra asks, turning around as we reach the front steps.

"Not yet."

"There's half a chicken pot pie in the fridge I can heat for you."

"Wouldn't say no to that." I follow them inside, kicking off my boots in the hallway before heading for the stairs.

"I can carry him up," Jaimie says waiting there.

"I'm good, just lead the way."

She does so spectacularly, giving me a great view as we head upstairs. In the boy's room, she flicks on a standing lamp beside the dressing table, spreading a soft light.

"Does he need a clean diaper?" I ask her when she peels off his little boots and snowsuit while I'm holding him.

"I just changed him at the restaurant before we left. I figured he'd be asleep by the time we got home. That seems to be the effect car rides have on him."

"Pj's?"

Her eyes flash to mine, but she shakes her head. "Just

put him in bed like this. I don't wanna risk waking him. He hasn't been sleeping well."

I walk over to the crib and bend over, carefully laying him down. His little face scrunches up, and for a moment I think he'll put up a protest, but then his features relax back into sleep. I step out of the way so Jaimie can tuck him in, before she turns to me. Her hands land on my chest as she lifts up on her toes and mine automatically reach for her hips.

"Hi," she mumbles, pressing her lips to mine.

"Hello yourself," I whisper back, before deepening the kiss.

A soft grunt from the crib reminds me where we are, and I release her mouth, a final quick kiss before letting her go.

"I've gotta grab the bags still," I mention, taking her hand and pulling her from the room. "You guys bought a shitload."

"I may have gone a little overboard," she admits, but does it smiling. "I'd forgotten how much fun shopping could be." She bursts out laughing when she sees the expression on my face. "Not your thing?"

"Fuck no. I'll take a root canal any day."

"You may not enjoy it, but I'm pretty sure you'll enjoy me shopping." She wiggles her eyebrows teasingly, and it's all I can do not to drag her into her bedroom.

"Bags, James," I growl, reminding her.

"Right. I can't wait to show you."

The sparkle in her blue eyes tells me she's not done teasing.

Sandra has me installed at the kitchen table with a heaping plate and a cold beer, while Jaimie empties bag after bag, showing me her purchases. Some outfits for the baby, clothes for her, and a couple of things for the kitchen. Most of it I couldn't give a rat's ass about, but my body takes notice when she pulls a pile of lace from the last bag.

"*Mercy*," I mutter under my breath, glaring at her. She's making it hard for me to concentrate on my food.

"I got these for a steal." She holds up a pair of barely-there lace panties, a smirk on her face and a challenging eyebrow raised. Revenge for the pair I ruined last night, I'm sure. She has me ready to ruin another pair, but her mother's soft chuckle behind me curbs that urge quite effectively.

"This one I'm saving for New York," she announces, lifting an almost see-through, baby blue nightie with frilly stuff at the top.

I drop my fork on my plate and scowl at her. "Like hell that's going to New York." In response she cocks a hip and tilts her head defiantly.

"Oh, give it up, Jaimie. You've tortured the man enough." Sandra sounds amused behind me.

"You're killing all the fun, Mom," the little minx says, while stuffing the lace confections back in the bag. "I'm just gonna put these away."

I manage to finish my food while she's upstairs and get up to put my plate away when a phone rings. It's not mine. Sandra moves to pick up the landline on the kitchen counter.

I listen with half an ear as she answers.

"Hello?...Yes, Agent Gomez, I remember."

JAIMIE

THAT WAS MEAN.

I snicker as I pull the underwear and nightie from the bag, draping them on my bed.

I spent a whack, but I figure I was due. The last sexy lingerie I bought was right before my wedding. The lace undies Trunk ripped last night had been all I had left. I'd saved them for a special occasion, which is why it didn't bother me when he tore them off. They'd served their purpose.

Rob didn't have much interest in what I was wearing once the honeymoon was over, both literally and figuratively. Where he'd been romantic and chivalrous prior to marriage, he was mostly absent and preoccupied after.

I blame myself. I'd been fast approaching thirty-five when he swept me off my feet, and could hear that clock ticking. Tall, handsome, with a successful business to his name, he was a dream compared to some of my previous loser boyfriends. Mom always said it was my core of steel that attracted the weakest guys out there, but even she had declared Rob a 'keeper.'

There'd been signs—even early on—I chose to ignore. The fact he took more time than me getting ready in the bathroom should've been one. The frequent hunting or fishing trips with his buddies another. Then of course the constant arguing about me working outside the house when he preferred me at home. I'd been waiting for the last straw to walk out of the house, when I discovered I was pregnant with River.

Rob had been over the moon, and for the first time since we got married, his focus was entirely on me. Attentive, he insisted on going to each and every doctor's appointment with me. He made sure I ate right, didn't take off with his buddies for weeks at a time while I was pregnant, and it felt like we'd turned a corner. He held my hand during River's delivery, and when I caught him brushing away tears after our son was born, I thought I couldn't be happier.

That happy bubble popped three weeks later when he left for one of his hunting trips in Montana. He was gone for a month. His next trip, which had been last summer, was finally the last straw for me.

Asshole.

Not at all like the man downstairs, who may be a little rougher around the edges at first glance—and is far from the smooth charmer my ex could be—but is more of a man than Rob ever had the right to claim.

There may not be flowers and foot rubs waiting for me, but who needs those when all the simple, caring things he does add up to so much more.

My son already adores him, and my mom is not far behind. I've crushed on him from a distance so long; the slide into real feelings seems to have come naturally. I don't want to mess this up by being stubborn and unappreciative.

As I hang my new suede skirt on a hanger in my closet, I decide I should tell him about the package. His mention of River's pj's reminded me. Better he hear it from me than someone else.

I flip off the lights, sneaking a peek into River's room to find him still sleeping in the same position, and head downstairs.

"Agent Gomez just called," Mom announces when I hit the bottom step. I'd heard the phone ring, and figured Mom would answer. "He asked if he could pop in tomorrow morning. He has a few more questions. I told him that was fine. That okay?"

I glance over Mom's shoulder into the kitchen and find Trunk's immobile form glaring at me. Well, so much for good intentions.

Mom seems to pick up on the angry energy coming off him and mouths an apology, before saying out loud, "I think that's my cue."

"Night, Mom," I call after her, my eyes never leaving Trunk's, even as he mumbles his own goodnight.

"I was just about to tell you."

"That sounds like a brilliant idea," he snarls sarcastically.

"Look," I start defensively. "This all happened when you were on your way to Monticello. There was no point in—"

"Tell me," he grinds out, cutting me off.

Fuck. This is not going well.

I quickly give him the whole story about the box, the pj's, and even the note. "I called Keith Blackfoot right away. He was here within half an hour with Agent Gomez." I watch Trunk's nostrils flare and quickly add to reassure him, "It's all under control. Luna mentioned last night, they're keeping close tabs on Rob."

I realize my mistake when I see his eyebrows shoot up. "Let me get this straight," he starts deceptively restrained. "A week and a half ago, you find a package from your cock-sucking ex, with a sick message for your boy—the same baby I just put to bed upstairs—it worries you enough to call the cops, who bring in the FBI." I wince as his voice keeps rising. "You even talk about it last night at *my* club, with the wife of *my* president, but at no time during this past week-and-a-*fucking*-half, did you think I might like to know?" he thunders, and for just the beat of a second, I'm glad he's standing on the other side of the counter.

"I was about to. You had so much going on already. I wasn't entirely sure…"

"What weren't you sure of, Jaimie? Me?"

"No! I mean, yes…I mean, it's all new, I'm still trying to figure out what all is happening."

The side door opens and Mom sticks her head in. "Everything all right?"

"It's fine, Mom. Go to bed." She glances at Trunk, whose glare hasn't wavered from me, before giving me a nod and closing the door.

"Was it my truck parked outside your door last night?" he snaps, the moment she's gone. "My hands on your body? My dick pounding inside you?"

"Trunk…" I start, but he's not done yet.

"I'm no fucking expert on relationships, Jaimie, but when a woman talks to everyone but her man, the message is clear. Even for me."

With long strides he walks right by me, shoving his feet in his boots, and grabbing his coat before he's out the door, slamming it behind him.

Upstairs, River starts crying loudly.

Yup. I fucked that up good.

N
nw
ne
W
E
ARROW'S EDGE MC

15

TRUNK

FUCK ME.

I run my hands over my face before glancing at my phone on the nightstand.

Three *fucking* forty-five and I haven't slept a wink.

I shouldn't have left like that. I'd been home for only about twenty minutes before I clued in to that. Sure, she should've told me, but I didn't even give her a chance to explain why she didn't. Not that there is any excuse to justify keeping something like that from me, but I could've listened. Instead I blew up, left Jaimie upset, her mom freaked, and I could hear River wailing when I walked away from the house. That shit looks real good on me.

I can come up with a laundry list of excuses why my

fuse was so damn short, but in the end, I still lost it.

It's the middle of the goddamn night, I doubt I'll get any sleep, and there's nothing I can do to try and fix things right now. Frustrated and pissed at myself, I swing my legs over the edge and pull my jeans back on.

Heading down the hall, I notice the mess. I've barely been home these past two weeks and piles of dirty laundry have formed everywhere. The sink is full of dirty dishes, and I'm pretty sure whatever I have in the fridge is by now well past its expiration date. Thank God I drink my coffee black.

With the Keurig doing its thing, I start picking up dirty shirts and socks I seem to have left all over my living room. I gave up on boxers years ago, ever since Tahlula got her own apartment after she graduated.

I'm not a slob—exactly—I just like being efficient with my time. I spend as long picking one day's worth of shit up as a week's worth. Doing it once a week makes more sense, except I seem to have missed a few weeks.

I toss everything in the laundry room and fetch the rest from the bathroom and bedroom. My coffee is brewed by the time I have the first load running, and I take a big swig, letting the strong liquid slide down my throat.

Three hours later, I'm bouncing on the balls of my feet—wired—as I fry up a couple of frozen burger patties on the stove. It was the only edible thing I could find and I'm starving. I scarf down breakfast while watching the news on TV.

I'm feeling pretty good; my house hasn't been this clean since I moved in last year, and as soon as the food settles in my stomach, the plan is to hop in the shower and drive over to Jaimie's to grovel.

"YOU'RE FUCKIN' LATE," Ouray barks when I rush into the meeting at five past eleven.

I grunt in response as I take my seat, still breathing hard.

I fucking woke up fifteen minutes ago in front of some infomercial, took a three-minute freezing shower cause I didn't have time to wait for the water to heat, and beelined it over here. What started off as a good morning is going to shit fast. I haven't even called or messaged Jaimie, so nothing's been fixed there. The more time I let pass, the more difficult that's going to be.

Yuma storms in seconds after me.

"Someone else who can't fuckin' tell time. Now that we're all here, let's get to business," Ouray continues. "The good news: the gym and studio have been up and running and don't seem to have suffered much in the way of revenue. The bad news is that Brewer's Pub has suffered. Even after the health inspector cleared the restaurant, we did less than half our regular business in the past weeks. It's gonna take a long fucking time to rebuild the good reputation we had in this community." He turns to Yuma. "Did you get the figures for the apartments?"

"Yeah. Of the twenty-two leases, five are coming up for renewal first of May. Four of those tenants don't plan on renewing. Two others have not returned and are threatening to take it to court if we force them to pay the penalty for breaking their lease."

"What you're saying is we haven't just depleted our reserves, but we've lost a substantial chunk of our income. We're fucked," Paco complains.

"We're knocked down, not out. Which brings me to the next item on the agenda…"

Ouray proceeds to describe Chains's proposal to loud shouts of objection in colorful language. He slams his hammer down on the table to get some order in the room.

"Keep your shorts on. Not a chance in hell I'm going to fuckin' risk what we've built this past decade," he continues. "Talked to Tink last night. Just making sure he's actually backing his vice president on this. Found out he's got stage four liver cancer."

"Death sentence," Honon mutters.

"Right," Ouray agrees. "Took the fire out of him. Short of it is, he's left the running of the club in Chains's hands."

"That fucking sucks," Paco grumbles. "Chains is gonna be a loose cannon without Tink's leash around his neck."

"At least we know what we're dealing with," Lusio, who's one of the quieter brothers, suggests.

"How do you figure that?" Paco snaps.

"Chains may be a loose cannon, but he's clever. I'd bet my left nut, he made sure he had some leverage on Arrow's Edge before approaching the chief."

"Not much of a fuckin' bet; just your left nut," Honon

points out.

"That one's my favorite," Lusio jokes, grabbing his crotch.

Ouray ignores the banter. "He's right. Weaken your enemy, before engaging them in battle."

"You saying this is war, Chief?"

"No, we should be prepared for anything, but we're gonna handle this smart. We're gonna strengthen our ranks and expand our business."

The next forty-five minutes are spent discussing the addition of an auto shop to the compound, and how to increase membership.

"One last thing," Ouray calls everyone to attention. "I want you to be alert. Keep in mind Arrow's Edge is only as strong as our weakest brother. To divide is to conquer."

I catch the quick flick of his eyes in Yuma's direction, who is closely studying the wood grain in the table. Not hard to figure out why they were locked here last night.

With the meeting dismissed, everyone files out of the office, but Ouray calls me back.

"A minute?" I stay behind and take my seat again. "Luna mentioned you got Ahiga to talk to you."

"Yeah. He says he got tired of Matt making fun of him so he let his fists fly."

"Okay, but why didn't he just say so?"

I shrug. "He claims it's because he didn't want anyone making a big deal out of it. Says he can handle things himself."

Ouray tents his fingers under his chin. "And what do

you think?"

"He may have a point. Lord knows we're getting nowhere with Matt and if we call him out on this, he'll likely dig in even deeper, only making things worse for Ahiga. I think we're better off keeping a close eye out and making sure those two are not left alone together. Let them sort it out."

Ouray nods. "Agreed."

"Your son has respect from the other kids—both because he's the oldest and you're his father. Coming in fresh off the street, it may be a natural response for Matt to try and challenge him for that position."

"What about the other situation?" I know he's referring to the talk I had with Istu.

"Same deal. I can try and feel some of the kids out during our regular talks, but let's not push too hard and just keep an eye out. These kids feel cornered, their knee-jerk response is gonna be to bolt. That's gonna create more problems than it'll solve."

It's after one when I walk out of the clubhouse. Other than Matt and Ahiga, who are working at the kitchen table under Momma's supervision, the kids will be in school until three thirty.

It doesn't give me a lot of time, but maybe just enough to kick down a few bricks in that wall I know Jaimie is building.

I'm second-guessing that thought when I pull up and spot a little scrap of baby blue sticking out of the garbage can at the end of the driveway.

Jaimie

Maybe it's for the best.

I started telling myself that when I woke up this morning after a restless night tossing and turning. *Maybe it's for the best.* It sounds so adult and sensible, even if those are the last things I actually feel.

It's not exactly 'adult' to shove your face into a pillow and scream out your frustration, nor is it particularly 'sensible' to toss your hundred thirty-five dollar sexy nightie in the garbage can outside.

I hid out in my office space upstairs all morning, avoiding Mom's inquiring glances. I don't feel ready to respond to. It's a little after one when I surface for something to eat. I wasn't hungry this morning but by now my stomach feels like it's gnawing on me from the inside out.

I bump into Mom and River at the bottom of the stairs. My son is sleeping in her arms.

"I was just going to put him down for a bit," she says. "He fell asleep in his high chair." I bend down to kiss his soft, downy hair. "I left some chicken noodle soup on the stove for you. It should still be warm."

"Thanks, Mom."

She continues up as I head to the kitchen. My mother makes the best chicken soup; it fixes whatever ails you. Sadly I've never been able to master it quite the way she makes it. As I close my eyes on the first spoonful, I wonder if she made it with fixing me in mind today.

"I think I'm going to have a nap as well," she says,

walking into the kitchen. "Call if you need me."

I feel guilty when she disappears out the side door; I haven't exactly been nice to her today. She's been an absolute lifesaver; uprooting the city she'd lived in all her life just so she could help me find my feet. At sixty-two, she had an active life, gave it all up for us, and I've been taking her for granted.

I turn when the kitchen door opens again, thinking it's Mom, but I'm shocked to find Trunk walking in, my new nightie in his large fist.

"What are you doing here?"

I wince, realizing how aggressive those words sound leaving my mouth. The only excuse I have is that I didn't expect him. I thought I'd chased him off for good.

"Saving you from making a huge mistake," he says, the deep rumble of his voice washing over me like a warm shower. "This still has the tag on it." He holds the nightie up while kicking the door shut with the heel of his boot. "Seems a waste to toss it out. I was looking forward to peeling it off you."

The last noodle I try to swallow goes down the wrong hole and I find myself choking on it. The next second a glass of water appears in front of me as a large hand starts rubbing my back. If I didn't have tears running down my face as I try to suck in air, I might've purred.

"I'm sorry," I finally manage, as he tosses his coat over a kitchen chair only to sit down right beside me.

"For?" He seems genuinely confused.

"For not telling you about the box right away. For making you think I don't trust you. Although in my defense, at the time you had your hands full and I wasn't exactly clear on where we stood at the time."

"They were clear to me. They've been clear for a while, which makes the way I reacted even worse." Now it's my time to be a little confused, especially when he frames my face in his hands. "It's always worked for me; use my anger to deflect fear, or pain…or vulnerability. There aren't many people able to make me feel any of those things."

It takes me a moment to understand what he is saying, but when I do; I grab onto his wrists and close my eyes. "Trunk…"

"Sorry if I scared you, or your mom, and it fucking kills me knowing I made your boy cry." He rests his forehead against mine. "I'm learning as I go here, Little Mama, but I want you to know you've got nothing to fear from me. Ever."

"Shhh…" I press a finger to his lips before replacing it with my mouth, kissing him sweetly. We may be in over our heads at times, and don't do so well communicating, but our bodies seem to have no trouble at all falling into sync.

All too soon Trunk ends the kiss, his dark eyes warm and liquid.

"Shee-it, James. You drive me to the edge of reason."

16

Trunk

IT'S ALMOST WARM tonight. Surprisingly so for the end of March.

"Let me bum one," Ouray says, joining me outside the clubhouse where I'm having my after dinner smoke. I hand him my pack and lighter.

"Does your wife know you sneak off bumming smokes?"

"My wife knows better than anyone how imperfect I am. Besides, she's an FBI agent; she knows everything."

She probably does too. There's not much that escapes Luna.

"Hear anything from Chains since the weekend?"

He shakes his head. "All quiet on that front, for now. We'll hear from him eventually, I have no doubt."

His eyes drift over my shoulder to the three-stall garage that housed the gym until a few days ago. Kaga's buddy Brick, the mechanic, is heading down from Grand Junction this coming weekend to have a look, and Ouray wanted to make sure he'd be able to see the full potential. So when I got back here on Monday after stopping over at Jaimie's to set things straight, it was all hands on deck.

The clubhouse basement, which apparently had been a catchall for all kinds of crap over the years, was suggested for the new gym. Not a bad idea, if you ask me. Makes far more sense to have it easily accessible. Especially in the winter.

Still, I could see why they hadn't gotten around to moving it there before. The large space was packed with crap. The only accessible part was right at the bottom of the stairs, where the club's industrial-sized washer and dryer were housed. The prior washer and dryer were still there, simply shoved out of the way. Boxes, broken furniture, bike parts, an old pool table, mattresses, it looked like crap had just been tossed down there without rhyme or reason.

It had taken every available hand a day and a half, plus a huge rented dumpster in front of the clubhouse, to empty out the space. It had been my suggestion to get the boys involved, thinking that working side by side on something that'll benefit everyone might be good for them. Ouray had easily agreed, provided I supervise the kids.

Of course that meant I've barely had a chance to breathe, let alone hang out with Jaimie, who's leaving for New York with my sister tomorrow.

"We're almost done painting the garage. One more coat tomorrow should do it," I share with Ouray.

"Good. Don't know why we didn't move the gym down there years ago. It's seen more action just last night and this morning than the entire month before."

"I'm sure it'll slow down again once the newness wears off."

A grunt is his response as he tosses his cigarette butt in the old coffee can and pulls the door open. "You coming in?"

"Nah, gonna head over to Jaimie's, haven't seen her since Monday. Wapi's got the kids."

Ouray grins. "Gettin' serious then?" I don't know how to answer that, so I shrug instead.

No denying, she's taking up most of my thoughts, but I find it a bit unsettling. Or maybe unfamiliar is a better description. I'm a guy who lives in the moment. I'm not used to making plans or thinking ahead too far, but I do now. In fact, it's all I do and almost everything revolves around Jaimie. I barely recognize myself.

"Word of advice? Don't think too hard." He lightly punches a fist in his stomach. "Go with the gut." With that he disappears inside, the door slamming shut behind him.

WELL, MY GUT takes me all the way to Jaimie's front step.

"Hey."

Her warm smile is all the welcome I need. With a hand on her hip, I crowd her backward into the house. The blue of her eyes deepens when I bend down for a taste.

"Hi, Trunk." Her mother's voice holds me back from the hot kiss I was about to lay on her, limiting me to a barely-there brush of lips.

"Sandra," I return, looking away from Jaimie's deepening blush at her mother, who scrambles to her feet.

"River's sleeping, so I was just about to head over to my place," she shares with a little smile.

"Don't leave on my account," I lie boldfaced. She knows it too, the smile turning into a smirk.

"Oh, I'm not. I have a few phone calls to make before I turn in. Night, guys."

"Night, Mom."

"Sandra."

When the door closes behind her, I turn back to Jaimie who is biting her bottom lip, instantly ramping up the fire in my blood.

"Have you eaten?" Suddenly self-conscious, she pulls away and walks toward the kitchen. I follow behind, keeping the distance she's trying to gain to a minimum.

"Yup."

"Wanna beer?"

She's already got her head in the fridge, and instead of answering; I grab her hips and press my hard cock against her ass. Her head snaps around.

“Not thirsty, James.”

Fire flashes in her eyes as she suddenly straightens up, twisting from my hold. “That’s too bad,” she bites off. “Food and a beer, it’s all that’s up for offer tonight. Sorry if you were looking for something else.” She shoves the cold beer she grabbed in my hands and stalks to the living room, plopping down on the couch.

Taking a deep breath in, and a swig of beer I hope will cool me down a bit, I join her, keeping a safe distance between us. This is the part where I should probably practice my social skills, because she’s right. Time to put my money where my mouth is. I almost messed up a guy last weekend for showing her no respect, but I’m no better myself, walking in the door without so much as a hello before I’m rutting against her like some animal.

“Any good movies?”

Her eyes open wide as she swings around to face me. “You wanna watch a movie?”

“Sure.” I shrug.

“I thought you wanted to…” She doesn’t need to finish the sentence.

I twist my body toward her. “Oh, I wanna. All I have to do is think of you and I wanna. All the fucking time. That doesn’t mean it’s *all* I want.” I see her face soften a little, and set my beer on the table so I have my hands free to grab hers, rubbing my thumbs over her knuckles. “Haven’t seen you for a bit, Little Mama. It’s been a crazy week, like every other goddamn week it seems. I wanted to see you before you take off tomorrow.”

The soft look is now a smile as she frees a hand and

grabs the remote before scooting over and settling in beside me. "Tell me about your crazy week first?" she asks, lifting my arm over her shoulder.

Normally club business stays in the club, but I know Ouray talks with Luna and I'm sure Kaga does the same with his wife. For the simple reason club business impacts their families. It clearly impacts whatever Jaimie and I've got going on, so I only hesitate a second before telling her. I leave out the offer Chains and the Moab Reds put on the table, or the suspicion they're the ones behind the recent mishaps, but I tell her everything else.

"What a great idea," she says, leaning her head against my chest. "It'll be great for those boys to work together on fixing up some old car or something. Gives them a common purpose, not to mention that it keeps them away from electronics. That's one thing I worry about when River gets older; there will come a point where I won't be able to keep the intrusion of gaming and internet away from him," she rambles.

I chuckle which has her look up at me. "Babe, the kid's just one."

"It'll go fast," she says, her face dead serious, and really fucking cute. I have no choice but to lean down and kiss her.

One moment she's sitting beside me, the next she's on my lap, her legs on either side of me, and her arms wrapped tightly around my neck. My fingers dig into her perfectly padded hips, as her tongue teases and tangles with mine. It's easy to get lost in her to the point where nothing else exists.

"James, baby," I mumble, keeping her hips still when she starts grinding on me. "Take me upstairs."

Two minutes later we're in her bedroom, ripping off clothes in a frenzy. When I see her standing naked in front of the bed, though, I purposely slow down.

"Fuck, you're so beautiful."

Her eyes get that heavy-lidded look as she backs up to the bed and sits down, beckoning me over by crooking her index finger. The moment I'm close enough to reach, she has one hand on my hip, while fisting my dick with the other. Before I can even think, her perfectly pink mouth slides over the tip.

It's like a million charges fire off through my body at once and all I can do is hiss with pleasure. So hot, watching my black cock slide between her lips as her blonde hair falls around her face. When she lifts those blue eyes to me from under her lashes, I know if I don't stop her now I'm done.

"I wasn't done," she pouts when I pull myself free.

"I know, but I almost was. You wanna blow me some other time, I'm not gonna stop you, but tonight I wanna come inside you." I retrieve a condom from my jeans.

"I'm clean and I'm on the pill," she says, surprising me in a good way. Only thing better than being inside her is being inside her ungloved.

"I've gotta clean bill." My voice is almost hoarse.

She doesn't say anything, but scoots back on the mattress, dropping her legs open in invitation. She's as near perfection as I've ever seen. Her face an angel's, ripe full tits and rounded belly, and then those soft, milky-white thighs perfect for cushioning my power when I drive inside her.

"Shee-it, James, you're a fucking siren."

I wipe the satisfied smile off her face when I set a knee on the mattress, and bend down and press the flat of my tongue to her heat. I lick my way up her body until my hips are wedged between her legs and our eyes are in line. Using one hand I carefully guide myself inside her.

My eyes almost roll to the back of my head at the tight, wet heat clamping around me.

Oh yeah, sheer fucking perfection.

JAIMIE

I WAKE UP almost on my stomach, a heavy body wrapped around me from behind. The muscular leg draped over one of mine, and a strong arm lodged underneath my torso, render me immobile. The moment I try to move at the sound of River crying, the arm tightens around me.

"Don't go," Trunk grunts sleepily.

"River's crying."

"I'll go," he says, and before I can protest, his weight leaves me.

By the time I turn over and sit up, he's already on his way out of the bedroom, his jeans hanging low on his spectacular ass. I have to pinch myself to make sure I'm not dreaming, although the tender feeling between my legs should've clued me in.

Unlike the first time—which was fast and wild—last night was slow, thorough, and delicious. The man drove me to the edge time and time again, only to freeze each time I was about to tip over. It felt like an eternity before he let me come on a keening cry, his own explosive release following right behind.

I can't hear crying anymore, but I hear water turned on in the bathroom down the hall. It's quiet for a while, and I'm about to go investigate, when Trunk walks in with a bright-eyed and bushy-tailed River on his arm wearing nothing but a diaper.

"Where's his pj's?" I ask, noticing the scowl on Trunk's face.

"Bathroom," he grunts, handing a very happy River to me.

"What are you doing up, buddy? You're way too happy for…" I check the clock on the nightstand. "… five fifteen in the morning."

"He's happy now. What'd you feed the kid?" Trunk grumbles as he gets back into bed. Wearing his jeans and staying on top of the covers, but still as if he belongs here as he settles against the headboard, stretching his long legs.

"Feed him? Did he throw up?"

"Blew up is more like it."

"Oh no." I try hard not to laugh at Trunk's disgruntled tone. "You should've called me." He grunts something unintelligible, and I feel compelled to lean over and kiss him. "Thank you, honey."

"Welcome," he mumbles, throwing his arm around me and tucking me to his side. River throws his body at Trunk, who catches him with one large hand under his booty. “Easy, Little Man.”

“Unk!”

“I’m guessing we’re done sleeping?”

He looks at me with an eyebrow raised and I press my face into his pec to stifle my snicker.

“YOU’RE UP EARLY,” Mom says, when she finds me in the kitchen cooking breakfast for a change.

“River had a blowout.”

“Oh no,” she commiserates, tossing her coat on the kitchen chair before looking around. “Where is he?”

“Coming.” I turn back to the bacon frying in the pan, smiling. Trunk offered to get him dressed in trade for me cooking him breakfast.

“What do you—Ohh.”

“Morning, Sandra,” Trunk’s deep rumble has me turn my head. He’s just coming down the stairs, fully dressed—thank God—carrying River on a hip. I watch as he passes the baby off to a surprised Mom’s hands and walks my way. He slips an arm around me from behind and kisses the nape of my neck before resting his chin on my shoulder. “Scrambled, Little Mama.”

“You’ve got it, honey.”

I get another kiss behind my ear before I feel him step away.

I’m not sure precisely what happened between last night and this morning, but any concerns I may have had, any uncertainty around what is going on, seem to have disappeared.

Actually, that's a lie: I know exactly what happened. Trunk happened. After the initial bump last night, he's proceeded to show me in a variety of ways how invested he is willing to be, and not just in bed.

When I set the pan of scrambled eggs and the plate of stacked bacon on the table, he is telling Mom about Ezrah.

"Aiming to go see him tomorrow. I talked to his foster mom and he's having a bit of a hard time."

"Poor kid," Mom says softly.

"Hard to believe someone would do that to a little boy," I contribute, sitting down beside River's high chair and handing him the toast I cut in strips.

When we're with done breakfast, it's Trunk who gets up and clears the table. I ignore Mom's bulging eyes and focus instead on cleaning egg off my son.

I feel hands settle on my shoulders.

"Good eggs, James."

I tilt my head up and smile at him. "Thanks, honey, but my mother's are better."

I glance over at Mom, who is looking from me to Trunk. I swear she has stars in her eyes.

"I've gotta head out," he says, plucking River from his chair. "You gonna behave? Your mama's gonna give Gramma my number, and you step outta line even once, I'm gonna hear about it, Little Man."

River giggles, pumps his little legs, and slaps his hands on Trunk's face. "Unk!"

"Just you remember that, boy." He hands my baby to

Mom and grabs my hand. “Walk me out?”

On the front step he pulls me close, giving me a hard kiss.

“Call me when you land, and make sure you give your mother my number.”

“That’s not nece—”

“Give her my number, James.”

“Fine.”

He tugs on a strand of my hair before cupping my face in his hand.

“Had a good night, Little Mama. Fucking great night.”

“Me too.”

Another kiss, this one sweeter, before he turns and starts walking, only to stop again.

“Call me.”

N
nw
ne
W
E
ARROW'S EDGE MC

17

TRUNK

"HOW ARE YOU doing, buddy?"

Ezrah, who doesn't seem to want to meet my eyes, looks down as he picks at his nails.

"Okay," he finally mumbles, but I get nothing more.

The boy's nails are chewed down to the point of bleeding. I look up at Deandra, Ezrah's foster mom, who looks on in concern. When I got here, she took me aside to let me know the police had been by again, trying to get answers from the boy. Without his cooperation they have nothing to go on, other than it was clearly a hate crime.

"Ezrah, can you look at me a minute?" I focus on the boy. "I know you're tired of people asking you questions. Especially cops, am I right?"

The kid lifts his head slightly and peeks tentatively

at me from under dreads that are falling in his eyes. His shoulders give a barely-there shrug. "Pigs," he mumbles. I hear Deandra inhale sharply in reaction. I throw her a quick glance and a curt shake of my head to ward off the admonishment I'm sure is coming. Her already half-opened mouth snaps shut.

"When I was a boy, I didn't think much of the police either. Always on the run from them. Course, they'd be after me for good reason." Ezrah looks up with curiosity and I take it as encouragement. "I used to hang with a group of kids, we'd get in trouble a lot. Spent most our time running the streets, looking for something to do, and we'd usually find it, or it found us. Weren't that many of us brothers around, so we were tight. Went at it with anyone lookin' at us funny." I see something flicker behind his eyes, and decide to probe a little, purposely letting some of the old familiar street language slip through in an effort to connect. "You got any homies, kid? They gonna wonder where you at?"

He shakes his head. "Nah. Prolly think I'm dead."

"You're not, though. You're right here, livin' and breathin'. Think maybe they'd wanna know?"

Again he shakes his head, his messy dreads bouncing around his face. "Dey don't care."

It hurts my heart to hear a young boy say that with such conviction, but I get it. I was there once myself. "I used to think that. Wasn't true, though. Did I tell you about my little sister?" His eyes show surprise, suddenly keenly interested. "She's three years younger than me. Growing up we were all the other had. You got a brother or sister?"

He hesitates for a moment, taking in a deep shaky breath. "Sister."

Grabbing on to the piece of information like a lifeline, I press. "Younger?"

"Kiara be four now."

I try to keep my cool while I work to keep the trickle of information flowing. "That's still little. She look like you?"

He shrugs, staring blindly at some point over my shoulder. "Ah guess. Ain't seen her for a while."

"I bet she misses you."

Ezrah's suddenly blinking at the tears welling in his eyes. "She'll forget."

"Why do you think that?"

"Better for her." I can almost see the shutters slam down. His eyes return to his hands, fingers restlessly picking at his nails.

"You may believe that, Ezrah, but I'm not sure that's true." I wasn't expecting a response and I don't get one. Figuring I've pushed him as far as he's willing to go for now, I get up from my seat. "I should be heading back. Do you still have my phone number?" His head barely moves. "Good. If you wanna talk—any time, kid—you call. Don't care if it's day or night. And I'll come back soon for a visit."

His head comes up then. "When?"

"Not sure yet, but how about I give you a call this week?"

He answers with another shrug, but I'll take it.

Deandra walks me to the door and quietly thanks me for coming out, admitting she feels a bit out of her depth with Ezrah. I reassure her she's doing all she can, and remind her she can call me any time as well, if she thinks I can be of any help.

The sun sets during my trip back to Durango. I notice driving into the mountains, with the temperatures warming up in recent days, the snow is quickly disappearing. It's high time to get my bike back on the road. The truck's an okay ride, but there's nothing better than feeling that wind hit your face. Except perhaps having Jaimie behind me, holding on tight.

She called last night from the hotel when they got settled in. We didn't talk long, she'd been wiped, and today I know they have a lot of stuff going on, so I'll hold off and call tomorrow before they head back to the airport.

Driving through town, I quickly give the club a call. I get Paco on the line.

"Things quiet there?"

"For the most part. Boys are. Yuma was being an ass earlier, but Ouray set him straight. "

"What was that about?"

"You know he's got this thing with Red and his old lady?"

Yes, we all know. I was an unlucky witness last year at a club cookout. Red, the president of the Mesa Riders MC—his wife, Ginger, riding him—and fucking Yuma pounding her ass. Sadly I haven't been able to bleach that picture from my head.

"Don't remind me," I grumble.

"Ouray got wind he invited them for a visit this coming week. Chief went ballistic."

"Good. Not really a good time for a fucking social call."

"Booty call is more like it," Paco corrects me. "Anyway, he got told. Momma got in on the action, which wasn't pretty. Anyway, Yuma left, Ouray went across the road, Momma's gone to bed, and all is quiet."

"Gonna head straight home in that case. I'll probably be by tomorrow."

"Yup. Sounds good."

As I drive up the mountain, I notice the water is running in Junction Creek where the road cuts close. Last week it was still frozen. Another sign we may be in for an early spring.

The house is dark when I pull up. As much as I love it up here, I'm getting tired of coming home to an empty house. Not so I'd want to be back in the clubhouse, but I wouldn't mind finding Jaimie waiting for me.

I slap a sandwich together in the kitchen, watch a bit of TV, and after the late news head to bed.

I'm not sure what wakes me in the middle of the night, but when I turn to look at my alarm clock, I notice a weird glow reflecting off the wall. What the fuck?

Kicking my feet over the side, I blindly grope around for the jeans I dropped beside the bed before getting in. Quickly pulling them on, I walk to the window where the orange glow is coming from.

Don't know why, but I'm not even shocked when I

see the fire in my driveway. I'm too fucking enraged to register what it is that's burning, and focus instead on the man standing in front of the fire, wearing dark clothing, a balaclava covering his face.

In seconds, I've pulled my gun from the nightstand, stuffed my phone in my pocket, and shoved my feet in boots, before storming out the front door.

"Hey! Fucking piece of shit!"

The figure doesn't appear to react when I raise my gun, but when I fire off a round in front of his feet, he turns and runs into the trees on the side of the driveway. I take off after him. He's fast, but so am I.

I don't even notice the cold on my bare torso; the hot rage inside me keeps me warm as I barrel through the underbrush after the motherfucker. From the corner of my eye, I see something coming at me and I quickly turn, but it's too late.

The bat hits me to the side of the head and I'm knocked off my feet. The first kick is to my arm and I feel a bone snap as the gun drops uselessly from my hand.

There are two of them. At least I think it's two. Hard to tell when you're on your back, getting worked over by what feels like a handful of bats and ten pairs of steel-toed boots.

I'm a big man. I'm not afraid to fight and often win, but I'm no match for these guys. Blood is running in my eyes, almost blinding me, as I try to block the blows that pummel my body with my one good arm. I roll on my side, curling my knees up to protect some vital parts, but that leaves my back exposed. They don't hesitate to take aim at my kidneys and with every blow landed; I feel the fight drain out of me.

"Finish him," I hear, before a glimpse of a boot coming at my head is the last thing I see.

JAIMIE

"I DIDN'T THINK it was possible to be this tired," Tahlula says, kicking off her shoes and putting her feet on the coffee table in our suite as Evan hands her the baby.

I agree with her. It's been a hell of a day. Fun and exciting, but exhausting as well. Karen Dove, Tahlula's editor, insisted on taking us out to dinner after the last interview, when all we wanted was to roll into bed.

Evan stayed in our joint two-bedroom suite with Hanna, who provided a good excuse to leave the restaurant without coffee or dessert, since T is still nursing.

"Why don't I run you a bath while she's feeding?" Evan suggests and, not for the first time this weekend, I consider what a lucky bitch my boss and best friend really is.

"Ahhh. That would be so nice," T groans. When her husband disappears into their bedroom, she turns to me. "If you wanna hit the sack, you should go right ahead. I'm heading there right after my bath, if I don't fall asleep in the tub first."

A quick glance at my phone shows it's already eleven thirty by the time I slip between the sheets. My case is packed, my clothes for tomorrow are laid out, and all I have left to do before we head to the airport early in the morning, is stuff my nightie and toiletries in my bag.

As much fun as this was, the New York pace is a little too high for me. I can't wait to get back to Durango and see my boy. I miss him.

Still, the last thought before I drift off is when I'll get to see Trunk.

"HAVE YOU HEARD from my brother?" T asks when we sit down in our seats on the flight from Denver to Durango.

"I tried a few times before we left New York, but it keeps going straight to voicemail. I ended up sending a text instead, but I haven't heard anything back." I grab my phone and check again. Nothing. It doesn't look like he's even seen my message yet.

"Weird. I've tried too. Maybe he's on the road."

"Could be. He did say he was going to Monticello this weekend."

"He's probably driving then," Tahlula concludes, tucking her phone away. "He's usually pretty good about answering, I'm sure that's what it is."

She and Evan start discussing groceries they need to get this afternoon, but my mind is still on Trunk. I'm sure he mentioned going to see Ezrah on Saturday, but it's always possible he ended up staying the night before returning home. It's still weird the calls go straight to voicemail. I quickly shoot off another message.

***Me*: Haven't heard. Text me so I know you're okay.**

Luckily the flight into Durango is only an hour. I only have my carry-on to grab, but we have to wait for Hanna's stroller to get offloaded.

I see Luna the moment we walk into the terminal, and I can tell from the tight look on her face something's wrong. Immediately my stomach starts churning.

"What's Luna doing here?" Evan wonders out loud, but I'm already rushing toward her.

"What's wrong?" I ask as I approach her.

Instead of answering she glances over my shoulder, and waits for T and Evan to catch up.

"There was an incident early this morning," she starts.

"Trunk…" I whisper. Evan tucks Tahlula close and wraps his free arm around my shoulders.

"Fire and rescue was called out this morning. A neighbor reported a fire at your brother's house. When they got there most of the house was engulfed. His truck was parked outside, also on fire."

"Trunk?"

Luna takes a deep breath in before she answers, but in those few seconds I've already died a thousand deaths. "They haven't found him yet, but that could be good news," she quickly adds, but already Tahlula lets out a keening cry, and I feel Evan's arm letting me go to tend to his wife.

"Why are you here?" I manage in an effort to hold panic at bay.

"Because it was an obvious case of arson. Whoever did it left a fairly prominent calling card burning in the driveway."

"What?" T snaps, wiping at her eyes as she lifts her head from Evan's chest and turns to the agent. "A fucking cross?"

"Actually, not a cross. It looks more like a large, rudimentary swastika."

"Jesus," Evan hisses.

"We're hoping Trunk is hiding, so Ouray is out there with the guys, roaming the woods."

"That makes no sense, he would've shown up by now," I suggest.

"The other possibility is that they took him."

"Or hurt him," T offers.

"I need to go look," I tell Luna, dragging my carry-on past her to the exit. The swastika reminded me immediately of Rob and his merry band of crazy nationalists. What if it's my fault Trunk was targeted? What if this is my motherfucking ex's doing?

"Hold up, Jaimie." She grabs me by the arm. "You can't go running off."

"Why the hell not?"

"Because about the same time we arrived at Trunk's house, your mother was banging on your landlord's door. She and your baby are fine," she quickly assures me when she reads the fear off my face. "Your garage door, not so much."

Luna insists I ride with her, and I don't object after hearing someone left 'bitch your MINE' spray-painted on my garage door. Apparently Evan's mother, Joan, picked Mom and River up from the Benedetti house across the street.

Luna wants to bring me to Joan's place so I can see my baby, but I'm torn, I want to look for Trunk as well.

"Think, Jaimie: what are you going to do that the club or the cops and the FBI can't? Best thing you can do for everyone right now is lay low and look after your family."

We've barely pulled out of the parking spot when Luna's phone rings.

"You're on speaker phone, honey," she warns her husband.

"We've got him. Heading to Mercy."

18

Trunk

"HANG IN THERE, brother."

I'm being jostled, and it's all I can do not to yell out at the excruciating pain shooting through my body. Attempts to open my eyes fail; so I have to go by sound alone. I hear the rustling of footsteps through underbrush and heavy breathing of those carrying me. I can't see them, but I know it's my brothers carrying me out of the woods. Ouray's voice is evidence of that.

I may have passed out again, because the next things I hear are sirens and the sharp scent of disinfectant penetrates my senses.

"You're gonna be okay." The soft feminine voice is a surprise, and this time when I try, I manage to open my eyes. "I'm Bella," the pretty, dark-haired, and vaguely familiar EMT explains. "You're a bit of a mess, but I'll take good care of you. We're on our way to the hospital."

I sense someone else and try to turn my head, but that triggers sharp pain all the way down my neck, which appears to be trapped in a brace.

"I'm right here," I hear Ouray's voice right before he moves himself in my line of vision. "Just relax and let Bella do her job."

Battling a sudden wave of nausea, I close my eyes.

"Trunk?" Bella asks. "Can you tell me where it hurts?"

I try, but it's impossible to pinpoint. My entire body feels like it's on fire. "Everywhere," I manage to croak.

"They worked you over pretty good, my man," Ouray volunteers.

"I know. I was there."

That earns me a chuckle but his subsequent question is serious. "Can you tell me anything?"

"Just a poke," I hear Bella say, before feeling the stick of a needle in my arm. "Giving you something for the pain."

That would be great.

"I think two of them. Saw the one. Black clothes, balaclava covering his face. White. I know that much. Went after him. Other guy took me out from behind. Trap."

"They say anything?"

"Finish him." I may not remember everything, but I remember those words. Don't think I'll ever forget. I had just a fraction of a second to think after they were said, but it was enough to fill with a lifetime of regrets. Not the least of which was waiting so long to make my move on Jaimie. It was her face I saw when that boot connected with my head.

I hear Ouray curse under his breath before he says out loud, "Good news is; they failed. But it sure as fuck wasn't for lack of trying."

Nothing to say to that; except, "Boots. Steel-toed boots, both of them. Baseball bat." As I feel myself starting to float on whatever shit Bella's putting in my system, something else occurs to me. "Find my gun?" I can hear my own voice slur the words.

"What did he say?" I hear Ouray's voice ask as I float farther away.

"Something about a gun."

JAIMIE

WE'RE WAITING JUST inside the doors when the ambulance pulls up to the hospital.

Luna drove straight here from the airport—just a five minute drive—while I called Tahlula. She and Evan were just seconds behind us.

Ouray is the first to jump out of the back, and my breath catches in my throat when I see the blood covering his front.

"Oh my God," T whispers, and I blindly reach for her hand.

Then they unload the gurney, my heart stops when I see his large, immobile form strapped down. I never even noticed Ouray walking up until he blocks my view of Trunk, pulling me in his arms. I smell leather and smoke, along with the metal scent of what I assume is Trunk's blood.

"Looks worse than he is. He was talking earlier." I try to let the words reassure me, as he steps aside in time for me to see Trunk's barely recognizable face pass by.

The next hour and fifteen minutes is spent waiting, Tahlula's hand still squeezing mine when a doctor finally walks into the now full waiting room. Conversations taking place around us all come to a grinding halt.

"Family for Titus Rae?"

"I'm his sister," Tahlula says getting up and pulling me with her. "We're his family."

The doctor looks around the room, before focusing back on T. "Very well, your brother was brought in with a variety of injuries. The most concerning right now is a high-impact fracture to the back of his skull. We'll be monitoring him closely in the next twenty-four hours for any signs of bleeding or swelling of the brain. Our next major concern is an open fracture of his right forearm. Both the radius and ulna have been displaced. Because it is an open fracture, this will require surgery immediately to minimize the risk of infection." The tight squeeze of Tahlula's hand around mine is almost painful, but I don't let go as I try to absorb the information. "In addition, he has several broken ribs, a fractured orbital bone, and a broken nose, along with a number of lacerations—some of which will need stitches—and bruises. Those should heal on their own."

"Is he already in surgery?" Evan asks.

"Within the next half hour or so he will be."

"Would it be possible to see him before? Not me," Evan quickly adds. "But I'm sure his sister and fiancée would like a chance."

I don't even flinch at his descriptor for me, I'm simply grateful he's going to bat for us, but I feel compelled to point something out. "Even if only his sister can see him, that would be helpful."

"Let me see what I can do."

In the end, we both get to spend a few minutes with him. If not for his familiar large form, it would be hard to recognize him.

I find a safe spot on the top of his left hand to press a kiss. Not that he feels it—he's not conscious—but I need that sliver of a connection. Tahlula is bent over, whispering close to his ear, and I hope between the two of us we've managed to convey he's not here alone.

Somehow that feels important.

Minutes later, we watch as his bed is wheeled out and follow him into the hallway, where emotions finally get the best of us when he disappears into the elevator.

"OH, SWEETHEART, HOW is he?"

My mom's concerned voice brings out the tears again. I feel five years old, needing the magical comfort of my mother's arms. It takes me a while to compose myself while Mom waits patiently on the other end of the line.

I briefly stepped out of the crowded waiting room,

after the surgeon reported on his outcome, to check in with my mother. I hadn't spoken to her yet.

"Surgery went well. He has plates in his arm and they're keeping a close eye out for signs of infection since the bone broke through his skin, but barring that, the doctor thinks it should heal fine."

"Is he awake?"

"No. He's still in recovery, they're keeping him sedated for now." A sob escapes. "Mom, you should see him. He's so broken."

"Bullhickey!" Mom's vehemence startles me. "That man is far from broken. I don't even have to see him to believe that. They may have done damage to his body, but I promise you there's nothing that could break his spirit. Mark my words, sweetheart, Trunk will come through just fine."

I take comfort in her words, even though I'd prefer her arms.

"How's my boy?"

"Spoiled with all the attention Joan and Tahlula's dog are plying him with." Her words remind me she's not at the house, and why.

"What happened at home, Mom?"

"That can wait, Jaimie."

"It'll only make things worse in my mind, Mom. Just tell me."

Her deep sigh tells me she's not happy about it, but she tells me anyway. I already knew about the words spray-painted on my garage, but I'm shocked to hear there was also a brick thrown through the living room window. That's what alerted Mom, who'd been upstairs giving River a bath.

"But I don't want you to worry about anything. Joan picked me up and took me to her place, and Joe followed us all the way there. He's got everything under control."

"Do you think Rob was responsible for all this, Mom?" I voice the thoughts whirling around in my head. "For the house…for Trunk? It seems too much of a coincidence not to be connected. I don't think I could live with—"

"That's enough," she snaps. "Whether or not he is has nothing to do with you."

"How can you say that? It would have everything to do with me," I sob.

"Bullhickey. That's like saying a victim of abuse is guilty. No one thinks that and you shouldn't either. You'd be playing right into his hands if you take any responsibility for this on your shoulders. You're smarter than that."

Trunk

THE FIRST THING I notice is the scent of vanilla.

The next is the throbbing pain that seems to drum through my body from head to toe.

Then I hear the sniffles and I force my eyes open. When they adjust to the light streaming in from a window, I see Jaimie's blonde head resting on the mattress beside my hand. I straighten my fingers to touch the silky strands, but the moment they connect her tear-streaked face snaps up.

"Oh my God, you're awake."

She wraps her fingers around mine and holds on so tight I'm afraid she'll break them, but I welcome *that* pain.

"Hey, Little Mama." My voice sounds rough and weak.

"Are you thirsty?" She's already reaching for the Styrofoam cup with a straw and fits it between my lips. I take a sip, and then another one, the cool water instantly soothing. "Not too much at once," she says, pulling it away from me.

"Thanks." My voice is a little smoother this time.

"Shit, I need to call a nurse. Call T. She just went home for a nap. Evan almost had to drag her out of here. Where is that damn button?" I watch as she frantically looks around.

"It'll wait."

"But I…"

"It'll wait. Come here so I can see you." I wait for her to sit back down; her eyes wide and worried, and I reach for her hand. My other arm is immobile and strapped to my chest. "I'ma be fine, James. Gonna need more than a baseball bat to take a Trunk out."

Her fingers close around mine. "They sure tried hard," she says in a shaky voice as her eyes scan my face, and I realize I probably don't look too pretty.

"Tried, but didn't succeed. Before you know it, I'll be back home." I know immediately I've said something wrong when her face crumples. "Hey, I will, just you wait."

She shakes her head. "There's not a lot left of your home, Titus. They tried burning it all. I'm so sorry."

I'd be lying if I said it didn't sour my gut, but seeing the guilt on her face is worse. "Nothing for you to be sorry for, James. Not like any of this is your fault. Besides, it's just a house. I always have a bed at the club. Or I can just share yours." To my surprise new tears roll down her cheeks as she tries to avert her face, but I tug at her hand. "Hey, talk to me."

"I don't know if I should," she mumbles.

"You hafta now. Can't leave me hanging."

"You need to stay calm, okay?"

I immediately tense up. Something tells me I'm not going to like what I hear. "'Kay."

"Um, well, I wasn't home, but apparently someone kinda left a message for me."

"Spit it out, James," I bite off, struggling to keep my cool, and that doesn't get any easier when she finally tells me what some motherfucker did to her house.

I close my eyes and take a few deep breaths in through my nose. I've always heard strong emotions can drown out even the worst of pain, but I've never actually experienced it until now. Hot rage replaces the painful throbbing as it courses through my veins.

"You don't look too calm, honey."

"Trying," I grind out.

"Are you in pain? Should I call a nurse?"

I ignore her questions and ask my own. "Ouray still here?"

"In the waiting room."

"Good. Don't go anywhere without his say so."

I can feel the sudden frost coming off her in waves before her mouth forms the first word of objection. "Excuse me? I'm not an idiot, Trunk. I can figure out on my own I need to be careful, quite well, thank you."

She moves to pull back her hand but I hold firm. "Come here, baby." I can tell she wants to struggle, but she bends closer anyway. "Need a kiss."

"Your face…"

"My lips are fine."

I'm amused when she rolls her eyes, but still closes the distance. I move my hand to the side of her face when she brushes my lips with hers. I'm frustrated when she pulls back, but I keep her close.

"Gotta bear with me, James," I whisper, my swollen eyes on her clear blue ones. "Was picturing your face when I thought I was done for. Means something your face was the first thing I saw just now, when I woke up. I like that face. I wanna see a fuckofalot more of it. Lose my mind to think of something happening to you. Lose my mind knowing I'm in here with no way to protect you." I see understanding grow in her eyes and I push my point. "I trust my brother to do my job until I'm able to, Little Mama. Can you give that to me?"

At some point the tears started rolling again, but she smiles when she looks at me. "I'll do my best."

"That'd be good."

"Trunk?"

"Yeah?"

"I think I like you."

I can't control the chuckle, but wince at the same time: that fucking hurts.

"Think we passed *like* a while back, James."

19

JAMIE

"MAH-MAH-MAMA."

I chuckle as River gnaws on my jaw.

I love my early morning cuddles with my baby. Waking up to his little warm body snuggled up to me in bed this past week has been an unexpected bonus to staying with Ouray and Luna.

Their house is gorgeous, and not at all what I would've expected from the president of an MC. Big windows, large open spaces, a stylish interior, and a beautiful view. I'd been reluctant to leave the hospital, I would much rather have stayed right by Trunk's bed, but I'd promised him I'd let Ouray look out for me. Clearly he took that job seriously, drove me to pick up my son and brought me to his home. Mom had been invited too, but she opted to stay with Evan's mother.

A temporary situation while my house is being put back in order.

Every day, either Ouray, Kaga, or Paco, drive me over to Joan's to drop River with her for a few hours before taking me to the hospital to see Trunk. He's doing much better, and yesterday there was talk he might be coming home. Although, where that might be is up in the air.

I'm starting to feel guilty for my lack of productivity since we got back from New York, but T keeps reminding me that with *Mens Rae* out on the shelves, we don't have anything pressing for the moment. Still, with the email notification of the payroll deposit in my account last night, guilt flared up again.

Seems that's all I do these days, feel responsible. There's a whole laundry list to feel guilty for, impacting a lot of people. Luna mentioned a few times they weren't even sure any of it has to do with Rob, they haven't found anything concrete to connect him with any of it yet, but I know better.

I should probably get out of bed. River is getting restless, climbing all over me and his diaper feels heavy.

"Come on, buddy. Time to get this day started."

"Gah!"

"Exactly."

"MORNIN'."

I look up to find Tony Ramirez approach us in the

hospital parking lot.

"Ramirez," Ouray rumbles in greeting.

"Hi."

"I was just in to see him. He looks a lot better," Tony shares. "Sounds like they might be cutting him loose today."

"Really?"

"That's what I hear. Perfect timing too."

"How's that?" Ouray wants to know, but Tony directs his answer to me.

"Benedetti mentioned this morning your place is ready. Clean up is done, new window is in, and the security system is up and running."

I knew the place had a security system before they had the fire, Ollie mentioned that herself before I moved in. At the time, I didn't feel it necessary to go to the expense of having it rewired, and I'd forgotten about it since.

"Good." Ouray's response makes me wonder if he knew they were working on that. "Greene monitoring?"

"Yup. Live feed to the station as well."

"Excuse me…" I hold up my index finger. "Who is Greene, and what live feed to what station, exactly?"

The men exchange a look before Ouray turns to me. "Jasper Greene is Luna's team member and the FBI tech specialist. He'll be keeping an eye out, along with Durango PD."

"Easier to have you all covered in one place," Tony adds.

I shake my head to clear it. "Okay, so am I to deduct from that I'm going back home? Does Trunk know about this?"

"Maybe you should talk to him about it," Tony suggests, looking a little uncomfortable.

"Maybe you should just answer the question," I fire back, more than a little annoyed at being handled. "Correct me if I'm wrong, but I believe it's my house—my *life*—we're discussing here."

I resist shaking off the hand Ouray places on my shoulder. "Trunk's idea, Jaimie, and it's the one that makes most sense."

"That may well be, it still doesn't give *any* of you the fucking right to be making *any* decisions without my involvement."

Pissed, I start walking toward the main doors at a good clip, ignoring the curious glances thrown my way from innocent bystanders. I wasn't exactly whispering. I don't know if the guys are following me or not and, at this point, I frankly don't care. Anyone who tries to mess with me when I'm this fired up is at least going to get damaged in the process. I barely acknowledge the nurse coming out of his room and barge right past her.

He's sitting up in a chair by the window, dressed in street clothes. I try not to be affected by the dimpled smile on his face when he sees me walk in, but it disappears fast when he catches my look.

"What's wrong?"

"When I conceded to stick with Ouray so you could have peace of mind, it wasn't an open invitation to take over my life."

"Keeping you safe," he counters immediately.

"Is talking behind my back in any way helping to keep me safe?"

"I wasn't—"

"You were." I cut him off, poking a finger in his chest. "Justify it all you like, but you totally were. You ask me to put my faith in you, but apparently that's a one-way street."

"James…that ain't true." I don't even bother responding to that, I simply raise an eyebrow. He's not a stupid man, he'll clue in. "Fuck," he finally mutters, dropping his head.

"This isn't gonna work if you shut me out."

"I hear ya." He reaches out with his free hand and grabs mine. "Little late, but you good with me stayin' at your place? Had the guys look into making sure your house is secure. I can stay at the clubhouse, but I'd rather stick close to you. Besides, that way it takes less resources to keep everyone safe."

"Now was that so hard?" I tease, seems I've blown most of my steam.

He tilts his head and looks up at me, a twitch at the corner of his mouth. "You bustin' my balls, James? I'm just used to taking care of things."

"As am I," I return, smirking back.

"Point taken. Now we got that outta the way, how about a proper hello?"

Nothing but a hint of amusement and a whole lot of warmth in his deep-brown eyes, so I lean down to kiss him.

"Better?"

"Much." I get a glimpse of the dimple before his face straightens out. "I'm a work in progress, Little Mama."

"Don't mind the work, Titus Maximus Rae, as long as I get my progress."

TRUNK

JESUS, IT'S GOOD to be out of that place.

I lift my feet on Jaimie's coffee table and relax back into the pillows. Listening to her and Sandra talking softly in the kitchen, I close my eyes.

It was noon before I walked out of the hospital, with sheets of instructions and an appointment for a follow-up with the orthopedic surgeon five weeks from now. Ouray drove us home, and Tahlula arrived shortly after, with Sandra and River, who had to be held back from climbing all over me.

Gonna be the longest five weeks ever, with my useless right arm in a cast. No rides for me in the near future, which is gonna seriously suck. Especially since the club is planning the first ride of the season for next weekend.

This is the one we hope will drum up some new prospects, since it's open to motorcycle enthusiasts. It's a day-ride, hitting all of the Four Corner states before cruising north to Moab, where the Mesa Riders are hosting a club party before the shorter ride home the next day. Undoubtedly Yuma's doing. Guess he'll get his time with Red and Ginger after all.

I won't be able to go, at least not on my bike. Maybe if I can convince Jaimie to come with me, we could drive up just for the party.

"Are you hungry?"

It takes me a few seconds to clue in where I am. Jaimie is sitting next to me, her hand on my face. "How long was I out for?"

"Too long if you ask River." I turn my head to the dining table where he's sitting in his high chair, smacking a spoon on the table. "A couple of hours. Deceptive, isn't it? You think you're all good in the hospital and then you crash hard when you get home."

"No shit."

"Wanna sit at the table with us? Or should I make a plate for you."

She's cute as fuck, playing nurse. I hook my good hand behind her neck, pulling her toward me to plant a kiss on her. "I'll come sit."

"Unk!"

"Hey, Little Man." I bend down to kiss his forehead as he smiles up at me. "You gettin' any of that in your mouth? You're making a mess."

Dinnertime is as comfortable as it was the previous two times I was over here for a meal. I look over at River, who looks to be getting tired again. He's a lucky kid. Can't remember many times I had dinner at a table with my family. Mostly my sister and I scrounged around for something to eat while our mother was off somewhere, or passed out on the couch. So different from these two women who, despite the shit life throws at them, will do anything to make sure that little boy has a normal life.

They have no idea they're doing the same for me.

Making me believe a normal life is even possible.

"Not hungry?" Sandra's voice breaks into my thoughts, and I look up to find her warm eyes on me.

"Starving," I tell her, my voice thick.

We're just done with dinner when Joe Benedetti knocks on the door.

"Thanks, but I'm not staying long," he tells Sandra, who offers him a beer, before he turns to me. "Ouray says he'll have someone outside overnight?"

"Yeah," I grunt.

I wasn't thrilled when Ouray told me he'd arranged that, but seeing as I'm not exactly in fighting form, I couldn't argue with him. I figure I'll be on my feet soon enough.

"I'll let my guys know. They're gonna do a few extra drive-bys, wouldn't want them to think one of your boys is a bad guy."

"That'd be good. Any news on those tires?"

The only usable evidence they found at my house was a set of tire prints along the road, just south of my driveway. As luck would have it, the ground had been soaked with the runoff, so the prints were a decent quality. Still, that kind of evidence is only useful if you have something to compare it to.

"They're Goodyear Premium All-Terrain. The size for a large truck. Pretty distinct and not cheap. You wouldn't put those on an old clunker."

"Great, so we're looking for a newer truck. That'll be helpful."

"Not so fast; one of the neighbors down the street

remembers what he thinks was an F250—extended cab, dark blue or black—drive past his house at a high rate of speed that morning. If we work from the assumption the same people were responsible for the damage here; that might be helpful. We're keeping an eye out."

My mind immediately starts filing through all the trucks I know, but I can't recall a dark, newer F250 crew cab. "I can't think of anyone who owns one, but I'll ask around."

"Sounds good." He looks at Jaimie. "Ollie says she's doing a grocery run tomorrow. She'll swing by before she goes, if you want to get a list ready for her."

"She doesn't have to do that," Jaimie protests.

"It's not a problem. She wants to help. Afraid you won't be able to talk her out of it anyway," he says, grinning. "Let me get out of your hair. I'll be in touch."

Sandra shows him out and immediately excuses herself to her apartment.

I watch some news until Jaimie's done cleaning up the kitchen. She walks in with a glass of water and comes to sit beside me, handing me a few pills.

"What's that?"

"Ibuprofen. It's what they've been giving you at night at the hospital. It takes the edge of the pain so you'll be more comfortable sleeping."

I don't bother telling her, I haven't taken anything since day two in the hospital. Don't like pills of any kind, but I have a feeling that wouldn't satisfy her.

"I'll take them right before."

She glares at me through slitted eyes. "You're not

gonna take them at all, are you?"

"I didn't say that."

"You didn't have to. It's written all over your face."

"Come here." I grin at her, using what spare charm I have. "Come on, Little Mama."

With a dramatic sigh, she settles in against my good side while I flip through channels, settling on an old episode of *Criminal Minds.* It doesn't take more than fifteen minutes before Jaimie is asleep beside me. I watch the end of the show before waking her.

"Time for bed."

She stretches, almost hitting me in the head. "You can take the bed, I'll take the couch. Don't wanna risk bumping you in the middle of the night," she mumbles sleepily.

"Sleep best in a sitting position, James. I'll stay here. You head up to bed, but kiss me first."

"Are you sure?"

"Yeah, baby," I whisper when she leans close, her eyes heavy with sleep.

She kisses me sweetly, before getting up of the couch and stumbling to the stairs.

"Night, Jaimie."

"Night, Trunk," she returns, yawning. "Love you."

N
nw
ne
W
E
ARROW'S EDGE MC

20

Jaimie

"You can cook?"

Trunk turns at my voice with a flash of that dimple. "Just because I don't, doesn't mean I can't."

I thought Mom had an early morning when I woke up a few minutes ago to sounds from downstairs—only five o'clock and River isn't even awake yet—but it's Trunk, shirtless in my kitchen. There is a God.

"You know, now the cat's out of the bag, you're creating expectations, right?"

"You haven't tasted it yet," he points out astutely, and I look at all the ingredients he has out on the counter.

"What are you making?"

He puts the knife down he's one-handedly chopping vegetables with and turns around. "Think I deserve a good morning first, Little Mama."

I look a mess, like I do most mornings, but Trunk hasn't run away screaming yet these past days. When I'm within range, he pulls me close with his free arm.

"Morning, honey," I manage before his mouth is on mine.

The growl from deep in his throat when my tongue brushes his raises goosebumps on my skin. He shoves his hand down the back of my flannel pajama pants and digs his fingers in my ass cheek.

"Careful," I caution, tearing my lips from his. "You drive me crazy enough, I'll forget you're hurt."

"I'm fine."

That's been his standard answer all along, but I don't trust it any more now than I did back in the hospital.

"I can see that," I tease, looking at the bulge behind his fly.

"You lookin' only makes it worse."

"Sorry."

"Tonight I'm sleepin' in your bed," he growls, his dark eyes glittering.

"But…"

"Woman, I'm not gonna argue about it."

After five nights of him sleeping on the couch, I don't think I want to argue about it either. In fact, I'm not in the mood for talking at all.

I let my hands resting on his chest slide down to his stomach. His sharp inhale, as I trace my fingers under his waistband, puts a smile on my face.

"Don't tease," his low voice rumbles.

"Who says I'm teasing?" I whisper, sinking down on my knees in front of him.

With quick fingers I have his fly open and his heavy erection drops in my hand. I stroke him once from tip to base, enjoying the feel of silk over hot steel, before closing my lips over the crown. He mutters a curse under his breath as his fingers slide in my hair.

He's beautiful: from the muscles bulging under his dark skin, to his gleaming, ebony cock. I tilt my eyes up to his face, taking him in with my fist, tongue, and lips working in concert. Seeing his eyes go hungry and his mouth slack, as I watch the effect I'm having on him, is an incredible turn-on. When I cup his balls with my other hand and lightly tug, his head falls back and he groans my name.

"James…" His fingers clench in my hair. "Baby, I'm…"

He doesn't get to finish the thought before his body jerks and hot semen coats my mouth.

"Jesus," he hisses when I let him slip from between my lips. He immediately reaches down to hook me under my arm and pull me up, folding me tight to his front. "You knock me on my ass, Little Mama. Like no one else can."

A declaration of love, it's not, but it makes my stomach flutter all the same.

I haven't forgotten the words that formed in my sleep-drugged head and inadvertently slipped from my mouth the first night he was home. The shock of hearing myself say them had kept me awake half that night. I'd been apprehensive going down in the morning, but finding Mom chatting with Trunk at the kitchen table when I walked in with River, and the casual good morning kiss he pulled me into had gone a long way to settling the nerves in my stomach.

The subject never came up, thank God, but these words hit me as deeply as the return sentiment would have.

I feel his lips against my forehead as his hand slides down my pants again. He seems to like the feel of my chunky ass. But just as his long fingers slip down my crease, a familiar cry sounds from upstairs.

"Mah!"

"Gonna have to talk to that boy about timing," Trunk mutters, pulling his hand free. "Was just about to give his mama her turn on the kitchen counter." A bone-deep shiver courses through my body at the thought. "You like that," he concludes accurately.

"Mmmm. Can't think of that though, duty calls," I mumble, as he bends his head to press a hard kiss on my lips.

"Tonight. Your bed. You sitting on my face."

I unwittingly squeeze my thighs together. "Deal," I croak, before slipping from his arms and darting upstairs.

By the time I come down, River babbling a mile a minute in my arms, Mom is sitting at the kitchen table watching Trunk at the stove. Her eyes bulge at me and I snicker.

"Trunk is cooking breakfast," she clarifies unnecessarily.

“I see that, Mom. Good morning.”

Breakfast is a hearty omelet with vegetables and lots of cheese. River eats some, but spits out the mushrooms. He’s a good little eater, but I guess we can’t have it all.

“I need to get to the clubhouse today,” Trunk says when we’re done. “I’ll get one of the brothers to pick me up.”

“Sure you’re up to it?” I want to know, and he looks at me with an eyebrow raised.

“I’m up for anything this morning.” The double entendre is not lost on me and I feel myself blush.

“In that case, why don’t I drive you? I’m getting a little cabin-fevered here.”

“You sure?”

“Yeah. Do you mind, Mom?”

Mom is already shaking her head when Trunk suggests, “We can take the boy. I’m sure Momma would like to meet him. Gives your mom a chance to do whatever she doesn’t get a chance to with his little butt underfoot.”

“Fine by me. I can get started on some laundry and make a few phone calls I’ve been putting off,” she readily agrees.

We take off after lunch. River is secure in the child seat in the back, and Trunk grumbles about having to get in the passenger side of my CRV. Clearly he’s not used to being chauffeured, because we haven’t even left the street before he’s already pointing out the flaws in my driving.

“One more word and you’re walking,” I finally snap when he points out the red light I’m already braking for.

"I'm buying a new truck tomorrow," he grumbles.

"Perfect," I fire back. "And while you're at it, you can figure out how you'll drive by yourself to Moab one-handed."

"Shee-it."

River, who's been babbling along in the back seat, his volume rising along with ours, suddenly yells, "Sheet, Unk!"

"That's right, Little Man. Shee-it."

I glare over Trunk who starts laughing. "You teach him cusswords, you're gonna pay for it, mister."

My heart isn't really in it, because he's so damn gorgeous when he laughs. Dimples and white teeth showing and all. The last bit of anger dissipates when he grabs my hand and presses a kiss in my palm.

"Don't be mad, Little Mama. I'll check it."

"Just make sure you do," I add primly.

It doesn't stop Trunk from chuckling all the way up the mountain.

At least he's leaving my driving alone.

Trunk

Momma is on River the second she spots us walking in.

"Gimme that baby."

Jaimie barely has a chance to put the seat on the closest table when Momma unclips his harness and plucks the boy from his confines.

River, who seems to love everyone who pays him any attention, immediately grabs for her pendant. The silver arrowhead the club had commissioned for her seventieth birthday last December. I haven't seen her without it since.

She takes him to sit on the couch and Jaimie stays close. Matt, who is doing schoolwork at the dining room table nearby, seems so fascinated with the baby; Momma has to remind him to finish his math.

"Good to see you up and about," Paco says, walking in from the hallway at the back.

"Doin' better. Day started off good."

I glance over at Jaimie, who caught that, and her eyes are almost bulging from her head. Fuck, I love it when she's rattled. All that fire is a definite turn-on.

Who the fuck am I kidding? Everything about her is a turn-on.

"Beer?" Paco asks.

"Water is fine."

He comes walking from behind the bar, carrying four bottles of beer and handing the water to me. "You coming?"

I follow him to Ouray's office, where he, Kaga, and a guy with a full beard and a do-rag tied around his head, sit around the large table.

Paco hands out the beers and takes a seat.

"Good to see you, brother," Ouray says, while Kaga lifts his fist for a bump. "This is Brick. He's Kaga's mechanic buddy from Grand Junction. Brick, meet Trunk, our resident shrink."

When the guy gets up I see he's a bit shorter, maybe six feet, if that. Good firm handshake and calm gray eyes.

He's probably not much younger than I am.

"Your president tells me you had some ideas about me setting up shop here. I'd like to hear them."

"Chief," Paco corrects him. "We do things a little different here than most clubs. Ouray's our chief, and we call our prospects cubs."

"Good to know," Brick acknowledges before turning back to me. "So your ideas?"

I take a seat across from him and outline my thoughts for an after-school program for the boys, and broach the possibility of apprenticeships.

"So what do you think?" Ouray asks him.

"Sounds interesting. You certainly have the space for it, but how are you gonna get customers up here? You're quite a bit outta town."

"We run a number of legit businesses in town," Kaga explains. "One is a boxing gym where half the male population of Durango hangs out at one point or another during any given week. Grapevine is pretty well established there. We also have the gun range, which reopens for the season in a few weeks, which draws a lot of folks up here."

"I talked to my wife, she works with the La Plata County FBI office," Ouray continues. "She mentioned their current fleet maintenance contract is up in May."

"Then there's the club. All the brothers have at least one, if not two, vehicles," I add. "Although, right now, all I have is my bike. Thank fuck I kept it here, but I won't be able to ride it for a while."

"I was gonna tell you," Ouray interrupts. "The

insurance company called yesterday. They're cutting a check for the truck."

Since my vehicles are insured through the club, he'd handled things with the insurance adjuster. My house insurance is a little more complicated as I've found out this past week. They're holding off until they have the full fire and police reports. Since it's an ongoing investigation, I'm pretty sure I won't see that money for a while.

"What kinda truck was it?" Brick wants to know.

"2019 GMC Sierra 1500 SLE. Bought it less than a year ago."

"Nice. I can look around for ya. I usually hit up a few auctions around Grand Junction. Can see if I can find something similar, give or take a year."

"Ain't gonna say no to that. But not some sissy color: I'll take black or gray."

Brick chuckles behind his beard. "Like that wasn't obvious already."

After exchanging phone numbers, Kaga takes him for a tour of the clubhouse and garage, leaving me with Paco and Ouray. I'm always surprised how these two seem so tight, but Kaga is his official right-hand man. The story is Paco never had the drive to take charge, but from what I've seen this past year, he's pretty hands-on.

"Talked to Chains a few days ago," Ouray volunteers.

"How did that go?"

He shrugs. "Just about as well as could be expected. Wasn't happy to hear we wouldn't be able to take him up on his offer."

"Downright hostile, if you ask me," Paco contributes.

"Yeah, he wasn't particularly receptive, but when I explained the FBI would be moving some of their parkour training to the club grounds and had eyes on the empty warehouse for an indoor shooting course, he backed down a little."

"You think that's the end of it?"

"Fuck no—that much was clear—but at least this way it wasn't an all-out declaration of war on our part. More a case of our-hands-are-tied."

"Smart."

"We'll see," he returns. "I'm hoping there are still some guys left with common sense in that club. Guys who don't want to take the risk messing with the feds, even indirectly."

"You're assuming Chains would put anything to a vote. He may not," Paco contributes.

He's got a point, from what I've seen of the piece of shit, he doesn't care too much about the rules of brotherhood. After all, he disrespected my woman in front of me.

Talking about my woman, it's about time I go check to see how she's holding up with Momma.

"What time are you riding out tomorrow?"

"Eight. We stop at the Hesperus cutoff to Farmington, wait for a few riders from Cortez to join, and get on the road from there at nine. Should roll up to the Mesa's clubhouse mid-afternoon, you still hoping to be there?"

"Possibly. I'd like to stop off in Monticello to see how Ezrah's doing. Haven't talked to him in almost two weeks. I'll shoot you a text."

I go to find Jaimie, who has moved to one of the small tables with Momma. The two seem to be deep in conversation. I look around to see where River is and find him sitting on Matt's lap on the couch. I still know too little about that kid, so I don't particularly trust him with the baby. Hell, I don't think I'd trust any of the kids with River. I aim straight for them.

The baby sees me coming and almost launches himself at me. I just manage to catch him one-armed and prop him up in the crook of my elbow.

"Unk!"

"Miss me, kid? I wasn't that long. Whatta you say we go see what your mama is up to?"

21

Jaimie

I HAVE TO give it to him; he hasn't said a word about my driving since we left home.

Not that I've given him much of a chance, I've fired off a million and one questions about Ezrah—who we're on our way to see—and about the party at the Mesa Riders this afternoon. He wasn't much help on the latter, since he's never been at one, but he had plenty to say about Ezrah.

It's clear he's worried about the boy. More so after he spoke with his foster mother yesterday, who is concerned he doesn't seem to be making any progress. In fact, she said he seems to be doing worse: hides out in his room, refusing to go outside. He doesn't interact with her two kids, seems scared of her husband, and barely eats. Trunk was upstairs in my office on the phone for a while last night, talking to someone at Child Protective Services.

"So let me get this straight, CPS is suggesting he be institutionalized?" If I sound incredulous, it's because I am.

"He's not thriving with his foster family, James. He's not thriving, period. The boy needs more."

"He's a scared little boy. How is sticking him in a place with more unfamiliar faces gonna help that? Why can't the club take him in?"

"Shit, Little Mama, the club is not exactly a stable environment right now. Also, it's full of white men, who do you think carved that mark on his body? Sure wasn't anyone black."

"I know that," I argue. "But trying to isolate him from what he fears is only going to make that fear stronger. He needs to see not everyone who happens to have a different skin color from his is like those cowards who did that to him."

"Appreciate what you're saying, but you don't understand. You don't live on his side of the coin."

I take a deep breath and consider my words carefully. "You're right, I don't. I can't pretend to know what it's like to grow up having people judge you simply for the color of your skin. But giving an eight-year-old boy a chance to maybe see the other side of that coin, to recognize not everyone is the enemy, to take some of the weight of centuries of oppression from his small shoulders, may give him the confidence and the belief he has every right to claim his own place in this world and help move it forward."

It's silent for a long time after my statement and I eventually chance a glance at him. His face is stony and his eyes are focused on the road in front of us. I can't help wonder if I've overstepped, but I haven't said anything I don't mean.

"Trunk?" I finally cave, unable to stand the heavy silence in the vehicle.

"I'm here," he rumbles. "I'm thinking."

"Did I make you mad?"

"Fuck, no. I'm just sitting here, thinkin' about the point you're making. Wondering how much of the baggage I haul is mine, and how much was cultivated in me." He falls silent again and I wait him out. "Hard to tell," he continues eventually. "I like the idea it could be different for the boy—better."

"Yeah?"

"Mmm. Still don't think the club's a good place for him now."

"What about with us?"

From the corner of my eye, I see his head whipping around. Granted the words slipped out before I had a chance to really think them through, but I went with my gut.

"With us?"

"For now. For one thing, he'll have you, and he'll have two women and a baby to show him a different side of what he seems to fear. Less threatening maybe than a bunch of men."

"You would do that?"

I shrug. “He’s a little lost boy, Trunk. There really isn’t a question if there’s a chance for us to help him.”

“Pull over.” I glance over at his barked order. “Now. Pull over, James.”

I scan the road ahead. We’re close to crossing over state lines into Utah and there isn’t much but fields on either side of the road, except for a rundown restaurant coming up on our side. I pull off into the empty parking lot. The moment I put the SUV in park and turn to face Trunk, he leans over the center console to cover my mouth with his in a hard, bruising kiss.

“Shee-it, woman,” he mumbles when he pulls back, leaving us both breathing hard. “Too fucking good to be true.”

I’m about to respond when he sits back in his seat, wrestles his phone from his pocket, and makes a call.

“Joyce….Yeah, on our way now. What would it take for us to take him? Us meaning my woman and me: nice home, family neighborhood. She’s got a little one, sixteen months old…”

As I listen to him outline our living arrangements, I smile when I realize he’s describing us as a family unit. One that includes him.

“Whatever you need signed, bring it. No use dragging this out if we’re here anyway. If you could give her a heads up? Right, see you soon.” He ends the call and quickly dials again.

“Where are you guys? Breaking for lunch?...Good. Listen, we won’t make it to Moab today. Something’s come up with Ezrah. Yeah, I’ll explain later.”

“Was that Ouray?” I ask when he hangs up.

“Yeah. Let’s move. Let’s go get Ezrah, baby.”

It only takes another twenty minutes to pull up to the modest home. I’m suddenly nervous, wondering how the little boy is going to react to me.

“Thanks for coming,” the pretty young woman opening the door says, eyeing me curiously.

“Deandra, this is Jaimie. Jaimie, Deandra.”

“Nice to meet you.”

She smiles and nods, stepping to the side to let us in. “Have a seat. I’ll go get Ezrah.”

“Hold on a second,” Trunk stops her. “Did Joyce talk to you?”

“She did. I feel terrible we weren’t more help to him.”

“All we can do is try,” he reassures her. “There’s no saying how he’ll do anywhere else, but it’s worth a shot.”

She nods in reply before indicating his cast and the remainders of his attack still visible on his face. “What happened to you?”

“Someone didn’t like the way I look.”

Her eyes dart immediately to me, and the guilt I thought I had under control flares up. “Something you and he have in common then,” she concludes. “Who knows, maybe it’ll help. Let me go get him. I haven’t mentioned anything yet.”

“Why don’t you let me?” Trunk suggests.

“Be my guest,” she answers. “Second door to the left is his room.”

The woman seems a bit uncomfortable when Trunk’s broad back disappears up the stairs. “Can I get you something?"

"No thank you, I'm fine. But perhaps you wouldn't mind giving me some pointers. Simple things, maybe foods you know he likes, does he watch TV?"

Trunk

I CAN HEAR the women talk when I walk up the stairs.

I'm surprised to find Ezrah's door open and him sitting on his bed, a full grocery bag beside him.

"What happened to you?" is his first question, and I tell him the same thing I told Deandra and can see he's drawing his own conclusions before I quickly change the subject.

"What's in your bag?"

"My stuff."

A life contained in one grocery back is sad. Even if the life spans only eight years.

"You're packed? Did Deandra talk to you?" His foster mother hadn't let on she'd prepared him already.

He shakes his head. "Heard her on the phone."

"You mean you were listening in," I conclude, and he doesn't argue, but looks straight at me. "So what did you hear?"

"I'm going wit you."

"If that's okay with you, yeah. For now you're gonna stay with Jaimie, Sandra, River, and me."

He instantly has a worried look on his face. "Who's that?"

"Jaimie's my girlfriend. River is her baby boy, and

Sandra is her mom. You'll like them. They're nice."

"Are they here too?"

"Jaimie is. I can't drive..." I lift my cast. "...So she's our ride."

I consider telling him this is not a black family, but that would give the racial difference more emphasis than I want it to have. Instead I'm gonna show him how little it matters.

"Ready to go?"

For moment I think he's not going to, but then he resolutely grabs his bag and gets up. I follow him out of the room. He's down to the last few steps when he freezes, and I know he just spotted Jaimie.

"Keep moving, buddy," I tell him, giving him a little nudge in the back. He moves, but the moment he hits the hallway he steps aside to let me pass. I do, but not without putting my hand on his neck and guiding him along.

"Oh, hey," Jaimie says casually. "You must be Ezrah, you're all Trunk's talked about." I bite off a smile at her exaggeration but it seems to have an effect on the boy, who turns his head back to look at me confused.

"That's Jaimie, boy. I've told her about you."

An hour later we're on our way back to Durango, with Ezrah still quiet in the back seat. He hasn't said anything at all, other than to say goodbye to Deandra. She'd hugged him and he just stood there, his plastic bag in his hand. He barely acknowledged when Joyce showed up with the paperwork

Jaimie does her best to fill the silence in the car, but

eventually just turns the radio on and softly sings along with the music. It's already seven when we drive through Cortez and she suggests stopping for dinner. It's over a massive plate of nachos that Ezrah first addresses her.

"Where is your baby?"

All credit to Jaimie, she barely flinches and continues to eat her dinner as if he's been talking to her all along. "Home with my mom. The car ride would be a bit long for him. You'll get to meet him soon."

I wish I knew what was going through the kid's head as he seems to be observing Jaimie closely, who does her best not to react to his scrutiny. At least he's eating something.

When the waitress shows up with the bill, Jaimie grabs her wallet from her purse.

"What are you doing?"

She looks at me surprised. "Paying for dinner."

"No, you're not." I fish my money clip from my pocket and toss a few bills on the table. I should know from the tight pinch of her lips that's not the last of it.

She proves me right the moment we step out of the restaurant.

"That was rude," she snaps. "I'm the one who suggested dinner. I wanted to pay for it."

"When you're eating with me you're not paying for dinner." I pull open the back door for Ezrah, who climbs in, and get in the passenger seat myself.

"That's ridiculous," she continues, as she slips behind the wheel. "Archaic even. What kind of example are you setting for him?" She cocks her thumb to the back seat.

"He needs to know women can look after themselves. This is the twentieth century, and…"

I know we'll never get out of the parking lot if I engage in this argument, so I lean over the center console and cut off her word flow with a hard close-mouthed kiss that seems to have the required effect.

"Boy's gotta know how to take care of the people he loves." I sit back in my seat and buckle in. Jaimie is frozen, staring at me with her mouth open. "Start the car, Little Mama."

That seems to snap her out of her daze, and I catch a flash of annoyance from her eyes before she fires up the engine.

"Bat-shit crazy," Ezrah mumbles in the back seat.

"Language, boy," I correct him, keeping my eyes on the road.

Jaimie snorts loudly beside me.

We've just passed Hesperus when my phone rings.

"Yeah."

"Need you to get to the compound," Ouray barks without explanation.

"I'm about fifteen minutes out."

"Fuck! Wapi called, someone shot up the clubhouse. We're rolling out now, but we'll be hours."

"I'll get there as fast as I can." I feel Jaimie's eyes on me when I end the call. "Step on it, James. Trouble at the clubhouse. I need to get there."

"What's going on?"

I give a little shake of my head. I don't want to get into it with Ezrah sitting right behind us.

A sudden rush of panic has me dial Jaimie's mother.

"Sandra, everything quiet there?" I ask when she answers.

"Joe knocked on the door to check on us a few minutes ago. Is something going on?"

"Nothing for you to worry about, Jaimie is dropping me off somewhere and then she'll be home." I don't want to get into explanations for Ezrah's presence, so I leave that for Jaimie to deal with when she gets home. "Unless it's Joe, don't answer the door, okay? Little Man okay?"

"I just put him down. Should I be worried?"

"No. Not worried, just careful. There's been some trouble at the clubhouse. It's being taken care of. This is for my own peace of mind."

"I'll be careful. You be too, honey."

I have renewed respect for Jaimie when she gets us up the mountain in record time without asking any more questions, although I'm sure she's burning with them. I'd much rather she and Ezrah were already safely at home, since I have no idea what we're going to find at the compound.

Even before we turn up the driveway, I see the flashing lights of emergency vehicles.

Luna is manning the gate, looking badass in full gear.

"Good. You're here," she says when I roll down the window. "Ouray said you were on your way. It's a mess, Trunk. The boys are in a state." I catch her shooting a concerned glance in Jaimie's direction.

"Jaimie's dropping me off. Anyone who can see she gets home okay?"

Luna doesn't need any explanation and immediately nods. "Sure thing. You can drive up, but stay to the right of the emergency vehicles. The boys are in the dorm."

I give Jaimie directions, while trying to get a glimpse of the state of the clubhouse. It looks like the entire front was blown out. First responders are trudging through glass and debris, and a cold fist squeezes my chest.

"Oh my God," Jaimie whispers beside me.

"Pull in here, babe. You can just back out and head back the same way." I direct her to the parking space outside the boys' barn. "I'll be in—"

"I know. Go do what you need to do. We'll be fine."

I nod and open my door when I remember Ezrah, and turn to him. "Gonna be okay, boy. Stick close to Jaimie, yeah?" He doesn't even look at me; his eyes are frozen on something outside. "Get home, baby," I urge Jaimie and slip out of the car. It's not until she backs out of the way that I see some of the boys have stuck their heads outside.

"Is Momma okay?" Istu asks tearfully when I reach them.

"Haven't seen anyone yet, kid. What happened to Momma?"

"She was hit."

22

Jaimie

I KEEP LOOKING in my rearview mirror at the unmarked police car following me home.

Tony Ramirez is behind the wheel; he just drove up, as I was coming up to the club gates and volunteered to see us home when Luna talked to him.

Ezrah hasn't said a word, but I can feel the anxiety coming off him in waves. Poor kid. As if things weren't already challenging enough for him, now he has to deal with this. I'm starting to reconsider the wisdom in taking him from his relatively safe placement in Monticello. I can only hope we haven't made things worse for him.

At home, I see all the lights are on and a patrol car is parked in the street. I pull in the driveway and Tony pulls his car in right beside me.

“This is us, Ezrah.” I turn in my seat and find his eyes wide and apprehensive. “I promise you we’ll be safe here, and Trunk will be home as soon as he can.”

Before I can get out of the vehicle, the front door opens and Mom steps out on the small porch.

“That’s my mom. She stayed here to look after River,” I ramble, as I coax him out of the back seat. “River is my little boy. I’m sure he’s already in bed. He’s only a baby still.”

With Ezrah so skittish I purposely ignore Tony, who gets out of his car at the same time, but luckily stays a few steps back while I guide the boy to the front door. Mom, who’s heard about Ezrah, quickly hides her surprise and adapts to the situation with lightning speed and keen insight.

“There you guys are. I was wondering when you were gonna get here. Come in. It’s chilly out.” She barely looks at Ezrah, but puts a light hand on his shoulder and leads him into the house, while keeping up a nonstop monologue. “I’m cold to the bone, I was just about to make some hot cocoa. You want marshmallows in yours too? I love marshmallows in my hot cocoa. Why don’t you drop that bag, we can take it up to your room in a bit. Hop on that stool and keep me company, will you?”

The poor kid doesn’t know what hit him. Almost stunned he takes a seat at the counter.

“Who’s that?” Tony asks softly behind me.

“A lost boy Trunk’s been helping out. He’ll be staying with us for now,” I inform him, keeping my voice low. “Another time for the full story?”

"That's fine. You gonna be okay?"

I turn and find genuine concern on his face. "We'll be fine. I see you already have someone parked outside. I'll arm the alarm, and Trunk will be home as soon as he can." Although, even as I say it, I realize he has no way to get home. "Are you going back to the clubhouse?"

"Yes."

"Could you do me a favor? Make sure Trunk has a way to get home? He can't drive."

The detective's smile is warm. "I hope he knows what a lucky bastard he is."

I watch him walk back to his car before I close the door, lock it, and set the alarm. By the time I join my mother and Ezrah in the kitchen, he's looking at her like she's from a different planet. There've been times I wondered that myself.

"Got any more of that?" I ask Mom when she slides a mug in front of Ezrah.

"Marshmallows?"

"You have to ask? And Mom? Don't be stingy."

From the corner of my eye I see Ezrah bending over his mug to hide his mumble, but I hear it anyway.

"Bat-shit crazy."

Awake in bed, my head churns over the events of the past hours.

Mom had coaxed Ezrah onto the couch in the living room and found a rerun of the first *Spider Man* movie while she putzed in the kitchen. I took the opportunity to dart upstairs and get the spare bed ready.

He's in there now. At least I hope so, although with the alarm armed, I'm sure to hear him should he decide to make a break for it. I'm grateful for my mom, who never even so much as blinked at the anxious little boy. Her easy chatter went a long way to creating a sense of normalcy amid what must be chaos for him. He seemed a bit more at ease with her, so I let her take the lead showing him upstairs and making sure he was set for the night.

We briefly spoke downstairs after, and I had a chance to fill her in on the scene at the clubhouse. I sent off a text to Trunk at some point, letting him know I'd set the alarm and asking for an update, but I haven't heard back yet. I'm sure he has his hands full, I just hope no one got hurt.

My mind jumps to what Trunk said to me earlier in the car, as we were about to leave the restaurant. *"Boy's gotta know how to take care of the people he loves."* I never had a chance to react, because that's right when Ouray called, but I'm pretty sure the return of the feelings I expressed last week was implied.

Or not.

I can't sleep and I'm driving myself crazy. I need a drink.

Kicking back the covers, I swing my feet to the floor, just as my phone rings on the nightstand. It's almost midnight.

"Hey." My voice is raspy.

"Shee-it, James. Did I wake ya?"

"No, couldn't sleep."

"How's the boy?"

"Sleeping, I hope. Mom was great with him. He didn't say much but he didn't run off screaming either."

His chuckle sounds tired, but warms me all the same. "That's good."

"What's happening there, honey?"

"A fucking mess. I was able to get the boys settled down, but Ouray and the guys are just rolling in, so it doesn't look like I'll be home anytime soon. I want you to get some sleep, though. Don't wait up for me."

"Is everyone okay?"

"Gotta run, baby, we'll talk tomorrow, yeah?"

Trunk

I HUSTLE TO catch Ouray before someone drops the bomb on him, but to my relief I see Luna is already approaching.

Yuma is another matter. He aims straight for his parents' place.

"Hold up, man," I call out, catching up with him. "They're not there."

Yuma stops in his tracks and swivels around. "What are you saying?"

"Brother, Momma got hurt. She was taken to Mercy. Nosh went with her."

In two steps he's nose-to-nose with me. "How bad?"

"Look, maybe we—"

He cuts me off when he grabs the front of my shirt. "How. Fucking. Bad!"

"Easy, brother." Ouray hurries over, putting a restraining hand on his shoulder.

"Bullet caught her in the gut. She was in rough shape but alive when they loaded her in the ambulance. That's all I can tell you, man." I don't tell him that with the quick glimpse I got of her grayish pallor, I thought for a moment she was already gone.

"Luna says she just spoke to the hospital," Ouray adds. "She was able to find out Momma is still in surgery. That's good news, brother."

Yuma's fist clenched in my shirt loosens as suddenly all the air seems to go out of him. He turns away, leans forward with his hands on his knees, and pukes. I don't blame him.

"I gotta go," he says, wiping his mouth with the back of his hand.

"I'll get Honon to drive you," Ouray suggests, taking the younger man by the arm and I follow behind.

Honon gets instructions to call Ouray as soon as he has updates not just on Momma, but on the other two injured. Tse—the brother who stayed behind while everyone else was off to Moab—and Shilah, one of the cubs. Neither one's injuries looked to be quite as serious as Momma's, but they were both hauled off to the hospital as well.

"What the fuck happened?" Ouray asks, when Honon's taillights disappear down the driveway. We turn to face the clubhouse. The front window is gone, as is a large section of wall, displaying the devastation inside.

Police and FBI have most of it cordoned off as their forensics guys sift through the rubble.

"Wapi says the moment the shots started flying, and he saw Momma go down, he corralled the boys and took off down the hallway to the basement stairs. Says it was rapid fire. Fully automatic. Lasted for a few minutes. He heard Tse yell something a moment before a loud bang shook the whole building. He was scared the place would come down on them, and risked taking the kids upstairs and out the back door. He called Luna from where they were hiding in the trees."

"How are the boys?"

"Asleep now, hopefully. Took a bit to get them settled. They were scared."

Luna walks up with Tony Ramirez and her boss, Damian Gomez, who addresses Ouray.

"So far we've found twenty-four shell casings, just outside the fence line, west of the gate. From the angles of impact of the bullets, I think we'll find another pile east of the gate. My guys are out there looking. M16s would be my guess. Plus, it looks like the front wall was blown out by a launched grenade. Someone with access to military grade weapons you pissed off recently?"

"Moab Reds?" Luna suggests.

Ouray flashes her a look. I understand his reluctance. Even though Arrow's Edge is walking the straight and narrow these days, there's still an unspoken understanding between clubs. You don't rat on each other. I'm guessing this is one of those fine lines he and Luna have to balance in their marriage. I don't envy them.

"Possible," he grudgingly admits.

"That the Norwood outfit?" Ramirez wants to know.

"Yeah. Tink, their president, has liver cancer and left the day-to-day running of the club to his vice president, Chains. Now that guy's a piece of work," Luna fills in ignoring her husband's glare.

"Need to know all you've got, Ouray," Gomez tells him almost apologetically.

"Fuck!" he barks, kicking at the dirt under his boots. "Gonna put a target on our back, Gomez."

"Got news for you, friend. That target's already there."

It's almost five in the morning before police and FBI vehicles start thinning out. We heard from Honon a few hours ago that Momma is in critical but stable condition. They had to take out her spleen, and a good length of her intestines to repair the damage from the bullet that hit her. Still, she's far from out of the woods.

Tse was hit with shrapnel in the explosion, his right side a mess. They'd operated on his leg, which took the brunt of the impact, but would likely need more surgery. Honon said he looked like he went through a meat grinder.

Shilah had come off relatively easy. He'd been cut by flying glass, had a few larger lacerations, which required stitching, and likely sustained a concussion when the blast knocked him to the floor behind the bar, but he'll probably be released in the morning.

I'm standing by uselessly as some of the guys are boarding up the hole left in the facade of the building, when Ouray walks up.

"You should go. Get home. One of the boys will give you a ride. Get some rest. We'll meet tomorrow at one. Give everyone a chance to get some shut-eye before we figure out what our next move is. We're covered for now."

"What if they come back?"

"They do, they'll find the full force of the club facing them. Hurtin' Momma was a big mistake. Big fucking mistake. The brothers are seeing blood. I can barely hold 'em back as it is. All they need is one good excuse."

The house is quiet when I walk in. I disarm the alarm and kick my boots off by the door. Part of me is exhausted, another part still wired while my brain processes this whole night. I open the fridge for a beer, and instead find a plate holding a thick sandwich, covered in plastic wrap, with a note on it.

thought you might be hungry. xoxo

I grin at the X's and O's in Jaimie's neat handwriting. Balancing the plate and a beer in my hand, I take a seat on the couch. Flipping the TV on, the volume low, I watch some news while chowing down my sandwich in record time.

I'm about to put my feet up and lay my head back when I hear a cry from upstairs.

River is excited to see me. The kid is good medicine as he smiles wide when I walk in. I quickly turn the monitor off, so we don't disturb Jaimie, before lifting him from his bed. I've discovered with only one usable hand, it's safest to lay him on the floor for his diaper change.

He's babbling away while I try to wrestle him in his diaper, when I see movement from the corner of my eye.

"Hey, kid."

Ezrah, who still looks pretty sleepy, shuffles inside. "That River?"

"Yup. He likes to start his day early."

"He a white boy." He sits down on the floor beside me.

I tilt my head. "So's his mama."

"You ain't," he states, looking at me.

"I'm not his daddy."

"Oh."

I grab the easy pull-on pants, which are not really that easy when you have only one hand to get them onto a baby who keeps trying to roll around.

"Boy's like an eel in a bucket of snot. Give me a hand, kid?"

Ezrah hesitates for a moment, but then he shrugs and grabs the pants from my hands. With surprisingly sure hands he lifts River off the floor and sets him on his butt between his legs, the baby's back to his front. With sure, practiced movements, he worms River's feet in the legs, puts him on his feet, and pulls the pants up the rest of the way. The baby is dressed in seconds.

"You're good at that."

"Looked after Kiara when Nana worked," he says without even thinking, providing me with another snippet of information.

"Bet you did a great job. Bet your gramma was proud."

The tough little street kid suddenly turns into a little boy when his eyes fill with tears. He tries to turn away, but River slaps his hands on Ezrah's cheeks and shakes his little head.

"Bah!"

"What is this?" Jaimie's voice sounds from the door. "All my guys having fun without me?"

Ezrah ducks his head as River makes a beeline for his mother, who scoops him up in her arms, blowing a raspberry kiss in his neck.

"Wouldn't mind some of that myself."

I get to my feet and wrap my good arm around her, River squeezed between us as I kiss her mouth.

"Morning, Little Mama."

"Morning, honey."

She turns to look at Ezrah, who is sitting at our feet, staring up. She reaches out a hand and ruffles his short dreads.

"Morning, buddy." He grunts something unintelligible. "How about you and me take this little guy downstairs so Trunk can get some sleep? Maybe you can help me make some waffles?"

That seems to catch the kid's interest and he's on his feet in a flash. It's the most animated I've seen him so far.

"Bed's still warm," she says over her shoulder at me.

"Won't have you though."

"That would not be conducive to sleep. You look about to drop. Get some rest, I'll come wake you in a few hours." With a wink she walks out the door, Ezrah sticking close behind her.

"Make sure you come alone," I call after her, grinning when I catch her eye roll.

N
nw
ne
W
E
ARROW'S EDGE MC

23

JAIMIE

"HELLO?"

"Jaimie? It's Special Agent Jasper Greene. Do not open the door."

"Sorry?"

The word is barely out of my mouth when the doorbell rings. Mom, who was folding laundry on the kitchen table gets up.

"I'm Luna's FBI partner. Do *not* open that door."

I swing around to see Mom reaching for the doorknob.

"Don't answer the door, Mom. Don't!"

The boys who are playing on the floor—Ezrah turns out to be amazing with River—both look up at my loud voice. Luckily Mom backs away.

"What on earth, Jaimie Lynn?"

"We're on our way, Jaimie. Hang tight," the agent says in my ear.

"Just come here, okay, Mom? Get the boys?" I smile my fakest smile for the benefit of Ezrah, who is not buying it for one minute. He darts worried looks at the door. "Hey, buddy, could you do something important for me? Would you go upstairs and wake Trunk?"

He nods in response and darts up the stairs.

"Good idea," Agent Greene says in my ear, just as the doorbell rings again. "You know we monitor the security cameras, right?"

"Yes."

"We noticed a courier van stopping along the curb outside your house. He got out with a package. Did you order anything?"

"No." My body starts to shake as I turn to Mom. "Did you order anything? Are you expecting a package?"

She shakes her head, tightening her hold on River, who is squirming to get down. Upstairs I can hear Trunk's deep voice. I can't hear what he's saying, but just the sound calms me down. Footsteps come down the stairs and my eyes focus there until I see him appear. He doesn't hesitate and comes right over, his concerned eyes scanning my face.

The doorbell rings again.

"Don't answer it," I tell him softly. "The FBI is on their way."

"That them?" he asks, pointing at the phone.

"Agent Greene."

He takes the phone from my hand. "Jasper. Talk

to me." His eyes dart to the front door as he listens. "Where's Joe?...Gotcha. Yeah, see you shortly." Then he ends the call.

"They're around the corner," he explains, tucking me under his arm. "Joe is stuck up at the clubhouse."

"This is crazy," I mumble, and he squeezes my shoulder.

"Why don't you get some coffee going?" he says calmly. "This could take a while." He brushes his lips over mine before letting me go.

I'm actually surprised at his calm, if not for the muscle ticking in his jaw, I might've thought he's not that concerned. Even River has stopped fidgeting in Mom's arms, for once not calling for his favorite person. His thumb has found its way to his mouth, his head has dropped to Mom's shoulder, and he observes us with wide eyes.

"Sit down, Mom," I suggest, indicating the kitchen table. "I'll get a pot going." Our eyes meet, and although I see concern in hers, she nods and pulls out a chair.

I turn to see Trunk has moved to Ezrah, who stopped on the bottom step of the stairs, a worried expression on his face. Once again Trunk's soft, deep rumble seems to calm the anxiety in the room, and it helps me focus on my task.

"You hungry?" I ask Ezrah when Trunk leads him into the kitchen, sitting him down at the table with Mom. I'm rewarded with a light shake of his head.

I'm about to join them when there's a knock at the side door. We all freeze, except for Trunk, who takes large strides and whips the blinds aside. Instinctively, I step behind Ezrah's chair and put a reassuring hand on his shoulder. He doesn't even seem to notice, he's so focused on the door.

Trunk shows in a tall man with dirty blond hair, wearing a navy jacket with FBI printed on his chest. The guy's eyes touch on everyone in the kitchen before settling on Trunk.

"Jasper."

So this is Agent Greene. Trunk steps aside to let him in.

"Hey, folks," the man says easily, addressing everyone. "Just wanted to let you know what's happening. My partner is asking the delivery guy a few questions, and then we're going to have a look at the package. It doesn't appear there's anything to be worried about, but we'll need a few minutes to make sure. Hang tight, okay?"

"How about an early lunch?" I suggest when the agent closes the door behind him. I give Ezrah's shoulder a little squeeze before moving to the fridge.

Twenty minutes later, the knock is on the front door and Trunk goes to answer.

"Could I borrow you for a minute?" Agent Greene zooms in on me.

I nod and get up. Trunk steps out behind me and closes the door. "What's going on?" he wants to know.

Greene hands me a Ziploc baggie with a note.

FINAL WARNING.

"This was in the box. We've been monitoring your ex-husband closely, as you know, but there's nothing we can find to connect him to this. He's had no communication with the outside world at all. Is there anybody else you can think of?"

"I have no idea," I tell him honestly.

"Any friends? Associates?"

"None that I know."

I hear Trunk make a sound as he leans over to look inside the box. I take a peek as well.

At first I don't quite know what I'm looking at. It appears to be some kind of tarp, and another plastic bag holding pieces of plastic. Actually, not just random pieces, but parts of what looks to have been a doll. A dark-skinned doll.

"Jesus. What is that?"

"It *was* an African American Ken," the second agent, a younger guy, dark hair, volunteers. "Now it's a bag of body parts."

Without looking away, my hand blindly searches for Trunk's, and I blow out a breath when I feel his fingers slip between mine.

"And the tarp?"

"Actually, that's not a tarp, it's a body bag." My mouth falls open. "I'm sorry to say you can apparently buy these on Amazon nowadays." Greene looks appropriately disgusted.

I pull my hand free and turn to Trunk. "You need to leave."

"James..."

"I'm dead serious. You need to go. Stay with your sister or something."

His hand snags mine and he yanks me close. "Not happening."

"But what if—"

"Empty threats, Little Mama. They can't touch me."

I twist out of his hold, immediately poking a finger in his chest. "Oh no? Have you forgotten they already did? Jesus, Trunk, you already got beaten within an inch of your life once. Do you really wanna tempt fate again? You have to leave."

"Not happening," I hear him, as I barge inside the house.

The only person there is Ezrah, who is still sitting at the kitchen table.

"What's in it?" he asks when I stomp into the kitchen looking for coffee. He startles me with the question. He hasn't exactly been chatty and this is probably the first time he initiates conversation. "The box, what's in it?"

"Nothing for you to worry about. Just a childish prank," I brush him off while I pour myself a refill. No way in hell I'm gonna tell the kid.

"Nana been sayin' that." I almost choke on my sip of coffee at his words, but quickly collect myself.

"Saying what?" I gently prompt him.

"Not to worry. She 'swrong too. I already know they here. I seen em. They hate us."

TRUNK

I JUST CATCH Ezrah's words when I walk in the door.

"Who hates you?" I hear Jaimie ask, but his eyes are on me as I approach.

"Who's here, Ezrah?"

Jaimie's head swings around at my voice, but I keep eye contact with the boy. I can almost see him disappear into silence.

"Don't matter," he mumbles before averting his eyes.

"Matters to me," I tell him, sitting down across from him at the table. "Matters to me a lot. I care, boy. About you, Jaimie and River, and about Sandra. Don't wanna see anything happen to any of ya. But I can't make sure'a that if I don't know who to watch for."

"Can't. They gonna hurt them," he says with regret all over his face as he glances at Jaimie.

I suppress the urge to slam my fist on the table in frustration, but that's not going to do any good.

"That's okay, sweetheart," Jaimie says, reaching out a hand to play through his hair. "We'll figure it out."

Sandra comes down the stairs without River. "Nap," she says by way of explanation.

I look at the clock and see it's already past noon. I'm gonna have to get one of the guys to pick me up for the meeting, because there's no way I want Jaimie out there right now. I quickly pull out my phone to see if Kaga can swing by when I notice a few messages from Ouray I missed. One to tell me Momma is hanging in—which is really fucking good to know—and the second one letting me know one of the guys will be by to pick me up. Saves me a phone call.

When Sandra asks Ezrah if he wants to help her bake

cookies, I get up and grab Jaimie's hand.

"Be right back," I tell her mom as I lead us to the stairs.

"Oh my God," Jaimie says twenty minutes later, sitting on the edge of the bed. "Poor Momma. Those poor boys, they must be so scared. What is going on, Trunk? I thought last year I ended up in some alternate universe when I found out about Rob, but this is…it's like the world's gone nuts overnight. And then this thing with Ezrah…I can't wrap my head around any of it."

"I know, baby." I pull her to my side. "I've got a meeting at the club shortly. Maybe we'll find out more. In the meantime, please don't go anywhere. Stay inside; keep the alarm on. Jasper was gonna talk to Benedetti, see if he can get a patrol car at the curb and if not, he knows some security guys he can call in."

"What if something happens to you? Again," she adds, her eyes shiny.

"It won't."

"How do you know that?" She sounds annoyed and I bite off a grin. I'd rather see her annoyed than scared or sad.

I wrap my fingers around the back of her neck and use my thumb to tilt up her chin.

"Because there's no fucking way I'd let anyone get in the way of collecting on that wake-up call you promised me this morning."

I'M SURPRISED TO see a group of guys already working on the clubhouse when we drive up. Even more so when I recognize my brother-in-law is one of them. I've only seen my sister a couple of times: once when I was still in the hospital, and then when she dropped by with Hanna and Joan at Jaimie's place last week. I never had a chance to call her about the latest, but I guess news travels fast.

"Showed up this morning," Kaga says beside me, as he pulls his truck beside the empty warehouse. There are already a good number of vehicles parked here. "Even got the boys into it. They're inside cleaning."

"Not a bad idea," I admit, getting out of the truck. "Meeting in here?"

"Yeah. More room."

I understand why when I walk in. Except for Nosh, Yuma and Tse—who are still at the hospital—all the brothers are assembled, along with Police Chief Benedetti, Detectives Blackfoot and Ramirez, as well as an FBI contingent of Damian Gomez, the young agent who was with Greene this morning, and of course Luna.

It's unconventional, to see law enforcement present at one of these meetings, but when Ouray invites Gomez to speak, I get why.

"Last year our office was alerted to an organization called the American Nationalist League. ANL for short. An anti-government militant group with a predominantly racist doctrine. They're affiliated with well-known white supremacy groups, and like to call themselves 'the chosen army.'"

The name is not unfamiliar to me, since my sister was

a target of one of their leaders: Rob Sutherland—Jaimie's ex-husband—who is currently in jail. What does surprise me is what this has to do with the club.

"We've been looking into this group, in depth," Gomez continues, "into their dealings, into their membership, and into their affiliations. One name in particular has come up a few times in relation to the supply of weapons; Bradley Fanshaw."

I look around for any recognition on the others' faces, because I sure as hell don't know who he's talking about.

"Never heard 'a him," Honon grumbles.

"You probably know him better as Chains."

"The fuck?"

Similar sentiments ripple through the cavernous space until Ouray calls for quiet.

"Let the man finish."

"Last night I found out the club had something of a disagreement with the Moab Reds. Or Chains. It's all the same, since he seems to be in charge at the moment. We've been sifting through the evidence we collected overnight to see if we could connect them to anything. One interesting thing jumped out. A tire print we found just west of your driveway actually matches the print recovered after the attack on Trunk." He stops, making sure he has everyone's attention before he continues. "Same tire, same flaw. We also have a witness account seeing a dark-colored F250 speed from Ms. Belcamp's house after her place was vandalized. Here is the kicker; Bradley Fanshaw purchased a black, 2018 Ford F250 crew cab last October with brand new tires the same make and model as the prints."

More shouting, but I shut it all out, letting the information tumble through my head.

Chains working with the ANL. I wonder if Sutherland still holds any power from jail. According to Jasper, he is being monitored closely, but people smuggle fucking guns and drugs into prison, sneaking out a message without detection shouldn't be all that hard.

It's possible.

"Hold on!" Gomez shouts, silencing my irate brothers. "Reason I've been forthcoming with information is so you can keep an eye out, as well as to stop you from going rogue; seeking some kind of revenge or justice on your own. Don't fucking make me regret it. We're gonna need time to put the pieces together. If you take down one man, you're just fighting one symptom, instead of the disease."

"He's right," Ouray contributes. "Everyone's gotta keep it together. We've got a clubhouse to fix, families to protect, businesses to run. Don't get me wrong, we're not going to stand by while someone tries to intimidate and decimate our club, but we sure as fuck are gonna do it smart."

Joe finds his way over to my side.

"I've got a guy on the house. Jasper called."

"Good to know. Thanks."

"Jaime okay?"

"Freaked. So fucking much going on at once, it's hard to wrap your head around it all."

"Don't forget to watch your back while you're looking out for everyone else's," he reminds me.

"I'll do my best."

24

JAIMIE

"GOD, IT SMELLS good in here."

I've been trying to keep myself busy, checking emails and doing some social media for Tahlula upstairs. Anything to keep myself from worrying and maintain some normalcy in the house, but after an hour or two my mind is drifting again.

Ezrah is helping Mom pack cookies in containers. So many cookies, you'd think she was getting ready for Christmas. The air is rich with the sweet smell of vanilla and a hint of cinnamon, and my mouth immediately starts to water.

"How many cookies do we need?"

"We don't *need* any," Mom responds, slapping my hand when I reach for a snickerdoodle. "We just got a little carried away. Didn't we, Ezrah?" It's good to see a little smile on the boy's face. I get the sense he hasn't done much of that.

"So why can't I have one?" I pout, with a wink for him.

"Because I'm making tea and you can wait."

"What are those?" I point to a rack of cookies covered in icing sugar.

"Snowballs," Ezrah answers. "Them's the best."

"I had to look up a recipe. I've never made them before," Mom admits. "But they're Ezrah's favorites and taste really good."

"So you got to taste them?"

Mom puts a hand on the boy's shoulder. "Well, of course. We made them."

The small smile on his face turns into a gap-toothed grin. Score for Mom. Again. She really seems to have a way with him.

When the water starts boiling and she turns to fill the teapot, I break a small piece off a snickerdoodle and pop it in my mouth.

"I saw that." My mother's voice holds a familiar tone, one that places me back at six or seven years old when I nicked a cookie behind her back. She scared the crap out of me then. She always used to say she had eyes in the back of her head. I remember thinking it must be true.

"You did not. You're just guessing."

"I was right, though, wasn't I?" She turns around and says to Ezrah, "Never could stay away from cookies, that one."

Sadly she's correct. I have a serious sweet tooth and a particular fondness for cookies, which is why I try not to have any in the house. My thighs don't need any more dimples, although Trunk doesn't seem to mind the padding I've accumulated over the years at all.

I grab sugar and milk while Ezrah fills a plate with an assortment on Mom's instructions.

"What's in these?" I ask the boy when I take my first taste of the snowball.

"White chocolate bits and nuts," he says, his own mouth full.

"Ezrah says his nana would use bits of toffee as well, but I didn't have any," Mom volunteers.

"Your nana must be a great baker."

"She's a cook in the big house."

My eyes dart to my mother, who takes the lead. "So she must be good at that too, if she's cooking for a lot of people."

He shrugs and looks down at his hands, fisted in his lap. "Lotta people."

"Are these the same people you think hate you?" I ask as gently as I can, but his head snaps up all the same.

"Theey do." His response is fierce.

"Are they the ones who hurt you?" Mom probes. He doesn't answer, but he doesn't have to, it's clear on his face. "And you're scared they'll hurt your nana or your sister."

He nods. "If I tell."

I put a hand on his arm. "Maybe you should talk to Trunk when he gets back, I bet you he could help." I have no idea, really, but I don't think pushing him to share more than he's comfortable with right now isn't going to do anyone any good in the long run.

I change the subject and ask Mom if she already has plans for dinner. She takes one sad look at Ezrah and quickly follows my cue.

By the time I hear a key in the lock, we're on our second cup of tea, finish the last of the cookies, and Ezrah is starting to look bored. Both he and River, who woke up during our dinner discussion, perk right up when Trunk walks in.

"Unk!"

I have to hold onto his high chair, littered with cookie crumbs, when he starts kicking his legs to get out. "Hold up, buddy," I caution him, doing a quick wipe of his face and hands with a tea towel before lifting him out.

The moment his feet hit the floor, he speed waddles to the front door, where Trunk is kicking off his boots.

Seeing their two heads bend together, as Trunk lifts my baby on one arm, never fails to make my insides melt. He walks into the kitchen, bending over Mom to kiss her cheek. Then he turns to Ezrah and holds out his injured arm for a fist bump. Finally he comes over to my side, leans down, and kisses me on the mouth. Something River feels he needs to be part of as he tries to horn in.

Despite the chaos of our lives, they seem to have blended together so naturally. Almost effortlessly. There are times I wonder if I should be more worried than I am. Maybe it's because what happens on the outside is so unpredictable, when that door closes us in, I'm left with this feeling of complete rightness. Like this is the way things are supposed to be.

Now if only we can get the rest of the world on board with this.

"What are those?" Trunk points at the baking rack with snowballs still sitting on the counter, popping one in his mouth in passing.

"Ezrah's nana's cookies. They're his favorite," Mom volunteers.

"That so?" He takes a seat at the head of the table between Ezrah and me, transferring River to his knee. "Your nana bake those for ya?"

"Sometimes."

"He says she's a good cook too," Mom prompts.

"Hmm. Not sure anyone can beat you, Sandra," he tells her with a wink.

"Nana can."

I hide a grin when Ezrah predictably jumps to his grandmother's defense. Likely what Trunk was after in the first place. Compared to the almost complete lack of communication from the boy at first, anything that keeps him talking is a bonus.

"Sounds like I need to up my game then," Mom picks up the gauntlet and runs with it. "Wanna give me a hand, Jaimie? I think I may need some help if I'm going to do better than Nana."

"Well done," I whisper, when I pass her on my way to pull supplies out of the fridge.

She throws me a saucy wink. "I haven't lost my touch. I remember a few particularly horrendous teenage years when I had to virtually stand on my head to get a word out of you."

"I remember no such thing," I lie, knowing full well I put my mom through the paces. I was an ornery teen, if I say so myself.

While we work in tandem in the kitchen—doing a little reminiscing while we prepare dinner—I notice Trunk and Ezrah have moved to the couch, River playing on the floor in front of the TV.

The two sit side by side, appearing to be deep in conversation.

Trunk

"They're not like the others."

I follow Ezrah's gaze into the kitchen where mother and daughter are chatting and chuckling while they work on dinner.

"No, they're not," I say, instinctively knowing what he's talking about. It prompts me to add, "I have good people in my life, Ezrah. Friends, who don't see or care about the color of our skin. I have a sister who is half white, club brothers who are Latino, or Asian. I know a Native American cop. All of them are good people, boy. I'm not sayin' everyone's like that, but there's enough of them."

The irony is not lost on me, since not that long ago it was me who looked at the world as a hostile place, and although I've been the subject of racism in my life, it was minor compared to what this boy's been through.

"The people Nana works for, they're not good."

"If they're the ones who hurt you, then no, they're not."

"They was mad. Nana told me run, so I run for a long time. I hid, but the nights were cold. They found me anyways." He slams his fist on his leg, clearly pissed at himself.

Since he was found the first week of March, it would've been cold out. I just wonder how long he'd been out there before he was found.

"How come your nana told you to run?"

He shrugs. "Saw somethin' I should'na."

"What'd you see, kid?"

He stares at me for a long time, probably as eager to unload as he is scared for the consequences.

"You'll be safe right here, Ezrah. I promise."

I'm reminded of Joe's words to me earlier, and hope I'm not biting off more than I can chew promising that.

"He what?"

I disappeared upstairs to Jaimie's bedroom when Sandra called Ezrah to set the table, after telling Jaimie I had to make a call.

"He says he saw a bunch of guys with motorcycles unload a large truck of crates into an old barn. He snuck up to take a closer look, saw guns in the crates and tried to back away when one of the men spotted him. Kid took off, found his grandma, and she told him to run."

Ouray curses under his breath. “Bikers? In Monticello?”

“No. In fucking Moab, or close to it.”

“How the hell did he get to Monticello then?”

I run a hand over my face, still rocked to the core with what the boy told me. “He ran.”

“Fuck me. It’s a fifty-mile drive. How the fuck long would that be on foot?”

“Says he stayed parallel to the highway. They almost caught him just outside of town, but he managed to elude them going through people’s backyards. They intercepted him when he was crossing the park. They beat him, carved him, and left him for dead. That was three days later.”

“Jesus, that poor kid.”

My sentiments exactly. Eight-year-old kid, three days and two nights on the run, scared out of his brain, near freezing overnight temperatures. It’s a miracle he even got that far. Makes me sick to my stomach.

“Did he see them?”

“If he did, he’s not telling. Scared for his grandma and four-year-old sister.”

“Motherfuckers. Was it the bikers? Don’t tell me it was the Mesa Riders, I’ll fucking lose my shit.”

“No. He keeps talking about the family. Didn’t say much about the bikers, other than one of them was wearing a bandana.”

“What color?”

“Black.” It was the first thing I asked when Ezrah mentioned it.

"Fucking Reds," Ouray concludes.

Aside from the obvious patches and rockers, you can identify some of the MCs by the specific color of their bandana. Black is the Moab Reds' color.

"Sounds like."

"Think maybe I should give Tink another call. Find out who in the Moab area they're in business with."

"That'd be good. Need to get that little girl and her grandma outta there."

I'm called down for dinner right after we end the call, and during the meal I keep a close eye on Ezrah, but if anything, he seems more relaxed. Maybe unburdening a little helped.

Since the women cooked, I insist on cleaning up and get the boy to help me, while Sandra watches *Jeopardy* and Jaimie takes River up for his bath. I'm about to sit on the couch with Sandra when Ezrah pulls on my arm.

"Yeah, kid?"

"Can you tuck me in?"

"You tired?"

"Yeah."

"Okay, then lead the way, my man." I catch Sandra's warm smile when I follow Ezrah.

Upstairs we get waylaid by River, who is coming out of the bathroom grinning wide. The kid's buck naked holding his mother's hand.

"Little dude, a little warning next time, okay? Woulda worn my shades."

Ezrah giggles next to me and I turn to him, surprised at the carefree sound. I catch Jaimie's eyes; who looks equally shocked.

"You heading to bed too?" she asks him, just as River tugs loose and waddles his naked butt into his room.

"Tired."

"No problem. Don't think any of us will make it too late tonight. I'd better get that baby in bed before he tears apart his room. Night, buddy."

She reaches out to ruffle his hair, but he ducks under her hand. He wraps his spindly arms around her waist, giving her an awkward hug before he darts into the bathroom, closing the door behind him.

"Did you see that? Ohmigod," she mumbles, her eyes shimmering.

I pull her against my body and kiss her forehead.

"Big strides, Little Mama."

"I know. I overheard some of what he said to you." She shakes her head. "Took everything out of me not to hug him tight." Her eyes are filled with liquid fire. "Promise me those people will pay for what they did to him."

"They will, baby."

I look down when I feel a tug on my pant leg and find River smiling up at me. I bend down and scoop him up with my hand under his bare booty.

"You really need to get some clothes on, Little Man."

"Ma-bah-oh-da unk!"

"Whatever you say, buddy."

Jaimie plucks him from my arm under loud protest, but when I bend my head to kiss his forehead and his mother's lips, he settles into the crook of her neck, his thumb in his mouth.

"Meet me in the bedroom after?"

She smiles. "It's a date."

It's almost an hour later before I walk into Jaimie's room.

Ezrah shocked me when he showed me the scar on his skinny chest and asked if I thought it would fade with time. I promised him we'd try to find a way to make it disappear altogether. That seemed to appease him. While he got comfortable in bed, I noticed the plastic bag holding his earthly possessions on the floor. One extra change of clothes, the flannel pj's he slipped into, and a few pairs of socks and underwear. That's got to change.

I just did a quick tour of the downstairs, and locked the door behind Sandra when she headed for her apartment, making sure we're secure for the night.

"Gorgeous," I mumble, my eyes glued to Jaimie's pale, lush, and very naked curves in the bed. "I'm a lucky dog."

"You're about to get luckier," she says with a sultry little smile that has my Johnson plead in urgency while I try to get out of my clothes in record time.

She scoots over to make room for me, but when I reach for her she pushes me on my back.

"Let me."

Swinging a leg over mine, she sits down on my thighs, her small hands playing over my chest.

"Kiss me, baby."

She gives me a sharp shake of her head when I reach for her. "Hands off, Titus Maximus Rae. This is my show."

"Shee-it."

Still, I grab onto the top of the headboard as she leans forward, her breasts brushing my chest as she kisses me. It takes almost superhuman strength not to take over as she explores my body with her hands and mouth, without even touching my dick.

By the time she does, firmly fisting my cock as she positions herself on top of me, I'm almost shaking with need. I have to squeeze my eyes shut when she teases the tip along her hot, wet slit.

"Open your eyes, honey," she whispers. She looks so goddamn beautiful as she slowly impales herself on me. "I love you, Titus."

I lose the battle and my hands settle on her hips, encouraging her to ride me. "Fuck, James. Love you like nothin' else."

N
nw
ne
W
E
ARROW'S EDGE MC

25

JAIMIE

"I'M NOT SURE it's a good idea right now."

Tahlula is silent for a moment on the other end. "Why?" she finally asks, and I hear disappointment in her voice.

Trunk was picked up this morning for a meeting at the club, and I left the boys with Mom to look for some ideas on homeschooling for Ezrah on my computer. Since we're still cooped up in the house, we may as well try to make the time useful. It's been well over a month since he's seen the inside of a school, and I don't want him to fall behind too far.

I was just about to print off some worksheets for him when Tahlula called about Trunk's upcoming birthday this weekend.

"There's a lot going on, T. The club, Momma and Tse still in the hospital, Ezrah…"

"I know, but it's his forty-fifth birthday. It's a big year. I don't wanna ignore it."

"I get that, but why don't we do something here? Something simple on the day of. Then when things settle down a little we can throw a big bash. It would be even better, since he wouldn't be expecting anything."

She's quiet, but I can hear the wheels turning.

"Maybe we could do it at the club, once they finish the reno."

"How about a big cookout? The weather will be a little warmer in a few weeks. That would be fun. I can talk to Luna, see if she'll talk to Ouray."

"That could work, but it can't be any later than early May. I'm already getting big as a house with this baby, and given what happened with Hanna, I don't wanna risk anything."

Tahlula gave birth to her daughter Hanna prematurely last year. I can understand her concern.

"A, you're not big as a house, and B, who's to say this one won't take his sweet time?"

"His? Do you know something I don't?"

I grin. She's been adamant not finding out the sex of the baby, wanting it to be a surprise. "Not really, you're just carrying differently than with Hanna. You were all out front with her."

"See? Big as a house. I swear this baby has taken over my entire body. I can't even shave my own legs."

"You could get waxed," I suggest.

"Actually…" I can hear a smile. "…Evan does it for me. He makes it fun."

"I bet he does."

We spend a few more minutes on idle chitchat before we end the call and I turn back to the lesson plans I found for Ezrah.

He's less than enthused when I set them in front of him at the kitchen table.

"Why? Why do I hafta do schoolwork?"

"Well, you need an education so you can be anything you want when you grow up."

He looks at me with a stubborn expression on his face. "I don't."

"How do you know that?" I challenge him.

"Good for no more'n working the pits."

"The pits?"

"Gravel pits."

"Who told you that?" He shrugs in response. "Well, they're wrong. You're smart, you're brave, and you can be anything you want to."

"Black people got no place in school."

"Oh no? What about Trunk? He grew up with nothing, and he didn't just help his sister to get an education, he got himself through college as well. He had to work really hard, but he had a goal and set out to get it. You can too."

He appears to think on that for a moment. I don't think he quite buys into it yet, but at least he pulls the top sheet toward him, and grabs the pencil I put down for him.

I turn to the living room, and Mom winks at me from

behind the book she's reading. River is babbling to himself as he tries to fit a triangular block into a round hole.

"Some more coffee, Mom?"

"Please."

Ezrah is bent over the worksheet, concentrating hard with his tongue between his teeth when I glance over. I printed off very basic stuff, just to gauge where he's at with his schooling, since we have no way to find out. Yet.

I pull my phone from my pocket and shoot off a text to Trunk.

Me: **Ezrah mentioned gravel pits. Think maybe he lived close to one?**

Trunk: **Will check. Good catch. Call later.**

Not sure if he means for me to call later, but I figure it's probably the other way around. I send him a thumbs-up and am about to put the phone down when it rings. Thinking maybe Trunk decided to call now, I blindly answer.

"Hey, you."

Silence.

"Trunk?"

More silence and a shiver runs down my back when I hear a deep inhale followed by dead air.

"Hello?" I try again, but I'm greeted with the sound of empty static.

"Everything okay, honey?" Mom asks, and I muster

up a smile for her.

"Yup, must be a wrong number." I quickly pour her a fresh cup and bring it to her. "Gonna run up for a minute. I forgot something."

Before she can call me on the lie—I've never been able to put much past her—I take off upstairs and close my bedroom door behind me. Scrolling through my phone I find the number.

"La Plata County FBI. Jaimie? It's Jasper Greene."

He throws me for a second when he calls me by name, but then I realize he probably recognizes the number.

"I'm probably overreacting," I start. "But I just got a weird call. I was expecting Trunk and didn't check. Are you still monitoring my ex? I mean, can you tell if he made a call?"

"No alert went up here, but let me see if there's a glitch. Tell me about the call?"

"It was probably nothing." I already feel silly contacting him over what likely was just a wrong number like I told Mom. "No one said anything."

"Nothing?"

"No. Except, I did hear someone breathing, but then they hung up."

"Calls from the jail are usually identified to the recipient first, warning them the call will be recorded."

"There was nothing like that. I guess it was just a wrong number. Never mind. Sorry to be a bother."

"There was a reason your mind went there, though," Jasper insists.

"It just made me feel unsettled, that's all."

"Can you read back the number to me? I'm just going to check into it."

Putting him on speaker I find incoming calls and recite the last number.

"Sounds like Denver number. Leave it with me, okay? I'll look into it and call you back."

Feeling all kinds of stupid, I apologize for wasting his time, but he waves me off and ends the call.

I meet Mom coming up the stairs with a sleepy River in her arms.

"Everything okay?"

"Yeah, it's fine. Let me take him, Mom." I reach for my son, who has his thumb firmly in his mouth.

"He doesn't go for his morning nap that often anymore," she says, a little concerned. "Feels a bit warm too. Maybe he's coming down with something?"

I press my lips to his forehead. He is a little warm. "Could be. Could also be he's teething again. He's been sucking his thumb a lot the last few days."

"True. Well, if you have him, I'll throw something together for lunch. Preferences?"

"Why don't you ask Ezrah? Doesn't matter to me."

She turns and starts walking down the stairs.

"Oh, and Mom?" She stops and turns her head. "I don't know what I'd do without you. I probably don't say it enough, but I love you lots."

"Nowhere else I'd rather be, honey. Love you too."

River is already asleep when I lay him down in his crib. So sweet.

My heart is full.

Trunk

"Where's Matt?"

I've looked at the boys' barn, checked outside, and just did a second walk-through of the clubhouse and gym, but I can't find him anywhere.

"Last time I saw him he was out here, helping cut wood for the framing," Wapi informs me.

They finished ripping down everything that was damaged yesterday, and this morning they're doing a complete rebuild of the front portion of the clubhouse, including part of the kitchen. There seem to be even more bodies here today than yesterday. It looks like an Amish barn raising. Not that I've ever seen one before, except on TV, but it sure looks like a community coming together.

It's a credit to the kind of club Ouray turned Arrow's Edge into.

This morning's meeting was more of an update.

Tse is scheduled for surgery on his face tomorrow. He has a piece of metal shrapnel in his head they're planning to remove, which is a little too close to his optical nerve. Momma is awake and talking but still kept in ICU, partially because of her age. She's apparently more pissed about the damage to her kitchen than anything else.

Ouray shared Ezrah's story with the brothers as well as his phone call last night with Tink. The man hadn't exactly been forthcoming, and suggested Ouray talk to Chains instead, but he was nowhere to be found, which shouldn't be a surprise.

Some of the guys were even more fired up to chase the man down, especially Yuma when he showed up. Poor guy looks like shit. From what I gather his relationship with his parents hasn't always been easy, but having your mother shot and almost killed in your own club has got to cut deep. I have a sneaky suspicion the fact—by some accounts—he was holed up with Red and Ginger going at it in their bedroom at the Mesa Riders' clubhouse, when this was going down, weighs heavy on his mind. Guilt is an ugly thing if you leave it unprocessed.

After the meeting, I pulled him aside to see if he needed to talk, but he blew me off.

I checked in with some of the boys after, making sure they were handling what happened. Helping with the work seems to be doing them some good.

I'd left Matt for last, but now I can't find him.

Thanking Wapi, I do another search of the clubhouse, the barn, and end up looking through all the outbuildings. He's nowhere to be found.

Finally I go find Ouray.

"Hold up guys!"

Slowly the clubhouse goes quiet as heads turn to Ouray.

"We're missing a kid. Matt. Fourteen, tall for his age, dirty blond hair, blue eyes. Anyone seen him?"

A couple of voices go up. Like Wapi said, he was seen outside helping with the wood. Someone else saw him head downstairs to the basement. Another guy says he thinks he might've seen him walking toward the barn.

During all of that I keep an eye on the group of boys standing by one of the club trucks.

Elan and Maska almost look like they're holding back Ezhno. My eyes scan for the youngest boy, Istu, and I find him standing close to Ouray's son, Ahiga, who seems to be observing the group of boys as well.

Something's up and I nudge Ouray, lifting my chin in the boys' direction.

"You take those three, I'll grab my boy and Istu," he says, leading the way.

The boys watch me approach and try to disperse, but one sharp shake of my head keeps them all rooted in place. Sometimes my size and menacing scowl can come in handy.

I grab Ezhno by the arm and to the other two I snap, "In my office. Now."

When the door closes behind the last of them, I pin each of them with a glare.

"Who's gonna start talking?" Ezhno is staring at his shoes and the other two have their heads turned to him. "Don't care if we're here all day, I *will* find out what is going on."

I sit down behind my desk and start writing random things on a pad of paper. I have two pages full of utter nonsense when I notice Ezhno starts shuffling his feet. It's when I turn over the next page of my notepad he finally caves.

"He has a phone and a—"

"Shut up," Maska hisses. "You're gonna get us all in trouble."

I look over at Elan, the quiet one, who is shaking his head while looking at the floor.

"And a what, Elan? He has a phone and a…what? A gun? You guys knew this and didn't tell us?"

The boy lifts his head and looks at me long and hard, until he finally opens his mouth. "Says he's gonna shoot one of us and we wouldn't see it coming, he could pick any one of us off."

"How'd he get his hands on those?"

"I dunno."

"What else haven't you told us?" I grill him, annoyed. "You know where he took off to? Did he say anything?"

"Not to me," this time it's Maska who answers. "And I hope this time he doesn't come back."

Ezhno snorts. "Same here."

It takes me a second, but then the penny drops.

"Whatta you mean, *this* time?"

N
nw
ne
W
E
ARROW'S EDGE MC

26

Trunk

I WATCH THE boys file out of the room.

Jesus. Wonder what Ouray found out from the other two kids.

Before I have a chance to get out of my chair, Ouray steps through the door.

"You got scotch or something in here?"

"Nope."

"Then get your ass in my office. We're gonna need that bottle."

I follow him across the hall where he steps aside to let me in, closing the door behind us. I take a seat at the big table, while he digs a bottle and two tumblers from a desk drawer. He doesn't skimp on the scotch and shoves an almost full glass my way.

"We've been had." He raises his glass and takes a deep swig. I follow suit.

"So it seems," I agree, feeling the smoky alcohol burn its way down to my stomach. "Guess they told you about Matt?"

"Mmm. My son did. Istu saw Matt sneak under a tarp in the back of a pickup truck that was leaving the compound and ended up telling Ahiga. I already have Kaga looking into finding out who the truck belongs to. See if we can track him down."

"Not gonna be hard for him to disappear in Durango."

"Maybe not, but he'll be cold on the street."

"Not so sure he'll be on the street long. Did they tell you about the phone and the gun?"

I can tell from his reaction that's news to him. "A fucking gun? How in hell?" He gets up and stalks to his desk, unlocking and pulling open the bottom drawer rifling through it. "None missing."

He walks to the door, yanks it open, and hollers for Kaga. A few seconds later his heavy footsteps come down the hall. "Chief?"

"Check with the guys, quietly. See if anyone's missing a gun." He hands Kaga a key ring. "Then check up at the firing range and see if any of the lockers were broken into."

"What's going on?" Kaga looks from Ouray to me and back.

"The boys say Matt had a gun and a phone. I wanna know how that's possible. Also send Wapi in."

The moment Kaga leaves, I turn to Ouray. "You

should probably know this isn't the first time the kid skipped out." That gets his attention. "Only once before, as far as the boys know. He snuck out at night and was back when they woke up in the morning. He threatened to shoot them if they told."

"Fuck, what a mistake it was taking that kid in. He caused discord among the boys right from the get-go."

Poor Wapi: the moment he walks in the door, Ouray is up one end of him and down the other. The guy walks out of here a few minutes later with instructions to find out how the hell this could happen, the weight of the world on his shoulders.

"We all missed it," I suggest to Ouray when he's gone. "Wouldn't be right to land it all on his doorstep. He works hard to get that patch."

"I know that, but I'm pissed now, brother. Let me have that. Been one thing after another, with no end in sight. It's wearin' on me."

I believe it. It's all been wearing on me too. Wish I could see the end of it, but the waters just get muddier and muddier the more we tread it to stay afloat.

By the time Honon drops me home on his way to the hospital to check in there; it's already getting dark.

No guns were found missing, the cops have been alerted to be on the lookout for the boy, and Wapi found a hiding place behind a loose floorboard underneath Matt's cot. The boys were subdued the rest of the day and will have a close eye kept on them.

Tomorrow, hopefully, we'll have some walls going up again in the clubhouse and unless more disaster strikes, we'll be painting after the weekend. The empty garage—which is heated—now houses the fridge and stove, as well as some of the salvaged furniture, so there's a warm place to eat.

Walking into Jaimie's house, a peaceful calm settles over me after the chaos at the clubhouse. I don't have much experience, but I'm guessing this is what coming home should feel like.

Sandra is watching her *Jeopardy* and turns my way when I close the door behind me.

"You look beat," she says, smiling kindly.

"That would be a correct assessment. Where is everyone?"

"Jaimie and the boys are upstairs. We saved you some dinner, left a plate in the fridge."

"Thanks, Sandra. Lemme go check on them first."

I can hear splashing and a few giggles that sound like they're coming from the boys, as I head up the stairs. River spots me first and slaps his hands on the water, splashing Ezrah, who's sitting in the bathtub across from him.

"Unk! Ba-rah!"

"I see that, boy. You're gettin' everyone soaked."

"Mama!"

I look at Jaimie who is smiling wide. "Ezrah taught him this afternoon. He can't stop saying it."

I grin back at her. River seemed stuck on single syllables and just called James, Ma. Unfortunately he also called a lot of other things *ma*. "About time, Little Mama."

"Mama!"

First I bend over and kiss her smiling mouth.

"Hey, honey," she mumbles against my lips. "Glad you're home."

That warm calm I felt walking in the door settles in my bones. "Hey yourself." I straighten up and look at the kids. "What are you two doing?"

River garbles in response and Ezrah just grins. I try hard not to look at the angry scars on his chest and focus on his smile instead.

It's Jaimie who ends up answering my question. "Ezrah was helping me give River a bath, and ended up soaked, so I told him he could get in there with him if he wanted. He's been trying to teach him how to wash himself, which—as you can see—has resulted in a waterfest."

"I see that. Need any help here? Otherwise, I'll grab a quick shower."

"Do you know how to twist dreadlocks? Ezrah says they're getting loose, but I don't wanna mess anything up."

"Your nana usually twist 'em for you, boy?" He nods. "Thinking it's time you learn for yourself then. Shouldn't do 'em wet, though. I'll show you tomorrow."

After my shower, when the boys are in bed, I head downstairs to get that plate from the fridge, but Jaimie already has it warmed on the table.

"Thanks." I sit down just as she walks over with a bottle of beer and a glass of wine for herself. "Where's your mom?"

"Gone up to do a little web surfing she says, but I think she doesn't want to be a fifth wheel."

I put my fork down and look across the table. "Hope I don't make her feel like that. Soon's we know which side is up, I can be outta your hair."

Something slides over her expression and when she speaks, her voice sounds tight.

"You don't, but if you want to go, I'm sure we'll be fine. You don't need—"

She stops talking when I get up and kick my chair back, before stalking around the table. "Don't," I growl, roughly turning, her along with her chair, so she faces me. I ignore the shock on her face and sink down on my knees in front of her.

"I need." Wedging myself between her knees, I snake my arm behind her and pull her close, burying my face in her shoulder. "Fuck, woman, you have no idea how much I need."

Her hand comes up to stroke my head, her voice whisper-quiet. "Tell me what you need."

I take in her vanilla scent, feel her soft curves pillow me, and soak up the love in her touch.

"This. You." I lift up and rest my forehead against hers, looking into those clear blue eyes. "I walk through your door and all the weight falls right off me. You're my island in a sea of chaos. Ask me to leave and I'm gone, just don't do it because you think I don't need to be right here, 'cause that'd be a lie."

"Then don't tell me you can get outta my hair," she sniffs. "I like you in my hair." I chuckle at the pout on her face. "And besides, you'd break my baby's heart. He thinks you hung the moon."

"Pretty crazy about the little rugrat myself."

"I love you," she says, her hands framing my face as she brushes her lips against mine. "Now finish your dinner, so I can show you how much."

She doesn't need to ask me twice.

Jaimie

It's still dark outside when I wake up to the muted rumble of Trunk's voice.

I roll over and see his back outlined against the window, his phone to his ear, naked and beautiful. I'm not really paying attention to what he's saying, but his mumbled, "See you soon," spikes my interest. I prop my hand under my head and wait for him to turn around.

"Sorry I woke ya. Was trying to be quiet," he says when he sees I'm awake.

"Don't worry about it. What's going on?" I ask, as he pulls on the jeans he dropped on the floor last night.

My clothes are probably there somewhere as well. They all went flying last night when we made it to the bedroom. I ended up bent over my dressing table, his large form dwarfing me, our eyes locked in the mirror as he took me from behind. It was intense and quite beautiful, filled with raw emotion flaring between us.

Afterward we let the air cool our heated, entwined bodies, lying on top of the bedcovers. We talked mostly about my day with the boys—he didn't want to discuss his "royally fucked up" one and ruin our mood.

"More club shit hitting the fan. I've gotta take off." He digs through the single bag of clothes he was able to salvage from his house to find a clean sweater. I'd emptied out a few drawers for him, but haven't mentioned those yet. Maybe this morning I'll put his stuff away.

"Anything I can do?"

He sits down on the edge of the mattress and braces on his good hand as he leans over me. "You can be right here, so I can look forward to coming home to you later."

I curl a hand around his neck and pull him into a kiss, a deep groan forced from his throat when I slip my tongue in his mouth. I love the weight of his body resting on my chest, the brush of his sweater against my nipples.

All too soon he pushes off me, both of us breathing hard.

"Gotta go, baby. Honon'll be here any minute, don't wanna keep him waiting."

"I know."

"Dunno when I'll be back, but I'll be in touch."

"Okay, honey."

He leans down for another brush of lips.

"Love you, James."

"Me too," I whisper, smiling.

TRUNK

"WHAT HAPPENED?" I ask as soon as I get in the truck.

It's just four in the morning and the street is deserted at this hour.

I hope Jaimie has a chance to get a couple more hours of sleep before River wakes up at his usual time. That's why I hesitated telling her about Yuma going AWOL. She'd be up worrying if she knew we're heading for the Moab Reds' clubhouse to try and stop him from doing something stupid. Or to back him up if he already did.

"Fuck if I know. He was already gone when I got to the hospital. Nosh said he was upset hearing Momma developed an infection yesterday afternoon. He spent a few hours by her bedside, not saying much. Then all of a sudden, he leaned over, kissed her, and walked out of the room. Nosh tried to stop him but couldn't catch up. Fucker won't answer his phone."

"That's why you think he's going after Chains."

"Yeah. Brother's been fighting it. Guess knowing Momma is back on the critical list just set him over the edge. Fuck, I shouldn't a let him go alone."

"Shee-it. Don't do that, man. With everything that's gone down, we all have more than one place we need to be at any fuckin' given time. We do what we can."

He grunts in response, not quite buying into it.

"How long a drive?"

"Two and a half hours."

"And how long before you got to the hospital did he leave?"

"About half an hour. Called Ouray right away, he sent some guys out to check his favorite drinking holes and this chick he's been banging on the side at the apartments. Fucking wasted another twenty or so minutes to find out he hasn't been seen. He's ahead by at least an hour."

No need to point out Yuma could get into a fuckload of trouble in an hour, or that there's no way we'd be able to catch up with him unless he gets a flat.

"He riding or driving?" I ask.

"Riding."

"Not too smart, not when he's riding alone, he'll be vulnerable and he'll be obvious."

"Doubt he was thinking much."

"True. What about the brothers?"

"Riding."

By the time the Arrow's Edge MC rolls into Norwood, not having the element of surprise might be too late to matter.

"Ouray call on the Mesa Riders?"

"Not sure. Dunno if he would. Not sure who they'd side with on this one. They still do a bit of business with the Reds."

"Maybe, but their president and his wife have this thing goin' on with Yuma. You don't think that counts for somethin'?"

"Fuck, I dunno."

I know Ouray is riding, but I'm hoping he'll have his Bluetooth turned on.

"Talk to me," he barks, and I can hear the loud rumble of engines in the background.

"Did you call Red?"

"Not sure it's the right play," he says.

"I think you should try. They probably wouldn't be in time to intercept him, but they might just get there before he turns up dead."

"Fuck."

N
nw
ne
W
E
ARROW'S EDGE MC

27

TRUNK

"YOU ARMED?"

I tear my eyes from the standoff we seem to be driving up on and look at Honon.

"No."

"Grab the one from the glove box."

"And then what? Aside from the fact I'm not a big fan of guns and the only one I owned was taken from me in the attack, I'm likely to do more damage than good trying to shoot with my left hand."

"Shit."

The Reds' compound is just south of town. A cluster of buildings set back from the road, about five hundred yards, with the only tree cover a row along one side of the dirt drive leading up to the steel gate. The north side of the compound is exposed, and on the south side a small cluster of trees borders the club. The entire grounds look to be surrounded by an eight-foot chain-link fence.

It's almost impossible to approach unseen.

The driveway is lined with bikes and from the sheer number, it's clear Ouray ended up calling in help from the Mesa Riders.

I may not have a gun to join the impressive firepower assembled, but I've always been more effective with words than bullets anyway. Hope that still holds true as I get out of the truck and walk to the gate where a small group of men is clustered. Ouray is one of them.

"…not fucking here!"

I catch the last part of what comes from a sickly-looking older guy on the other side of the gate. My guess is that's Tink, the MC's president. He looks like he should be in bed hooked up to life support and not engaged in a standoff.

"Fucking bullshit, Tink. I can see his bike from here."

I look where Ouray is pointing and spot Yuma's bike lying in low brush on the side of the driveway.

"I ain't seen 'em," the old man stubbornly persists.

"Don't wanna do this, my friend," Red, who's standing by Ouray's side, pipes up. "Things gonna get ugly in a hurry. I'm none too happy hearing your guys been doin' business on my turf. You hear me? My boys are outright pissed."

"I don't know anything about that," he sputters.

"Who's the fuck is president here, Tink? Who's holding the gavel? You want this for your club? War?

Cuz that's what it's gonna be."

"Chains is running the day-to-day—"

"Cancer make you a coward, Tink?" Ouray spits out. "You're hidin' behind that excuse a little too easily. You good with the path Chains is takin'? Your club good with that?"

I watch the three guys standing beside the old man exchanging glances. I'm guessing not everyone is good with it and decide to forge in.

"Something happens to Yuma, you know there's no getting back from that. Not for you, not for your club. Your guys know this? They realize flying the Moab Reds' colors will be as good as wearing a bull's-eye on their back?"

"Who the fuck are you?" he spits, regarding me with pure disdain.

"He's my brother," Ouray confirms.

"He's a fucking—"

"Say it and I'll put a fucking bullet between your eyes," Ouray spits, pulling his gun on him.

Instantly everyone goes on high alert, guns are drawn on both sides and the tension crackles. One wrong move, one twitchy trigger finger, and we're all in a world of trouble.

"Stand down, brother," I mutter to Ouray. "No use spilling blood over my honor. Stand down."

After a long pause he finally lowers his gun. Everyone else seems to follow suit.

"Clue in, Tink," Red speaks up. "The man speaks the truth and you fucking know it. This gonna be your legacy to the club you helped build?"

The starch seems to leave the old man's form as he slumps under the weight of the truth.

"Said there'd be no bloodshed. You're sittin' on a prime location, Ouray. Secluded, lotsa space, perfect for a trainin' and storage facility. Fuckin' waste 'a good money if y'ask me. Was just gonna apply a bit 'a pressure to get ya to play along."

"You call fuckin' shootin' up my clubhouse and injuring two 'a my men and gettin' Momma almost dead, a bit of pressure? There were fuckin' kids at the club, Tink!"

I watch as one of the guys has to move fast to hold the man up. The younger guy turns to Ouray. "He was here. Yuma."

"Shut up, Son," Tink sputters.

"No, Pops. We're done. This is done. You let Chains drag this club down long enough."

"As touching as this family moment is between you and your pops," Red says with a hefty dose of sarcasm. "You're wastin' time, Rooster. Where's Yuma?"

"Chains took him down. Shoulder shot." I grab onto Ouray, who looks like he's gonna draw again. "Taped him up, tossed him in the back of his truck and took off."

"Where the fuck to?"

"How the fuck am I s'posed ta know!" Rooster fires back at Ouray.

"He's got a place two miles south 'a here. You can see it from the road. White, run-down, single story with a large standalone garage," Tink says, sounding tired.

"Watch ya backs. His two closest brothers took off after him on their bikes. He won't be alone."

"You best pray my brother is in one piece and breathin'," Ouray hisses at Tink before turning on his heel to where the rest of the brothers are standing by. "Saddle up, boys!"

Twenty-five or so bikes rev up and tear out, Ouray leading the pack, before I even get to the truck where Honon is waiting for me. While he turns the truck around and follows the guys, I quickly shoot off a text to Jaimie who should be awake by now.

Jaimie

River blesses me with a rare opportunity to sleep in, waking me an hour later than usual.

Heading over to his room, I hear sounds coming from downstairs. Mom, I'm guessing, and probably Ezrah, since his bedroom door is open and the bed is empty.

River is making efforts to climb over the side of his crib. Something I've caught him doing twice before. Wonder how long it'll be before he gets out on his own.

He's all smiles and stretched arms when I walk in.

"Don't look so innocent, Little Man. I see what you're up to."

"Ma-ma-up-bah," he babbles, keeping up a steady stream of gibberish interspersed with the occasional recognizable word.

I have him changed and dressed in short order and lift him on my arm to take downstairs. Mom is putzing in the kitchen and Ezrah sits at the table, his head bent over one of the sheets I printed him out. He's concentrating so hard, the tip of his tongue pokes out between his lips and he doesn't even notice us.

It's not until River cries out, "Rah!" pumping his legs to be let down, Ezrah looks up.

"Morning, kid."

"Hey," he mumbles, but a tiny smile tugs at his mouth.

"You guys slept in," Mom says from the kitchen.

"Morning, Mom. Sorry about that."

"Don't apologize, sweetheart, you probably needed it." I narrow my eyes at her, looking for evidence of teasing, but if she is, she's hiding it well.

I tuck River in his high chair. "Ezrah, can you keep an eye on him while I grab a coffee?" Without a word, he moves to the chair right next to River, who immediately resumes his chatter now that he has a new audience.

"Where's Trunk?" the boy asks when I serve River his strips of toast and sit down to eat my own.

"He got called out early this morning. Something happened at the club."

"What happened?"

At the tone of his voice I glance up. He looks concerned. "Not sure what, buddy, could be anything. He said he'd be in touch."

Mom, who seems to sense the tension coming off Ezrah, strikes up a casual conversation updating me on a friend of hers in Denver, who is recovering from surgery. That leads to her asking if I've already scheduled River's doctor's appointment for his checkup.

“I haven’t. I should give them a call now.”

“Is he sick?” Ezrah wants to know.

“No,” Mom volunteers. “It’s just a regular checkup for babies. He’ll probably need a needle.”

Ezrah’s eyes grow big. “Needle?”

“His immunization. It’s to protect him from getting sick.”

“Oh.” He doesn’t look very convinced, and I wonder if he’s ever had his shots. Before I can ask him, though, he has his head bent over his paper again.

I wipe River down, who’s managed to get crumbs all over himself, before taking my stuff into the kitchen. “Mom, you’ve got him for a bit? Left my phone in the bedroom.” She nods and I take off upstairs.

When I pick it off the nightstand I notice a few messages from Trunk.

***Trunk:* Sleep well?**

***Trunk:* Not sure yet how long I’ll be but will let you know.**

I smile. Wasn’t long ago he would disappear days at a time without a word, making me wonder whether he’d forgotten about me, but it appears I don’t have to worry about that anymore. I quickly shoot one back to let him know I did, followed by a heart. But before I can locate the pediatrician’s number, the phone rings.

This time I check the caller before answering. It’s Jasper Greene.

"Don't tell me there's someone else outside my door."

His cheerful chuckle settles the knots that are twisting in my gut. "Hey, Jaimie. No. No one out there. I'm just calling to give you an update. That phone number you gave me is for a prepaid phone. Those are hard to trace because they don't require personal information. I was waiting for the call records from the provider, hoping they'd give some insight, when I had a light-bulb moment. I called the detention center, they tossed Sutherland's cell this morning, and found a phone hidden in his mattress."

"How the hell did he get a phone in there?"

"Trust me," Jasper informs me. "You don't wanna know." My all-too-vivid imagination comes up with a few scenarios, none of which are particularly appetizing. "The phone matches the number that called you. They also found a few other things that will put him in solitary for a nice chunk of time."

"Do I wanna know what?"

"Probably not. Good news is, he'll be very closely monitored—have no or very limited interaction with other inmates—and for the time being, will be restricted to only visits from his lawyer. At least until they've done a full investigation on how those things ended up in his cell."

"Does this mean it's over?"

He pauses before answering. "That would be nice, but I think it's premature to think so. The first box and the phone call he could've done from jail, but not that second delivery. And certainly not the vandalism to your house or the attack on Trunk, provided those are all connected."

I was afraid of that. I'd give anything for this to be over, but to be honest, I don't know if my ex is the kind who will ever give up.

"We won't rest until we get to the bottom of it, Jaimie. We still have those phone records, they may tell us something."

"Thank you, Jasper. For letting me know. I appreciate it."

After ending the call, I take a few minutes to shake it off before I call River's pediatrician and set up an appointment for mid-July. I sure as hell hope we'll be able to leave the house by then. I'm about to crawl up the walls.

"You got more a these?" Ezrah asks when I come downstairs.

I can hear Mom in the laundry room. Dropping my phone on the counter, I walk over to take a peek at the sheets I just printed off for him yesterday. They're all filled out neatly, and from a quick glance the answers look correct.

"Wow. I'm impressed. You're really smart, Ezrah." There's no missing the surprise followed by pride on his face.

"Easy," he says cockily, making me grin.

"I see. Well, then it's good I printed off some sheets at the fourth grade level as well. They're upstairs next to the printer in my bedroom."

He doesn't need to be told twice, he's off like a shot up the stairs. River comes waddling up, grabbing onto my jeans to be picked up. I just lift him in my arms when

I hear a soft knock at the side door.

Wondering if it's Ollie or Joe, I pull aside the blinds. Shocked, I quickly unlock the door and pull it open.

"Oh my God. What happened to you?" Blood runs down from his hairline and he looks near tears as I wave him inside. "Who did that to you?"

I can hear Mom's sharp inhale when she comes out of the laundry room. "Oh dear."

"Mom, can you get the first aid kit from my bathroom? Sit down, Matt," I order the boy, putting River down before turning to the kitchen to grab some towels and bowl of warm water. "How did you get here?"

When there's no answer, I turn around and promptly drop the bowl on the floor when I catch sight of him.

The boy who'd been so sweet and attentive with River when we were at the club, is now holding my son, pressing the barrel of a gun against his golden blond hair. I hardly hear it when my phone starts to ring, drowned out by the sound of my heart pounding in my ears.

"Please…" The plea automatically leaves my lips.

"Oh Lord," Mom's whisper comes from somewhere behind me.

"Please, give me my son. You can have me."

His laugh is maniacal and my heart stops when River cries out when he's shaken roughly. "Why'd we want you? You're nuttin' but a stupid vessel. The boy was ours all along."

Desperate, I take a step closer, reaching for my son, but Matt backs up, River screaming when he grinds the barrel into the baby's skull.

"Please don't hurt him," I plead, lifting my hands defensively.

"Then don't move."

Behind him the door opens and a blonde woman steps inside. "Give him to me."

My relief is instant when Matt turns the gun to point at me, but then he releases my child to the woman, who immediately disappears out the door, my baby in her arms.

"No!" I cry, my only thought for my son as I take off after her, when something heavy slams my chest and takes me off my feet.

The last thing I remember is my mother's screams.

28

TRUNK

ONCE AGAIN, WE'RE the last to arrive.

We couldn't have missed Chains's place if we tried. The guys rode their bikes right up to the house. Not exactly a cautious approach, but that would've been difficult anyway in the middle of the day.

"Give him up, Chains!" Ouray yells, standing beside his bike.

Kaga and Red flank him on either side, all three with their arms crossed over their chests. The rest of the men have taken up similar positions beside their bikes. A challenge, making for easy targets, but at the same time letting the men inside know they're facing a united front.

My phone vibrates in my pocket but I ignore it.

Movement from one of the front windows proves

they're keeping a close eye. I'm sure the men inside have their weapons at the ready, and it wouldn't take much for one of them to start shooting.

"Fuck off! Think I'll hold on to him until you agree to my proposal! Send him back to you in parts to keep you motivated."

"Not gonna happen," Ouray shouts back. "Push this agenda and you will go down."

"You're challenging my club?" The wild cackle that follows sends a shiver down my back. He sounds like a man who's so high on his own power; he's lost touch with reality.

"No. Just you. Your brothers aren't here, Chains, why do you think that is? You don't have the club behind you, how do you think we got here?"

Ouray is walking a fine line, challenging and provoking him. I'm not sure it's a smart move. Then I hear the sound of loud voices from inside the house.

Maybe Ouray is smarter than I gave him credit for—they're arguing. Divide and conquer, just like Chains tried with the Arrow's Edge.

The phone buzzes again.

"Any of you can walk away free and clear, no consequences." He's clearly addressing the two other guys inside.

"Bullshit!" Chains yells, followed by more arguing from inside.

Voices are raised and snippets of the loud exchange drift out: *"...I didn't sign up for this..."* and *"...do as I say..."*

Then suddenly the sharp cracks of gunshots have everyone instinctively ducking for cover. Immediately all guns are out and aimed at the house.

Sounds of a scuffle and then a voice we haven't heard before yells, "He's down! Don't fucking shoot! I'm coming out!"

I stay low behind the truck. This could easily be a ploy.

Then the front door opens and a bunch of guns get tossed out, right before one of the guys comes in view, his hands raised high. The second guy is close behind him. A few of the brothers rush up and quickly secure them, while Ouray and Red disappear into the house, guns drawn.

"Trunk! Get your ass in here!" I hear Ouray calling from inside.

There I find him leaning over Yuma's prone body, blood still actively flowing from a hole in his left shoulder. I vaguely register a second body nearby. "Whada you need?"

"You're a doctor, do something," he snaps, panic in his voice. I understand why, there's no color left in Yuma's face.

"I'm a fucking psychologist!" I yell, struggling to remember first aid basics.

Airway, check. Breathing, check, albeit shallow. Circulation…I try to find a pulse with the fingers of my left hand and locate a thready one. It isn't much, but better than none. Now to stop the fucking bleeding.

"Find me some towels."

Ouray rushes off but before he returns, a hand lands on my shoulder. One of Red's men is leaning over me. "Move out of the way, brother. I've got this. Army medical corps."

Relieved, I scramble to my feet and glance over at the body of Chains. Except he's not dead, yet. Blood bubbles up from his mouth as his body seems to fight for air, but his fucking eyes are wide open and staring at me. As I watch life slide from his eyes, once more my phone vibrates.

Someone is clearly trying to get in touch with me, and suddenly a cold fist closes around my heart. I pull it out to see Jaimie's home number.

"Yeah?"

"Trunk, it's Joe. Fuck, man."

I've never rode bitch before, but I'm grateful for the solid form in front of me.

Being the only one with a truck, Honon had to get Yuma over to the nearest emergency care, but Ouray immediately pulled me to his bike. Taking charge at a moment when I was frozen with indecision.

My mind conjures up images of Jaimie with a bullet hole in the chest, and I want to rush to her side, but I know Ouray is right: best thing we can do for her is find River. I'm sick at the thought of what might happen to James, or of that little man hurt or scared in any way.

I don't have the full story yet, but apparently Ezrah

hid out of sight when Matt showed up at the house. He knew who Matt was and was able to place the woman with him as well. He identified them as the seventeen-year-old son and an older daughter of the Hinckle family his nana works for. They weren't able to get much more from him—he was too scared and upset—other than to mention a gravel pit behind the *big house*. Joe told us local law enforcement in Moab and FBI had been dispatched and to let them do their job. He also mentioned Ramirez was taking Sandra and Ezrah to follow the ambulance to the hospital. The thought of Ramirez being there instead of me burned in my gut.

"Let's go get that baby," Ouray had said, despite the fact it would be about a two-hour ride from Moab, and I shook off the irrational jealousy.

Kaga stayed at the scene with a few of Red's men to get what information they can from the two Moab Reds, but the rest of the guys, both from the Arrow's Edge and the Mesa Riders, are right behind us.

With nothing better to keep my mind occupied than imagining a world without the woman who owns my heart, I attempt to distract myself with the bits and pieces of information, trying to fit them all in some coherent pattern, but there are still big holes and question marks.

I can only assume Matt landing on our doorstep was an intentional move. Especially after hearing that family name—Hinckle—the same family Jaimie's ex was associated with. The same family whose bat-shit crazy daughter Margaret had it in for my sister just last year. James Hinckle, a former member of the Utah Senate, was already well-known to the FBI for his associations with militant and white supremacist groups.

Couple him with Rob Sutherland and his American Nationalist League, and add the Moab Reds led by Chains, and the picture becomes downright scary.

Power, radicalism, and weapons. A deadly triad.

Jaimie

It feels like an elephant is sitting on my chest.

I groan at the pain when I try to suck in a deep breath of air.

"Oh, sweetheart," I hear my mother's voice nearby.

I blink my eyes open and squinting against the stark light, I can just make out her face looming over me.

"Mom?" I croak, and immediately her hand is there, brushing my cheek.

"It'll be okay, honey. It'll all be okay," she murmurs. "You were so lucky. The bullet hit your sternum and deflected into soft tissue. They were able to remove it easily. You have a few stitches here and there, and probably feel like you were hit by a truck—not to mention the bump where you hit your head hard going down—but you should be fine."

I'm confused at first but torturously slowly the memories return.

The boy's bloodied face, except it had been a ruse. The gun in his hand pressed against my son's silky, white-blond hair. The large, fearful eyes taking up all of River's little face. The strange woman taking him and running from my house. The sharp impact even before I heard the shot; followed by Mom's screams.

"River?"

I feel her hands wiping the tears from my face.

"They'll find him, sweetheart. You'll see. Trunk won't rest until we have our baby back."

"Trunk?" I'm desperately trying to grab onto any single one of the many things tumbling through my brain.

"Joe talked to him."

I nod, a sharp stab radiating from my head down my spine which I ignore as I try to sit up, working my unwilling legs over the edge of the mattress.

"Whoa, Jaimie. You need to stay put." In my dazed state, I'm not even surprised to see Tony Ramirez walk up to me. He firmly lifts my legs into bed and pushes me back down.

"I need to get out," I mumble, incoherent even to my own ears. "My baby," I try to explain.

"Listen to me," he says leaning over me. "Everyone is out there looking, and aside from that your mother is right: Trunk will not stop until he finds your son."

"You can't know that," I cry out, trying to push him away, but he grabs my hands and carefully brings them down to my sides.

"I can, because that's what I would do."

I don't have a chance to examine the sadness flashing in those normally playful brown eyes, when a nurse walks in and the detective takes a few steps back to make room for her.

"Good to see you awake," she says much too

cheerfully. “Let me have a quick look.”

“Where are you going?” I ask Mom, when I see her moving toward the door.

“I’ll be right back. Just checking on Ezrah.” Before I can protest she slips out of the door.

“He’s with Luna in the waiting room,” Tony clarifies, as the nurse straps a blood pressure cuff around my arm.

Guilt wars with the almost paralyzing fear, realizing I hadn’t even thought of him yet. “Jesus, Ezrah.”

“He’s fine.” I can only hear Tony’s voice since the nurse is shining a penlight in my eyes.

“The doctor will be in to check on you shortly,” she says as she leaves, apparently satisfied with her findings.

But my focus is on Tony, who continues talking the moment she disappears through the door. “Without that kid we wouldn’t have the first clue where to start.”

I listen in shock when he tells me what the boy shared. I recognize that name quite well and red-hot anger shoots through my veins, making my head throb. *Fucking Rob Sutherland.*

The flare of rage disappears when the door opens and Mom leads a scared-looking Ezrah in the room.

“I thought he should see for himself you’re going to be okay. He didn’t really believe me.”

My eyes fill when I see his do the same.

“I’m going to be fine,” I tell him. “I promise.” He nods his head, even as his bottom lip quivers and a thick tear rolls down his face. Poor kid is breaking my heart. “Come here, buddy.”

He shuffles toward me until I can reach his arm and

pull him closer. His head drops to my shoulder and I wince, but keep him right there, my hand resting on his dreads.

"S-sorry," he hiccups, his shoulders shaking.

"You have nothing to be sorry for, honey. Not a thing."

"Shoulda told ya, but I was scared."

Mom walks up and sits in the chair beside the bed, gently turning Ezrah toward her. "You heard Agent Roosberg, right? She's going to make sure nothing happens to your nana or your sister. You did good, telling her everything."

"What about River?" he asks.

I answer this time, letting the same confidence Tony and my mother feel fill my heart.

"Trunk will bring him home to us."

An impish little smile forms on his lips. "Yeah. He's badass."

Trunk

FUCKING CRIED LIKE a baby.

The moment we arrived at what looked more like a reformatory school than a house, Red was off talking to some police officers he apparently knew. The whole place was lit up like Christmas against a darkening sky, and the presence of law enforcement was visible everywhere.

An FBI agent with a familiar face walks up to us, lifting his chin to Ouray before focusing on me.

"We met at Ms. Belcamp's house," he says by way of introduction. "The Ken doll?"

Right, now I remember him.

He holds out his hand and I shake it. "Name's Dylan Barnes. I just got some good news I wanted to pass on, in case you haven't heard."

I could do with some good news.

"Agent Roosberg—Luna, he corrects himself—called to let us know it looks like Ms. Belcamp will be okay. She's awake and talking."

That's when it happened.

Shee-it.

Hot tears spill over and carve a path through the dirt accumulated on my face after two hours on the back of a bike, without protection from the elements, with the fear of Jaimie dead driving me to the edge of reason.

"I need a fucking smoke," I mutter, pulling the pack from my pocket and lighting it up.

"Gimme one," Ouray holds out his hand.

Inhaling deeply, I close my eyes and try to collect myself.

"Thanks, man. That's…that's a fucking relief," I tell the agent. "What about the baby? Any news?"

"Highway patrol, in conjunction with various other agencies, has set up roadblocks along Highway 191. It's a waiting game. I'll let you know if I hear anything."

He jogs away, just as Red returns. Ouray quickly fills him in.

"Fucking great news, brother," he booms, clapping me on the shoulder. "Ready for some more dirt? This place is insane. Hinckle has four kids. Three girls, one boy, all adults, and one of the girls is in jail. Yet they found five unidentified males between ten and sixteen in the house. All fuckin' dressed in some kind of camo uniform, and get this: they all fuckin' look identical. Blond hair, blue eyes, ice cold."

Just like Matt. That's the first thought that pops in my head. The next one is: *and like River*. A shiver runs down my spine, and I'm not sure whether it's this place or the bad weather that's been threatening all afternoon.

"…Some kind of training facility. They've set up some kind of parkour in the gravel pit behind the house, with moving targets for crying out loud."

I try to keep track of what Red is saying, but my mind drifts to Jaimie and how scared she must be. Fuck, I'm scared.

A black SUV comes down the drive a few minutes later. The passenger window rolling down as it stops beside us. Agent Barnes is behind the wheel.

"Hop in. Highway patrol just stopped them north of Monticello."

I don't have to think. I'm in the passenger seat in a flash, not even thinking about the brothers I leave standing beside their bikes.

My family comes first.

29

Trunk

"Fuck."

I feel Agent Barnes's eyes on me as I dig my phone from my pocket.

"What? Forget something?"

"You could say that."

These past hours my thoughts have been so preoccupied with Jaimie and River, I dropped the ball.

"Talk to me," Ouray answers.

"Ezrah's grandmother and baby sister. Find out about them? Can't believe I fucking forgot."

"Give yourself a break, brother. Been a hell of a day."

"Not over yet," I remind him, adding, "Hang on a sec," when Barnes holds up his hand.

"Tell him to get hold of Special Agent Grand. He's in

charge of the scene there."

I relay the information to Ouray, who promises to take care of it.

"How'd you get here so fast anyway?" I ask the agent when I end the call.

"I was already in Monticello. I've been part of a task force investigating the Hinckle family since your sister became a target last year. We already had search warrants ready to go, and were in the middle of strategizing our approach, when the call came in about the baby. It just moved our agenda up by a few days," he explains.

"Did you know about the kids?"

"Not until we went in there. We knew they had some kind of training facility, but had no idea it was kids they were preparing for warfare. Pretty disturbing. My wife and I have four boys, it hit a little too close to home."

No shit. My professional brain is trying to process what would be required to undo the psychological damage done to those kids. I can see it now, they'd likely targeted kids from broken families—maybe from the street—who craved some guidance, some place to belong. It wouldn't be hard to turn boys with that need for connection into a devoted army of men.

A ping on my phone has me look down at the screen.

Ouray: **Talked to Grand. Grandma and girl safe in FBI custody. Stickin around 'til I know where they'll be.**

We make it to the roadblock in half an hour. The

moment I see the large number of flashing lights up ahead, my heart is in my throat.

Barnes is stopped and shows his credentials.

"Where's the baby? I've got his father here," he says to the officer, who sticks his head in the window to look me over.

"You sure about that?" he asks Barnes, and I have to keep myself from reaching over and dragging him into the vehicle by his throat.

To his credit, the officer blanches at the glare Barnes sends him and quickly points out the ambulance on the other side of the roadblock. I'm out of the SUV before we've come to a complete stop and head straight for the closed doors in the back.

I hear crying from inside and release the breath I was holding before opening the door. I barely hear Barnes explaining who I am behind me. I only have eyes for River, who's giving his lungs a workout while an EMT tries to examine him.

The moment he spots me, his little arms reach.

"U-unk!" the poor kid hiccups.

I ignore the protesting EMT and scoop River off the stretcher. Poor kid immediately snuggles his head under my chin and pops his thumb in his mouth.

"Hey, Little Man," I whisper, feeling his small body tremble against me. "I've got you, kid."

The EMT still wants to check him out, but within fifteen minutes Barnes is ushering us into the back of his SUV.

"Already called ahead. Luna says she'll let Jaimie

know we're on our way," he says, climbing in behind the wheel. "Let's go home."

I'm suddenly wiped. I have a shitload of questions, but no energy to ask them. With River falling asleep on my chest, I drop my head back and take in the first full breath in many hours before closing my eyes.

Jaimie

"Little Mama."

For a minute I think I'm dreaming again when I hear Trunk's voice. I've been drifting in and out of sleep for the past two hours, since finding out he's bringing my baby home.

I realize it's real this time when I feel a soft brush of familiar downy hair against my cheek and breathe in a hint of baby shampoo. I turn my head and open my eyes to River's angelic sleeping face beside me in the hospital bed.

"Thank you," I whisper, my voice thick with emotion as I search out Trunk's soulful eyes.

"My pleasure, baby," he whispers back, his hand coming up to stroke my face with his fingers.

"Is he okay?"

"He's fine, just tired. He slept the whole drive here."

My eyes well up as the horror of the past day suddenly threatens to overwhelm me. "I've been so scared."

"I know. I'm so sorry I wasn't here," he mumbles, looking a little overwhelmed himself as he takes a seat next to the bed.

I reach over my son and take Trunk's hand resting on the mattress, squeezing his fingers. "Don't be. I would've gone mad if I didn't believe with everything in me you would bring him home."

He doesn't say anything, but leans over to kiss me ever so gently on the lips, before putting his head down on the other side of River's. We stare at each other over his blond hair, expressing all we can without the need for words.

I'm not sure how long we remain like that when the door opens, and a young nurse walks in who seems startled at the tableau we make.

"Visiting hours are over, sir," she announces when Trunk lifts his head and turns to her.

"Good to know," he rumbles. "But we're not going anywhere."

"I'm afraid those are hospital rules," she says primly.

"If they go, I'll be leaving too," I fire at her, meaning every word.

"But, ma'am, the doctor says you need to stay overn—"

"Either we stay together or we leave together. Your choice," Trunk challenges the young woman, entwining his fingers with mine.

On a huff she leaves, and Trunk turns back to me.

"I don't want you to go anywhere," I tell him.

"Ever?" he teases, his eyes lighting up with a spark of humor.

"You know what I mean."

His eyes soften. "Yeah. Feel the same way, James."

The door swings open again, but instead of the nurse I was expecting, it's Ezrah followed by Mom. Both of them freeze in the doorway.

"You're here," Ezrah beams at Trunk. "Where's the baby at?"

"Right here, kiddo," he rumbles, moving his body out of the way so he can see. A soft gasp has me look at Mom, who is losing it after being the rock holding me up.

Trunk lets go of my hand as he gets up and walks up to her, wrapping his arm around her. Overcome, she does a face plant in his chest.

"Happy tears, Ezrah," I quickly explain, as he looks a little worried at Mom's unfamiliar display of emotion. "These are all happy tears."

A few minutes later, Mom is sitting in the chair beside my bed, stroking her grandson's hair, when Ezrah turns to Trunk.

"What about my nana?"

"She's okay, buddy. So's your little sister," he says in a gentle voice. "My friend Ouray is looking out for them."

With a sob, the boy buries his face in Trunk's stomach and wraps his skinny arms around his hips.

"THIS IS UNREAL," I mutter, walking into my house on Trunk's arm.

He tried lifting me out of his sister's SUV, but I

reminded him there wasn't anything wrong with my legs. When that didn't stop him, I mentioned it would probably hurt more to be carried than to walk on my own two feet. That did the trick.

Evan had come to pick us up in Tahlula's Lexus, which easily fit us all.

Good thinking, because last night even Ezrah refused to leave, so everyone ended up staying the night. Mom and Ezrah sleeping on the couches in the waiting room across the hall, and Trunk dozing off and on, sitting in the bedside chair, with his head on the bed.

I don't think anyone had a particularly restful night, but it didn't seem to matter.

Tahlula and Evan had popped in last night for a quick, tearful visit. They didn't stay long, but offered to come back in the morning to drive us home.

I guess Tahlula decided to wait for us at home, because she's in my kitchen making coffee.

"Crazy, right?" she says, smiling wide. "I walked in with my bouquet and one from Joan, but the place was already overrun with them."

The house is filled with flowers on almost every available surface.

I let Trunk lead me to the couch, where he takes off my coat and the boots Evan brought over this morning. "Who are they from?" I ask, sitting down.

"Ollie, would be my wild guess," Evan says, walking over to kiss his wife.

"The sunflowers over there are hers, yeah," Tahlula points at a nice clay pot I don't recognize with a substantial number of the bright blooms. "It's the only one with a card."

"You read her cards?" Trunk grumbles.

"Only one, Trunk, pay attention," T corrects him.

"One too many," he fires back. "Always so nosy."

"Bite me, Titus."

"Shee-it, woman." He shakes his head in mock disgust, while the rest of us chuckle at their bickering.

Ezrah looks on like he sees water burning.

"I'm just gonna give this boy a quick bath and change," Mom pipes up, as she heads for the stairs with River. "Wanna come give me a hand, Ezrah?"

He shrugs like he's barely interested but when she starts going up; he's right on her heels.

I find myself staring at the spot where I hit the floor. Not quite twenty-four hours ago. It could've ended much differently, if the bullet had just been a fraction to either side, I probably wouldn't be sitting here. If Ezrah hadn't hidden, he may not have been alive to tell us who it was we were looking for. If anything had happened to my baby…

"Stop." Trunk's lips brush my hairline as he sits down beside me and gently tucks me to him. "It's over, Little Mama. Done. I don't want you to waste another second thinking about what might'a been. You're safe, you're home."

I lay my head against his shoulder and close my eyes, letting his words filter through. I can hear the boys' giggles accompanied by splashing from upstairs, and smile.

"Ready for some coffee?"

"Hell, yeah." My eyes pop open and I take the steaming mug T is offering. "Thanks." I take a sip before lifting my face to Trunk, kissing the underside of his jaw. "And thank you, honey."

"For what?"

"The flowers. Clever asking Ollie. She's got good taste."

His eyes drop down to mine. "Smartass," he mumbles pressing a kiss to my lips. "And you're welcome."

I glance over when I hear a sniffle and catch Tahlula looking near tears.

"What's wrong with you?"

She waves her hand. "Never mind."

"Hormones," Evan says calmly. "She's all over the place."

"I'm not!" T sits up straight and glares at her husband. "Don't you dare blame my hormones. It's my brother's fault."

"The fuck did I do now?" Trunk immediately reacts.

"You bought flowers. That's so not like you—it's so…sweet."

"Lawd," her brother moans, rolling his eyes to the ceiling.

Evan tries to hide his chuckle, but it's infectious and I'm soon snickering along with him.

TRUNK

"I'LL GET THEM set up in one of the vacant apartments."

The house is quiet. Everyone turned in early, but I wasn't tired yet, even though I've barely had any sleep in the past forty-eight hours.

Ouray's text came in a few minutes ago and rather than texting back I called.

"I'll cover them," I immediately respond.

"We'll worry about that later. I'm sure there'll be enough shit to shovel through in the next couple of days. Let's first get this family reunited tomorrow. I'll bring them over in the morning."

"Be prepared for waterworks," I warn him. "Doesn't take much to get those going."

"Seems to be goin' around," Ouray teases.

"Whatever."

He chuckles at my expense. "Bustin' your balls, brother. Been there myself. Around ten thirty good for ya?"

"Yeah."

"The sister is cute as a button, but wait 'til you get a load of Ezrah's nana."

"Whatta you mean?"

"You'll see."

After I hang up, I lock all the doors, turn off the lights, and head upstairs. Instead of going straight for the master, I first stop in to check on Ezrah, who is sleeping on his stomach, his head buried underneath his pillow. Don't know how the kid can breathe like that. I carefully lift it and watch his relaxed face.

Thrilled as I am he's going to have his family back tomorrow, I'm a little sad too. I've come to care about the kid and would've happily offered him a home. But he already has one—or will—and he has a sister to look out for and a nana to take care of them.

Next I look in on River, who has kicked off his blankets and just starts fussing. A quick touch to his diaper finds him soaking wet. Secretly glad for the excuse to pick him up, I take him to the dressing table and carefully lay him down. His long lashes flutter against his cheeks a few times before his blue eyes look up at me.

"Unk."

"Yeah, kid. Let's get you dry so you can go back to sleep, all right?"

The normally chatty toddler quietly observes me while I quickly change him. When I lift him up and sit down on the rocker, he snuggles against my chest. I listen to him mumble half asleep, his little fingers restlessly moving against my neck until he nods off.

I carefully put him back in his crib, cover him with the blanket, and turn to leave, finding Jaimie leaning against the doorway.

"Asleep?"

"Yeah."

I step up to her, brushing the tangled hair from her sleepy face.

"I love you, Titus Maximus Rae."

"Love you too, Jaimie Lynn Belcamp."

She takes my hand and leads me to the bedroom, where she lets go and gingerly slides under the covers. I strip in seconds and get in with her, rolling on my side to face her, with my hand on her belly. I would love nothing more than to slide inside her welcoming body, but watching her smile softly as her eyes get heavy with sleep is a close second.

I can wait until she's better.

We've got nothing but time.

N
nw
ne
W
E
ARROW'S EDGE MC

30

Jaimie

"I CAN'T WAIT for warm weather."

Mom looks up from her book and slides her reading glasses down her nose, peering at me over the frame.

"What is up with you? You've been moping around all morning. Are you hurting?"

I sneak a peek at the boys, playing on the floor. Ezrah is being very patient; trying to build something with blocks and River keeps knocking it down, giggling every time the blocks go tumbling. The older boy simply starts all over again.

I'm going to miss him.

Trunk told me about his nana and baby sister coming this morning. I'm so happy for Ezrah—he'll be over the moon—but I'm sad at the same time. He hasn't been with us that long, but he thrived. No longer the scared, suspicious little boy he was when he got here.

I admit part of me had hoped maybe he could stay here. I'm finding I like having a houseful.

"Not really, I'm just getting a little stir-crazy."

"Well," Mom pushes the glasses back up her nose, "give yourself the week the doctor said to take it easy. After that you can get back to your regular speed."

She returns her attention to her book and I once again am staring out the window, fiddling with a tassel on the throw Trunk covered me with.

He's upstairs, making some phone calls. He told me about the five boys who were found at the house in Moab. He's trying to get some psychological follow-up set up for them before they slip through the cracks and become scary adults. I don't blame him. The idea of more kids like Matt out there—manipulative and violent underneath that innocent veneer—is absolutely terrifying.

I can't even wrap my head around what little he's told me. The worst of it is, my baby was on his way to that place. The thought of my sweet boy—who adores Trunk and sees no differences—being brainwashed into hating him, makes me absolutely sick. The fact his father may have had a hand in that chills me to the bone.

Kids aren't born hating, they're taught to.

The sound of footfalls has me twist my head back to see Trunk coming down the stairs, his eyes fixed on me.

"Ouray's here," he announces, going straight for the door.

Guess he's been keeping an eye out too.

Sure enough, Ouray's big truck pulls into the driveway just as Trunk slips outside.

"Who dat?" Ezrah asks, his eyes sharp on me.

I realize I'm giving it away by intently staring out the window, so I force myself to look at the boy.

"Trunk's friend."

Luckily, River distracts him by knocking over his careful construction, his giggles turning into a full belly laugh when Ezrah pretends to be upset.

When I hear the door open behind me, I keep my eyes on Ezrah, watching him closely. Surprise is the first emotion that registers, but then his face crumples as he jumps to his feet.

"Nana!"

I stand up, turn, and just catch the boy throwing himself into the arms of a woman. A strikingly beautiful woman, who couldn't be much older than me. Forty tops.

Wait. This is Nana?

This whole time I'd imagined some plump old lady in an apron. My automatic mental image when I think of a grandmother. It occurs to me how unrealistic that is, given my mother—who is in her sixties—doesn't even fit that picture.

River starts crying at all the commotion and Mom picks him up. I notice her eyes are as wet as mine.

The woman goes down on her knees and pulls a little girl who was hiding behind her into her embrace as well.

I'm so focused on the scene before me, I don't notice Trunk until I feel his hand sliding around my stomach, pulling me back against his solid front.

"You good, Little Mama?" he whispers in my hair.

Unable to form words I simply nod.

"Well, where's our manners?" Mom suddenly says. "Trunk, honey, can you take River? I think this calls for a fresh pot of coffee."

While Mom bustles off to the kitchen, Ouray steps forward and makes the introductions. Nana's name is Lisa and her eyes are understandably suspicious when I shake her hand.

"I'm so glad you're here," I tell her. "Ezrah's been so worried."

She looks over my shoulder, taking in Trunk with my son on his arm, before she answers in a surprisingly soft voice. "Thank you for looking after him."

"Come on in," Mom calls out from behind me. "Have a seat. Here, I'll take your coat." She almost pulls the woman's coat off her and gives her a little shove into the living room. In true Mom-fashion, she normalizes a slightly awkward atmosphere. "Ouray, you sit too. I'll bring out the coffee."

We've all found seats—Lisa sitting in the club chair, both kids clinging to her side, while Ouray appropriated a kitchen stool, and Trunk is sitting right beside me, River on his lap—when Mom walks in carrying a large tray.

"Look," she says, grabbing the plate of cookies and showing them to Lisa. "Your grandson and I baked last week. I had to look up the recipe, but he insisted we make his nana's snowballs. We made enough cookies to last us 'til Christmas, didn't we, Ezrah?"

Mom busies herself serving everyone coffee and waves off any attempts at helping her. I notice Ezrah's precious little sister following her every move with blatant curiosity. Lisa's eyes keep drifting to Trunk and me.

"Lisa has agreed to help us out at the club while Momma recovers," Ouray breaks the silence.

"How is Momma?" I ask, mortified when I realize I should've asked sooner.

"Improving, but at her age it's taken its toll. I suspect it'll be a while before she's back on her feet."

"Yuma?" Trunk inquires.

"Will be released tomorrow or the day after. Looks like we'll have an entire sickbay at the clubhouse. Good thing we were able to get Mason Brothers Construction to fit us in on short notice. They should be done with the clubhouse before the end of the week."

"Good to have Lisa on board then," Trunk says with a smile in the woman's direction.

"Glad I can be of help," she replies to him with a brief flash of white teeth.

"We're moving Lisa and the kids into the Riverside Apartment building this afternoon. Kaga's wife and Luna have managed to pull together some furniture for them to start with."

"Need extra hands?" Trunk asks, and I stiffen beside him.

Ouray chuckles. "You only have one good one, brother, but it may not be a bad idea."

The two men seem to exchange some private message

I can't decipher.

I'm silent through most of the visit, listening to the conversation that seems to flow a little easier. Even Ezrah participates, grabbing the lesson sheets he's been working on to show his nana.

When it's time for them to leave, I suddenly realize Ezrah will be leaving with them and tears rise to the surface. He seems excited at the prospect so I swallow them down, only partially successful.

I stand with Mom at the door while Trunk accompanies them to Ouray's vehicle, carrying Ezrah's belongings. The boy is halfway to the SUV when he suddenly swings around and comes running back, throwing his arms around Mom for a hug before turning to me.

The moment his skinny arms come around me, I lose my battle with the tears. I bend down and kiss the top of his hat.

"Don' be cryin'. I'ma be back," he says looking up at me.

"Okay, buddy," I manage. "I'll be here anytime you wanna come visit." I force on a watery smile and watch him dart off again to where Lisa is waiting, before turning inside.

"You okay, sweetheart?" Mom asks.

"Yeah. Just tired," I lie. "Would you mind watching River? I think I'm gonna lie down for a bit."

"Of course."

I ignore her scrutinizing look and head straight upstairs, closing the bedroom door behind me. I lie down on top of the covers, grab Trunk's pillow, and press it to my face as I let my tears flow freely.

TRUNK

"WHERE IS SHE?"

Sandra is clearing away the cups when I walk in.

"She went to lie down for a bit. Tired."

Shee-it.

Tired my ass. I could feel her withdrawing from me even without her body moving away. Not sure what's in her head, but I can guess.

Ouray had not been wrong when he told me to wait until I got a load of Nana. She's somethin' all right. A beautiful, mature black sister in whom I have no more interest than I would if she looked like Aunt Jemima. More importantly, she's not Jaimie.

I'm guessing the fact she's still recovering, combined with the sadness over Ezrah leaving, has her pull back instead of stake her claim. The latter would be more her style. Either way, it looks like clarifying who belongs to who has to come from me.

I'm on my way upstairs to do exactly that when my phone rings.

"Yeah," I answer, sitting down on the steps.

"Dylan Barnes here. I thought I'd give you an update."

"'Preciated."

"The boy, Matthew James Hinckle, has been singing like a canary all morning. The rest of the family is sealed up tight, but that kid is so high on his own superiority, he doesn't think anyone can touch him. He's bringing everyone down. I had to take a break from all the self-righteous vitriol he's spewing."

"No shit?"

"Nope. Turns out the ANL, as well as the Hinckle family, were well aware we started looking into them last year. The Hinckle property had been used as arms storage and distribution facility for the ANL, but they got nervous when we were keeping a close eye. The Moab Reds were already part of their supply chain. James Hinckle approached Chains, hoping to get his input moving storage and distribution to an alternate location. He's the one who proposed the Arrow's Edge compound, making the mistake of equating Ouray's withdrawal from illegal dealings over the last decade as a weakness."

I have to chuckle at that. There's no way anyone with half a brain would mistake Ouray for weak.

"Matt was a plant," Dylan continues. "His objective was to feed useful information about the club's runnings, while creating internal distractions, as Chains put the pressure on from the outside."

"Trying to cut off our sources of legitimate income," I volunteer.

"Exactly. Hinckle wasn't happy with the slow progress and threatened to cut Chains off, which made him careless."

"The shooting," I conclude.

"That," he confirms. "But before that, the attack on you. Matt was pretty proud to claim his part in that. In fact, he thought it hilarious that the gun he shot Jaimie with, was yours. That's when I had to leave the room."

I swallow down the bile shooting up my throat. I already hated guns, but now I never want to own one again. I'll invest in a dozen or so fucking baseball bats to protect my home and my family.

"I don't get what purpose them burning down my place and beating the tar outta me served. Or how Sutherland fits into all of this," I force myself to ask.

"Unexpected twist, that. All those kids during their training are assigned a mentor. Sutherland apparently was Matt's. They stayed in touch, even after Sutherland was convicted; they found a way to stay connected. At first through Sutherland's lawyer, and later via the phone that was found in his cell."

"Jesus. Let me guess, all the shit that went down with Jaimie—the messages, the packages, taking River—all that was her ex?"

"Looks that way. We'll probably find out more when we bring in the lawyer, but the working theory is that Sutherland kept his fingers firmly lodged in the pie from behind bars through the Hinckle boy. There are a lot of small details still missing, but that looks to be the gist of it."

"Unreal."

"You have no idea. Some of what we've discovered is enough to give you nightmares. Did you know those kids were taught to hunt? Not animals—*people*. What was done to that boy you brought back from Monticello? They took pictures. Had them hanging on the walls of the sleeping quarters like trophies."

"Makes me sick," I mutter, my stomach twisting at the thought of Ezrah having been subjected to that.

"Me too, believe me. I think I told you we have four

kids, and I'm scared sick raising them in a world like this."

Curiosity as well as concern has me ask, "How deep does this shit go? The American Nationalist League, does it go down with Hinckle?"

There is a telling pause on the other side before Dylan answers. "Let's just say the organization is bleeding profusely. No way of knowing yet whether it turns out to be a fatal injury. What you need to know is that we're not going to rest until we can confirm the ANL has been eradicated."

"'Preciated, although it's unlikely we'll see the end of organizations like that in our lifetime, Barnes. If ever."

"One step at a time."

"Yeah."

I take a few minutes after ending the call to process the truckload of information before I resume my trek upstairs.

She's on top of the covers with my pillow pressed over her face, staying perfectly still. Too still. I don't believe for a second she's asleep.

"Hey." I get on the mattress beside her. "James."

There's no reaction, but when I try to remove the pillow, she holds on tight. Fine. I don't need to see her to tell her how it is.

"There'll likely always be people lookin' at us funny. Whose minds are so narrow, they can't see beyond the color of our skin the way we do. Fuck, baby, I never woulda thought I'd meet the woman for me, let alone one who's white. But here I am: gone, head over ass, completely and irrevocably in love with you."

Her chest starts heaving with the muffled crying coming from behind the pillow. This time when I pull it away she lets me. My hand immediately goes to her blotchy face, brushing at the tears rolling down her cheeks.

"What am I gonna do with you, Little Mama? It kills me you so easily doubt me."

"I d-don't d-doubt you," she says, grabbing onto my hand but keeping her eyes shut. "I just…I was thinking it would've been perfect for Ezrah, and for his sister: you and Lisa."

"Bullshit."

Her eyes fly open and I'm happy to see the familiar fire. "Don't tell me what I'm saying is bullshit. It's the truth."

I lean close so our noses almost touch. "It's a lie you told yourself, so you don't have to admit you're jealous over nothing."

"That's beyond ridiculous," she sputters with feigned indignation that makes me chuckle.

"The lady doth protest too much, methinks."

"Are you quoting *Hamlet* to me?"

"If the shoe fits." I grin at her.

"Great," she snaps, rolling her eyes. "We're on to fairy tales."

I'm now full on laughing with my face buried in her neck.

"And now you're laughing at me," she pouts, as I push myself up and quickly brush those puckered lips with mine.

"I'm not laughing at you," I gently correct her, letting my eyes roam her beautiful face.

"No?"

"I'm laughing because you make me incredibly fucking happy."

N
nw
ne
W
E
ARROW'S EDGE MC

31

Jaimie

"FUUUCK, JAMES. I'M there."

Trunk's eyes close as his neck arcs back, pressing his head in the pillow. His fingers dig into my hips, leaving bruises for sure.

I don't care. I revel in the hint of pain, knowing I've brought him to the edge of reason. He makes me feel whole—powerful—as he fights not to take control.

I grind myself on him, filled with his cock as he bucks underneath me, and I cry out when my body jerks with the force of my release.

"Baby," he whispers in my hair when I collapse on top of him, struggling to catch my breath. My face is pressed to his chest, where his heart beats erratically, and his large hand strokes my back, soothing the rapid pumping of my own.

It's been a long time coming.

He's been so careful with me in the three weeks since I came home from the hospital. So afraid to hurt me. It's taken this long for any evidence of bruising to disappear. He'd been gentle, using hands and mouth to please me, but he always stopped me before I was able to return the favor. I was starting to think perhaps he was turned off by the scars the bullet left behind.

Yesterday his cast came off and still he held back. But as much as I've appreciated his gentle control, I was ready for that man who before had been unable to keep his hands off me.

So when I woke up to a silent house, the early morning still dark, I took matters into my own hands.

"Did I hurt you?"

I lift my head and look at him with an eyebrow raised. "You've all but covered me in bubble wrap these past weeks. Are you kidding me?"

He rubs the pads of his thumbs along my hips. "I probably bruised you."

"Good." He seems surprised at my reaction. "About time. I'm not made of glass, Titus."

"You were hurt," he insists.

"Yes, I was, and so were you, but we're fine now." I note the stubborn scowl on his face. "I was starting to worry you were turned off by me. That somehow I'd lost my appeal."

His hands tighten on my hips and the next moment I'm on my back, Trunk looming over me with a dark scowl on his face. "Are you nuts?"

"Well, what was I supposed to think? Every time I tried to initiate something, you shut me down."

"Yeah, because you were *hurt*. Haven't whacked off that much since I was in high school," he grumbles.

"You didn't have to. I would've—"

"Baby," he whispers, brushing the backs of his fingers over my cheek as his eyes scan my face. "You could've been dead."

I grab onto his wrist. "I'm not. I'm very much alive, although at times I was so horny for my man I thought my head would explode."

He winces. "Don't give me another visual that's gonna take weeks to get rid of."

The monitor crackles and River's faint *"Mama,"* comes through. Pretty soon he'll be bellowing it at the top of his lungs, if one of us doesn't get to him.

"Let me get up, honey." I push uselessly against Trunk's chest.

"Gimme some sugar first."

I roll my eyes but kiss him anyway. Of course, River, the other demanding man in my life, quickly gets impatient.

"Mah! Mama! Up-Toce!"

Toce is what he calls breakfast, a new addition to his vocabulary, which has expanded in the last few weeks. He is starting to become particularly fond of *yes* and *no*, tries to mimic words we say, and loves saying *me,* slapping his little hand on his chest like a mini caveman.

"I'll go."

Trunk rolls off me and I take the opportunity to appreciate his fine ass as he bends over to grab his jeans and pads off to the bathroom.

Rolling on my side, I turn the volume up on the monitor. This is my secret pleasure; listening to the two most important men in my life interact.

"Unk!"

"Hey, kid. How come you're always up so early? You're messing with my playtime."

"Pway!"

"That's what I'm saying. Had to leave your mama in bed all hot and bothered."

"Mah-hot!"

"Exactly. Glad you're gettin' me. So tomorrow you sleep in, okay?"

"No sweep!"

"Shee-it, buddy. Stop squirming, how am I supposed to get a diaper on you when you keep movin' around?"

"No!"

"Yes. I know you prefer running around buck naked, but until you learn to do your business on the potty, we'll stick with diapers."

"Paw-tee."

"Potty."

"Paw-tee."

It's quiet for a moment, only the sound of rustling coming from the monitor.

"Let's go see you mama, okay, Little Man?"

"Mama?"

"Yes. Sounds like Grandma's up too."

"Gramma-toce."

"I'm sure Grandma will have toast ready..."

His voice trails off as I hear them coming down the hall. I quickly turn the monitor off and roll on my back, just in time to catch a giggling River, who launches himself from Trunk's arms onto the bed.

"Mah!"

"Morning, baby." I cuddle my son close, my nose in his hair. "Did you have a good sleep?"

"Toce!"

"In a minute."

Trunk lies down beside me and I snuggle under his arm, River on top of me.

My favorite part of every day.

"WHAT WAS THAT?" I ask Trunk after he hangs up.

"Home insurance. Looks like they're ready to cut a check."

"That's great news." Except, he doesn't look too happy. "What's wrong?"

"Not sure what to do about the house." He turns his dark eyes on me. "Got any bright ideas?"

"Uh…fix it?"

A small smile tugs at his mouth, giving me a glimpse of that dimple I love so much. "That part was pretty much a given, James, but after?"

It's probably silly since we've been living together for a while already, but we haven't officially talked about our housing arrangements yet. I like our status quo, and don't really want anything to change.

"I like waking up with you," I confess.

"Goes without saying," he replies, a cocky grin on his face. "Especially when I wake up to you riding me."

My eyes dart over to the kitchen table, where Mom is feeding River lunch. The plan is for her to put him down for a nap, while Trunk takes me for a ride on his motorcycle. I'm excited about that, but even more so about the surprise party later this afternoon. I'm supposed to keep him busy until four, when we're expected at the club. He thinks we're having a cookout celebrating the renovated clubhouse tonight, but he won't be expecting everyone to be there on his behalf.

His birthday was two weeks ago and other than a birthday cake Mom and I baked, and River decorated with his handprints, he didn't want any fuss.

Mom will load up River in my SUV when he wakes up and will hopefully be waiting at the clubhouse along with T, Evan and his mom, and a bunch of other friends, by the time we get there.

"Do you miss living on the mountain?" I ask him. He seems hesitant to answer, so I prompt him. "The truth, honey."

"I would miss living with you more, but yes, I miss it. Nothing beats the views, the lack of noise, the fresh air. It was nice to be around the corner from the clubhouse."

"Okay, then what if we move there with you?"

"Wait a minute," he stops me. "But you have work here, and your mom—"

"I work mostly from home anyway, so that's not really an issue. And there's lots of room for Mom."

"Actually, I'd like to stay here," Mom pipes up. "You guys don't need me underfoot and to be honest, I love this house and can't wait to get my hands dirty in the garden. Maybe it's time I go out and make some new friends. I can still babysit whenever you need me."

"But, Mom, you'll be alone."

She snickers. "You think that scares me? You forget, I lived alone since you went off to college. Until last Christmas that is."

I turn to Trunk, who has a questioning eyebrow up. "Sounds like it's up to you," he rumbles.

"When are we moving?"

Trunk

Fuck that feels good.

The brothers have been out a few times already. I haven't, unless you count the two hours or so I spent on the back of Ouray's bike, but those were hours I'd rather forget.

The wind in my face and the freedom of the road are welcome and familiar, but the feeling of Jaimie's body pressed tightly against my back is new. Better. Other than Tahlula on one or two occasions, I've never had another woman on the back of my bike. Never had a woman I wanted to share my life with, let alone my club and my brothers. Not until Jaimie.

"Can we go up there?" Jaimie yells in my ear, steering

me up yet another winding mountain road.

I grin. She's taken to the bike like it's second nature. Can't seem to get enough of it. At this rate we won't be back until late. Not that I care, I'd fucking drive her to Denver if she asked.

I follow the road to the top of the ridge and pull off at a lookout point. The moment I stop, she climbs off the bike, takes off her helmet, and walks up to the edge, throwing her arms out wide. Her blonde hair is getting longer, almost halfway down her back, shining like gold in the afternoon sun.

"I love this!" she yells, swinging around with a huge grin on her face. "It's so beautiful."

"*You're* beautiful."

She stops mid-swirl and looks at me, her arms slowly lowering to her side. "Trunk…"

"Come 'ere, baby."

Her gorgeous blue eyes turn silk as she slowly makes her way back. The moment she's within reach I tug her close.

"Do you have any fucking clue how much I love you?"

"Not as much as I love you," she says softly, running a hand along my jaw as she leans in for a kiss.

"Impossible," I mumble against her mouth, tasting the wind on her lips. "You own me, Little Mama."

"Titus…"

My hand tightens in her tousled hair as I kiss her like she's my next breath. "I want you to stop taking the pill."

"Uhm…what?" She pulls back but I hold her firmly.

"Baby, love you, love your boy, but the two of you've ruined me. Never even considered kids and now it's all I can think about; having a baby with you."

"Wow. I…uh…" she stammers, looking a little shell-shocked at first, but then her eyes narrow. "Having a baby *with* me, huh? Sounds good when you put it like that, but it'll be me trying to push another watermelon from my hooha. Have you seen the size of your head?"

"I'll be there every step of the way," I promise, trying to look serious, because I don't think she'd appreciate me laughing.

"You're serious," she mutters.

"Perfectly. I'm forty-five. You're going on forty."

"Forty? I'll be thirty-nine in July, thank you very much," she snips.

"I stand corrected," I concede. "Doesn't change the fact I want a baby with you before we get too old. Before River gets too old."

"We haven't been together that long," she protests.

"Long enough to know my feelings for you aren't gonna change," I tell her stubbornly. "Are yours?"

"No. That's not what I'm saying. I mean…we've barely figured out our living arrangements, okay?"

This time I let her slip from my hold and watch as she puts the helmet on, fastening it with jerky movements. "Then let's take care of that…but then we're making a baby."

"You're insufferable, you know that?"

Yeah, I know, but I'm not going to tell her that.

I grin all the way back to Durango.

"SURPRISE!"

The first face I see when I walk in is my sister's. From the smirk on her face, I know she's probably behind this and damn proud to have pulled one over on me. But before I can give her hell, she's in my arms.

"Happy birthday. Love you, Titus."

"Ditto, Sis," comes out instead.

My head is soon spinning with the congratulations coming fast and furious. Evan, Hanna and Joan, Sandra with River, who manages to jump from her arms to mine. Ollie is there with Joe, Dylan Barnes and a cute brunette with a gaggle of boys, and even Tony fucking Ramirez is grinning big as he claps me on the shoulder. Keith Blackfoot with his family, Kaga, his wife, and the twins.

I meander through the people until I get to the couch, where Momma—just released from the hospital last week—is holding court. I kiss her cheek.

"Good to have you back, Momma."

"Good to be back. See you haven't let any grass grow over it. She's a good girl, don't mess it up."

"Not planning to," I assure her.

I turn when someone taps me on the arm to find Ezrah, his grin big, standing behind me.

"Happy birthday."

"Thanks, buddy. Good to see you. I missed you." He almost knocks me over with the force of his hug.

River, who loves all the attention, immediately twists in my arm, trying to get at Ezrah's dreads.

"Can he come wit me?" the boy asks, holding his arms up for River.

"Where you takin' him?"

He points at the club's four remaining charges lounging on new beanbags in front of a large TV, playing some kind of movie.

"Don't let him eat or drink anything unless you clear it with Sandra or Jaimie, okay?"

"'Kay."

I grin when I see the effort it takes him to carry the little man over to the group of boys.

"Ready for a drink now?" Paco claps a hand on my shoulder and leads me to the brand-new bar, where Ouray and Luna, along with the rest of the brothers seem to be congregated.

A beer gets shoved in my hand and I take a swig, before turning to Tse. "How are you feeling?"

"Like someone went over me with a meat tenderizer and I fucking look like ground chuck, but I'm feeling a lot better now I have access to beer."

"Amen," Honon cheers, raising his bottle.

"Yuma?" I ask Ouray quietly, noting his absence.

"Couldn't get him to come out. Guy's messed up, brother. Won't see anyone, not even Momma can get through."

"Give him time. I'll check in with him next week."

Ouray nods.

I turn my back to the bar and scan the new clubhouse.

Still pretty basic, with some of the old furniture making a reappearance, but some new stuff too. I watch Jaimie come out of the kitchen across the room, carrying a tray of some kind of finger food. She sees me watching her and smiles, giving me that warm feeling in my chest.

"Feels good, don't it?" Ouray mumbles, having witnessed the exchange. "One minute you're doin' fine on your own—no complaints—and the next you can't figure out how the fuck you ever did without 'er."

"Feels great," I tell him, never taking my eyes off my woman.

From the corner of my eye, I see Barnes approaching.

"I just got a call from Gomez," he says, addressing me as much as he is his partner, Luna. "Sutherland was found dead. Shanked in the showers. Not even twelve hours since being put back in general population."

"Who?" Luna asks immediately.

"No one's seen anything, but if you ask me, the ANL is making sure not to leave any loose ends. Through his right eye, straight into his brain."

Ouray whistles between his teeth as I catch Jaimie's attention, motioning her over.

"I wasn't sure whether you wanted me to tell her, or—"

"She can do without the descriptives," I growl.

I'm not sure how she'll react, but there isn't a better place for any kind of news—good or bad—than among friends.

"Hey."

I hook her around the waist and pull her close.

"Sutherland's dead, Little Mama."

"Rob?" She looks confused.

"Someone got to him in the showers."

She closes her eyes and puts her hands on my chest. I give her a minute.

"James?"

She shakes her head. "I'm trying to figure out how I feel about that. He's River's dad."

"Sperm donor," I correct her and her eyes snap open, blue and fierce.

"Don't remind me."

"So how do you feel?" Luna asks.

Jaimie scrunches up her face and then shakes her head again. "Not a whole lot. Not enough to let him mess up this party."

"I'll drink to that," Honon volunteers.

"That's what you've been doin' all afternoon," Ouray grumbles.

Just like that the motherfucker, who'd never see his beautiful kid grow up, is gone from our minds.

It's late.

Sandra drove us home in Jaimie's Honda, because we both had a few too many. She offered to carry River to bed, but tonight I want to put the boy to bed.

Jaimie kisses him goodnight and shuffles into our bedroom, while I take him into his room.

"Good day, buddy?" I mutter mindlessly, as I peel off

his clothes and quickly grab a clean diaper and his pj's. He can barely keep his eyes open. "I know, I had fun too."

"Rah."

"Ezrah, I know. He looks good, right? Happy." I strip back the tabs of his diaper. "Shee-it, kid. Why you gotta save those butt bombs for me?"

"Butt!"

"That's right," I mutter, trying not to breathe through my nose as I clean him up. "Dirty butt bomb."

"Butt!"

"Exactly." I make quick work of getting him into a fresh diaper and his jammies, before lifting him off the table. "There, now you smell good."

River grins at me and slaps his hands on my cheeks, leaning close.

"Shee-it, Unk?"

I barely have a chance to chuckle when I hear Jaimie from the other room.

"Titus Maximus Rae!"

THE END

ABOUT THE AUTHOR

Award-winning author Freya Barker loves writing about ordinary people with extraordinary stories.

Driven to make her books about 'real' people; she creates characters who are perhaps less than perfect, each struggling to find their own slice of happy, but just as deserving of romance, thrills and chills in their lives.

Recipient of the ReadFREE.ly 2019 Best Book We've Read All Year Award for "Covering Ollie, the 2015 RomCon "Reader's Choice" Award for Best First Book, "Slim To None", and Finalist for the 2017 Kindle Book Award with "From Dust", Freya continues to add to her rapidly growing collection of published novels as she spins story after story with an endless supply of bruised and dented characters, vying for attention!

Lightning Source UK Ltd.
Milton Keynes UK
UKHW021122040522
402471UK00007B/1225